All Things End in Yes

Lily Barker

Published in 2013 by Caspian Press

A CIP catalogue record for this title is available from the British Library.

This novel is a work of fiction. Although some of the characters existed, the incidents portrayed are the work of the author's imagination.

Dedicated to: my father, Persian translator of fine literature; my mother, for bravely immersing herself in another culture; and Edward Fitzgerald who had the foresight to self-publish his inaugural interpretation of the Rubaiyat in 1859.

1

London, England 2003

In the past fortnight Manucher James Zand had frequented the most renowned restaurants in London and eaten the spiciest of meals: without success.

He had sampled the most pungent of cheeses and consumed the most aromatic foods. Nothing doing.

Even the sultan of dishes, his mother's Fesenjan stew, with ground walnuts and rich pomegranate syrup, was not enough to tempt the return of his faculties.

It was without question a disaster of immense proportions. All taste buds and nasal hairs (usually experts in their field) were unavailable for comment. Taste and smell were playing truant. They had gone into hiding. Missing. Snuffed out.

To his right, on the desk, was positioned a bulb of raw garlic - which he occasionally thrust to his nose in the frenzied hunt for a scent.

To his left, he had placed a small bowl of lemon juice into which he would occasionally dip his finger, to assess what condition his condition was in.

It was like being castrated of one's competence and one's compulsion in a single sitting.

'Impromptu-bout-of-sensory-impotence' and 'no-apparent-cause' had been the only memorable leftovers from his doctor's diagnosis.

"Been under any stress recently Mr Zand?" his physician had enquired.

The dimple in Manu's unshaven chin had twitched, catching a javelin of light from the surgery window in its aperture. Opaque eyebrows buckled above a rather obvious, but not wholly unattractive, nose. Fingers dived aggressively into a flourishing (and lately un-mown) lawn of coarse black hair.

Not to his knowledge, was his response.

Since then, life had been a journey from fridge-to-here, and fridge-to-there, in an ongoing test of his sensory aptitudes. A peculiar vision danced about his head. It was one of himself, twenty years hence: an acclaimed but disabled food critic. Society would marvel over the case of a man, devoid of the intrinsic possessions relating to his craft and fighting to continue his career despite such a major incapacity. Foodies would come for miles to study his methods of assessment, now based on calculation and probability rather than sensual prowess. Disability campaigners would hail him as their cause célèbre. But in private a woeful ache would overcome him: the Torment of Tantalus, an unattainable feast for the eyes only. It would be a destiny of two extremes: exquisite mastery and absolute misery.

He hammered some heated words into the keyboard with his spade-like fingers before coming to an emergency stop. The article in front of his crippled nose was taunting him with luscious edibles he might never again savour. *Best of British.* Its haughty undertones seemed misplaced. Should he re-write it? No, too painful. He cast a hungry eye over the wording. It was like hankering after an old flame. His salivary glands exploded reflexively. That was a result, at least.

"It was a pig's life being a butcher," declares Stan Cooper leaning over his redundant meat counter sporting an extra-tall chef's hat.

Once a proud best-end-of-neck man he's recently transformed himself into a rough-puff-pastry man. This metamorphosis from boner and trimmer to deft patissier has apparently done wonders for his marriage. "You ask the wife," he urges. "It's the offal or me she told me one day. And fair dues, (he laughs) it must've been like coppin' off with an old piece of mutton every night!"

Manu Zand took an editorial pause to suck in the extra 2 inches of girth which had been loitering above his belt since somewhere round his thirtieth birthday. Was it like that for Alice? Copping off with pot-belly every weekend?

Poor thing, no wonder she came around less frequently these days.

As for born-again-baker, Stan, he had been fortunate. No more entrails for him. And no more looking back, since the tale of his conversion to dough had surfaced on the collective lips of the Shoreditch set.

"Home made pies. Just lush!" says one follower.

So what's the attraction? A pie's a pie isn't it?

Not so, says Stan. "All down the Kingsland Road these days, everything is sundried this or tapenade that. Punters are looking for something simpler nowadays. It's a sort of genesis, mate: a re-birth of traditional English fayre."

He insists people are starting to see the light.

Illumination. That was something Manu Zand yearned for himself. Over the years he had been on a number of pilgrimages to explore the dialectics of life's little absurdities. Sleeping with a friend's wife had been one such romp. But these transgressions had not gone unnoticed by the self-righteous Morality Auditors, lurking in his conscience and hovering over every flaw. 'Rather a lot of entries under Living For Today, Mr Zand. And Personal Gratification seems to be proving to be a regular feature in your life. Where will they lead do you suppose?'

It was true. He had been wandering off course for some time now.

So, for those of you who have lost your way amongst the sea of courses, offered by too many continental eateries, this is an opportunity to sample a little bit of true Brit. Here you can nail your colours to a British mast (well Union Jack bunting anyway - you'll find it dripping from every wall) and revel in beer and bulldogs. But if you think we're talking school dinners, make no mistake. You might find yourself eating a slice of humble pie. And mighty tasty it is too. Stan's pig's liver and bacon crust, which locals refer to as the

'Pig's Purse' is a mixture of rough-cut, chopped liver and bacon in a red wine and rosemary gravy, wrapped in a thin bready pastry. The Stuffed Turkey and Cranberry slice comes a close second to the real festive deal, and you don't have to wait until Christmas to savour it. But if you can stomach the unashamedly patriotic surroundings, it's well worth a lunchtime visit. Be warned though, it's unmistakably more Drool than Cool Britannia.

Manu sighed loudly, turned off his computer and sauntered over to the steamed up window of his top floor flat. The Hampstead afternoon school run was in full throttle. A battery of young mothers driving metallic urban street tanks tried to manoeuvre them into the most inconvenient of territories. One driver appeared to be in heated combat with a traffic warden who had halted her advance. Manu found himself observing her tactics: polite; irritable; and finally belligerent, whilst her fist-sized terrier bounced itself off the windscreen in a fit of yapping rage.

Further down, across the road on a wall, sat two youths, one of each gender, engaged in an amorous coalition. Or was her tongue just caught in his nose ring? It was hard to tell. Why did everyone else's relationships look so simple and straightforward?

When the doorbell rang just after six, he was examining his nose in the mirror, looking for exterior manifestations of his ailment. Alice had come to pick him up. They were going to dinner at his parents' house.

Alice Perrywall was a serial career woman. A producer in network radio, she churned out little gems such as *Plush Pursuits,* a game-show, in which people guessed the hobbies of middle-ranking celebrities who happened to be passing through London that day on a publicity tour. "You'll never guess what x or y does in his spare time," was a frequent conversation opener.

Her impish, lanky body was covered in the usual tight little suit. Today it was emerald green. And her hair boasted fresh blonde highlights which reflected off the sharp angles of her gaunt face. There was something reassuringly constant about her though which Manu had never been able to put his finger on.

Their sex life was fair, although less frequent than either of them would have wished. Worryingly, she had in the recent past been canvassing his opinion on moving in, children, marriage and the like. He had accepted the subject politely, contemplated it with the sincerity of a Shakespearean farceur, and covertly filed it in the out-tray of his intention. The tray, however, having amassed such propositions for a good twelve months, was now a creaking weight demanding urgent attention.

"I saw Laure on my way round here this evening," said Alice on their drive to Richmond. "Just closing the café. She looked a little weary."

"Did you speak to her?" asked Manu.

"No, I was in the car. I couldn't stop. But it definitely looked as if she'd been up half the night."

"Last I heard her father wasn't very well. Perhaps that's it."

"Oh, I presumed it might be because she had a new man in her life," said she, dangling a verbal taunt.

"Really?"

"Well, I'm not sure. That's what I've heard."

"Who from?"

"Sally, one of the girls at work who keeps in touch with her."

"Are you sure it's not a rumour?"

"Would you like it to be?" asked Alice, turning momentarily to purse her thin lips in his direction.

"What does *that* mean?"

"I mean. Could you cope with it?"

"Well how ridiculous," said Manu. "She can do what she wants. She's a free agent."

Alice raised her eyebrows and smiled from the corner of her mouth. "Yes, some would say," she said under her breath. Manu ignored the comment and they drove for a long while in silence.

She eventually resumed the conversation. "How are your parents anyway? I spoke to your mother on the phone the other day and she says that there is a guest coming to dinner tonight."

"Apparently so. A neighbour of ours from the 'old country'. I knew her when I was very young but can't remember what she was like. Yet another evening raking over old coals," he sighed.

"Oh you're such a miserable sod!" exclaimed Alice as she pulled into his parents' drive and curtailed the conversation with a punctuatory hoist on the handbrake.

Manu tried to see his parents at least once a fortnight. They weren't getting any younger and, although they drove him to distraction with regular frequency, he had grown to tolerate their little foibles.

"Oh just ignore him my dears," his mother quipped as they walked down the pebbled drive. "He's *still* going on about the new neighbours."

"I tell you my son, they are a family of vultures," said his father loudly. "Three weeks they have been moved here and immediately he's building an extension. Bebeen! See! Just look at that monster shadowing over my greenhouse. And eenchieh? What is this? A pink pole! Who for God's sake puts a pink pole in the middle of their garden!"

"Mehdi dear, keep your voice down. We haven't even *met* them yet. They might be very pleasant. Anyway, I've seen the wife and she looks very well dressed," said Rebecca Zand.

"You see, pessaram! The woman is tricked by the devil with gold horns. It wears an Armani suit and everybody walks in its shadow!" cried Manu's father at the top of his voice. He threw both his hands to the sky as he was led inside by his wife and son.

Since retiring from his job as an importer of Iranian artefacts, Mehdi Zand had found it difficult to occupy himself, and his wife had found it equally impossible to keep him occupied. Happily, things had improved following the purchase of a pair of Porro Prism binoculars. The super optical intruder had refocused much of his persistent meddling from his own backyard to that of the adjoining neighbourhood. The joyous consequence was a modicum of peace for his wife. This self-appointment as community voyeur had given him a much needed inspectorial status, characteristic of a local constable, albeit an uncertified one. To the majority of St Margaret's, Richmond Upon Thames, however, he was simply the nuisance at Number Forty-Three.

"You look through this my son. Its lens is so powerful it can travel half a mile," said Mehdi Zand as he pushed Manu upstairs towards the landing window to try them out. "Chee meebini?"

"Well. I can see the time on that church clock on the hill," Manu responded looking through the lenses of the heavy contraption.

"Yes. Well. Now. Move your head a little this way. That's it. A bit more. Now. Do you see that top window. With the red curtain?"

"Ye-e-es."

"Now. Just a little to the right. Do you see that big black box in the corner of the room?"

"Yes, dad, but I'm not happy about doing this."

"Meedoony chieh?"

"I haven't a clue. It looks like an amplifier on a stand. A loud speaker or something."

"Exactly! What did I tell you! They are going to drive us all mad with the music! That box should be in a concert hall, not in my street!"

"I think that you may be overstepping the mark by using these," Manu said, handing the hefty binoculars back to his father. He snatched them back impatiently.

"It is *they* who are thrusting their obscenities into my face! If they remove them I will remove my lens," said Mehdi.

A shout from his mother alerted them to Mrs Garakian's arrival and to food on the table.

In the majority of cases Manu did not need to be aurally summoned to dinner. The fragrance of his mother's cooking was enough to lure him out of the most embroiling of preoccupations. This evening was an exception. For him there was no smell of fresh herbs, no smell of infused dried lime and lamb. There was no bouquet of cucumber yoghurt mixed with walnuts and sweet raisins. Even the aubergine and garlic pickles were not acidic enough to jump-start his olfactory machinery or his half-baked appetite.

"Perhaps you should see a specialist," suggested his mother as she dished out the rice. "I mean, what will I do without the compliments?"

Manu looked at his father.

"My congratulations are not necessary. She's been cooking long enough to know what I think," said Mehdi Zand with a mouthful of bread.

Rebecca Zand rolled her eyes and shrugged her shoulders. Despite her English heritage, years of living in Iran had made her as respectable as any Persian cook.

Mrs Garakian came to her aid. "I think it's delicious," she said plainly.

Old Mrs Garakian was an anguished Armenian wanderer whose face and gait exhibited a gallery of characteristics, shaped by generational persecutions at the hands of Arabs, Mongols, Turks, Soviets and Persians. She had spent a short time in Tehran, after fleeing Stalin's ethnic cleansing programme. After the revolution she had settled in London, at the same time as the Zands, in the nineteen eighties. Now, (due to the death of her husband) she was planning to return to her liberated, and for the time being, sovereign, country of birth. The purpose of her presence today was to offload some household artefacts she would not be able to transport overseas.

After they had eaten, the old woman set about retrieving a multitude of boxes and bags from her car. She politely rejected assistance from the assembled company and persevered in bringing each item into the house herself. Mrs Zand followed her to and from the car pleading with her to reconsider. Manu stood at the doorway watching the old woman's long, thin grey plait swinging like a pendulum above her buttocks as she waddled backwards and forwards. The small squat figure was hardy despite its age, he thought, as she approached him carrying a rug on her shoulder. A medley of wheezes and sighs accompanied each delivery, it being impossible to distinguish whether their genesis was emotional or physical.

The ornaments themselves ranged from traditional Middle Eastern trinkets, and metal-ware to modern-day imports, most likely acquired from a London market. A set of small interlocking brass goats, and an ornate silver goblet, depicting a barbarian hunting scene, exemplified the style of garish workmanship in which Manu took limited delight. It was clearly a doleful occasion for the old lady who fondled each article, embellishing it with a tale of this and that, before passing it over for inspection. A fog of awkwardness hung about in the air: obstinate, immobile and unrepentant.

The four intruders scrutinised, probed and prodded Mrs Garakian's (until now) private possessions. Manu wished they could have asked her to step outside the room so they could rifle mercilessly, even though he had no particular interest in anything much she had. In spite of this, he knew that he would be returning home with a token item, most probably earmarked for the dustbin or, at best, an unfortunate cupboard.

By now Alice was unrolling a small Persian rug which had been deposited at the side of the sofa. No, he wasn't really interested in that either. His small flat had a modern feel about it: Conran coffee table; the occasional Eames chair. Persian carpets were unquestionably not part of his interior design policy.

"Look Manu," said Alice. "It's beautiful don't you think?"

She unravelled the rectangular rug, the size of a large desktop, over the sofa on which they sat. It was an exquisite object, of this there was no doubt. Its beetroot red border embraced a scene of interlinked, delicate ochre-coloured flowers, which ran along the edge in a bold and complicated curvilinear pattern. At each corner rich black lines erupted into copper-coloured, leafy gatherings. And a large, and loud, diamond silhouette of geometric shapes, beleaguered by elaborate channels of goldish brown, sat valiantly at its centre. The overall design had a symmetrical Rorschachian appearance. And yet, if you looked closely enough, each flower or motif had its own peculiarities. Altogether the rich-red, gold and other sienna-type colours joined in concert to evoke a feeling of excited calm: like the restless tug between music and silence during an orchestra's warm-up before a concert.

He ran his hand over the fine velvet pile. A billion silky hairs greeted the tips of his fingers and proceeded to melt in all directions.

The old lady apologised for the rather musty smell. "It's been sitting in my attic for twenty years," she said ashamedly.

"It appears to have some writing woven into it here," said Alice getting out her glasses.

"Yes," said Mrs Garakian, "It is a strange inscription I do not understand it."

Manu examined the bottom right-hand corner of the rug. Woven, in small delicate English script, was an inscription. How strange that it was in English. It was difficult to fathom as the pile of the carpet distorted the lettering here and there. He smoothed his hand over the area attempting to flatten it. The black characters evolved into a sentence. "*All things end in yes.*"

"That phrase seems very familiar," said Rebecca Zand who was standing behind the sofa. "But I can't think why."

"Why on earth would an English phrase be woven into a Persian carpet?" asked Manu.

"This is astonishing," said Mehdi Zand. "I have never seen such a thing. And I have seen many Persian carpets. Where did you get it?" he asked the old woman.

Mrs Garakian had been waiting for another opportunity to tell a tale. "I bought this in 1951, when I was living in

Tehran," she said. "I remember exactly the year because it was a present for my husband's thirtieth birthday. It was newly woven and sold me by Mr Forooshi, a wonderful carpet seller in the bazaar. Ah yes, and he had the most charming son, who had a parakeet. He was a funny, funny character." She grinned widely, revealing a mass of unemployed gum leading to a small fortress of yellowing front teeth, which Manu found himself counting – nine in total.

"The parakeet lived in a cage hanging above the shop," she continued. "And at daytime they took him out and he would march up and down like a little soldier on his own little carpet outside the shop. What a funny thing he was!"

She picked up the edge of the rug and rolled it between her fingers. "But you see this, it's lovely. Good quality cotton and will last another few hundred years. No?"

"Look Mehdi, there's something on the back of it!" said Rebecca pointing to where Mrs Garakian was holding up the corner.

They turned it over. A thick scrawl of aging black ink attempted to cling to the rough knotted surface at the back.

"It's in Farsi," said Alice. "What does it mean?"

Zand's father inspected it. "It simply says: Abadan municipal swimming pool at noon," he said with a shrug.

"Where's that?" asked Alice.

"The pool I am unsure. But Abadan is the location of Iran's oil refinery," said Mehdi. "There's a date next to it also. October 4th."

"Your brother's birthday, darling!" said Rebecca looking into her husband's face with an exaggerated smile, whilst patting him on the back.

Mehdi Zand grunted and rose from the sofa. "I don't have a brother," he mumbled walking towards the kitchen.

"Oh dear. I've hit a nerve," said Rebecca biting her lip. "It's a gorgeous piece of work but I'm afraid it probably won't be welcome here. How about your flat Manu? It would look wonderful on your floorboards."

****

Much later that evening Manu was slumped in a leather armchair at his flat, his gaze entangled in the vivid complexity of hues and patterns of his new acquisition. To his horror the little rug had looked intensely charming on the wooden floorboards in front of the coal fire. In truth, the whole experience had been one of compulsion and coercion. Both his mother and Alice had used every morsel of persuasion and reasoning they could muster to chip away at his resistance. It was only a carpet after all; not a large one; and how wonderful it would be for him to own a little something symbolising a facet of his lost culture. Whilst his father would occasionally look up from his newspaper and make comments like: "Surrender to them my son. It is much simpler."

The capitulation, when it came, was more of a predicament than relief. Was there a space in the loft? Might it fit in the airing cupboard? Under the bed in the spare room was a possibility. In spite of this, he had found himself to be more gracious than he had imagined, agreeing a temporary settlement for the rug in his living room. His ability to tolerate its presence would remain to be seen. When all was said and done, however decorative and sumptuous it was, it remained the emblem of an itching discomfort with his primordial sense of self: an uneasiness with his inner oriental recesses.

He leaned forward to have a look at the inscription which had camouflaged itself back into an illegible scribble once more. He stroked the top of the black smudge with the base of his hand. It sharpened into significance.

All things end in yes.

His mother had, after much fussing, remembered where she had heard the phrase. This was followed by a trip to the attic, the emptying of a variety of cupboards and scanning a number of bookshelves before the answer was made fully clear.

Manu leaned over and retrieved from his coat pocket the tiny leather bound book his mother had given him before he left: *Edward Fitzgerald's English translation of the Rubaiyat of Omar Khayyam.* He flicked through the delicate pages. It was a hefty poem and took him a while to locate the appropriate quatrain. It read:

And if the wine you drink, the lip you press,
End in Nothing – all Things end in – Yes;
Think then you are today, what yesterday
You were, tomorrow you shall not be less

Why would a Persian carpet weaver, with no likely knowledge of the English language, weave an *English* translation of a poem from a revered Persian poet into a Persian carpet? It didn't make sense.

But sense had been missing from this life for quite a while. Missing from sober reality. Missing from circumstance. And missing from sensibility. Quite simply, life had capsized. And out of it had drained purpose and appetite.

Thus, Manu retired to bed with a smearing of Eucalyptus oil on his pillow and a sprig of dried lavender next to his nose. As usual, he hoped that accompanying the morning light would be his most dear and precious sensory companions, without whom life was not worth its salt. And as he drifted in an out of sleep he began to devise a recipe for apricot soup. He must talk to Laure about putting it on the menu. Was it true what Alice had said about her? He couldn't imagine Laure with another man. But it had been five years since the divorce. Perhaps it was time for her to move on. He would have to respect that.

2

Tehran, Iran 1949

When she first saw the naked ones they were promenading along the city's tree-lined boulevard. Faces chalky white and hair open to the elements. It was 1939 then, and the world had lately begun to fight itself. At home, her king waged war on women. He outlawed the veil; the curtain which kept them safe. And nowhere did its absence have more presence than in the capital, Tehran. She had been told what to expect. And she saw it when they arrived.

Parissa was nine then or ten perhaps. Her family had been travelling on foot for twelve days, the skeleton of their estate sitting proudly astride an old mule as it picked its way through the reticent mountains. Then, the moment they crossed the threshold of the city gates, the poor beast shuddered, grunted and expired. And for a long time she was convinced it was shock of the nakeds.

From that day she observed her mother gradually discharge herself from life, because her refuge had been peeled away. Each deeply personal expression, long hidden, became a raw emotion open to the collective air. She was compelled by the authorities to publish her face onto society. Obliged to advertise every smile or grimace. But eventually it stripped her mother's confidence and caused great suffering – untutored as she was in parading her character in public. Every male gaze or wink of the eye was an assault on her spirit.

Finally, her mother confined herself to the house. And from the window, with each spent year, she observed this new rule write, write and write itself into custom. Like an ongoing trickle of water endlessly cutting its groove into the landscape to establish dominance. In the end she died, a prisoner in her home, its thin white walls providing the closing cover of her final tortured years.

Today things were different. An equilibrium of sorts had been reached. Veiled and unveiled walked alongside each other in the streets. And the naked ones with their cherry lips no longer stole Parissa's breath but became her lantern; flushing specks of splendour into her enclosed world. And with every second that ticked her life forward, the specks grew more influential – urging her to join the sisterhood with its lacquered hair, taught corset and pointed shoe. To think she had once trembled in their presence!

It had been Afsaneh who had first pressed the seed of fear into her conscience, drawing vivid pictures of the type of depravity awaiting them in the capital.

"In the meydan," she said creeping up behind her and blowing in her ear, "old men snatch children and sell them to the farangis because they fetch a high price!" she contorted her fingers into two claw-shaped omens in front of Parissa's face. "Did your uncle tell you that as well?" her eight year-old self had asked.

"No, my cousin. But he knows because his friend went to Tehran and never returned. They say he is now working as a slave in the West!"

She never saw Afsaneh again and wondered what future tales of misery she had gone on to construct about the plight of her childhood friend Parissa.

Before the migration there had been much to be grateful for. What daughter would not thank God for a life of tranquillity and contentment when all around was infected with poverty and starvation? If her father had not caught the good providence of the blessed Mohammad they would have been forced to cling to the hem of the prosperous.

Back then, in her father's workshops in the city of Tabriz, women and girls sat aside each other in rows of four or five on long wooden scaffolds, knotting carpets from sunrise to sunset, taking intermissions only to eat and pray.

Occasionally Parissa was given permission to sit at the end of the scaffold and assist, for her mother was one of the ustads. Idle chatter about husbands, children and ailments would pepper the air. The sound of clicking combs as they knocked each weft into place became a lullaby which was to remain with her, and comfort her, for years to come.

Her fondest pastime was watching the myriad of patterns slowly advancing up the warp of the loom in an eruption of turbulent colour, like the creeping flush of an angry dawn, awoken before its allotted time. Even now, she still marvelled at how inconspicuous strands of wool, once married together, could acquire an aptitude far beyond their singular capacities. And to this day the smell of stacked wool: damp and musty in the winter; coarse and sweet-smelling in the summer, frequently tossed her back into the workshop as though she had never left.

It was commonplace in those days for many carpet merchants to treat their workers with harshness and disrespect, but her father did not. He was one of the few that would not employ children less than nine years old, even though their tiny fingers produced the tightest Ghiordian Knots known to the trade. Despairing parents implored him to offer their daughters a place on the scaffold but he always refused, as the long hours on a plank left them with bandy and twisted legs.

"They will only produce un-consenting knots," he would say. "Those mothers will thank me later when their children can do a proper day's work."

She was close to her father in those days. He was a fine and caring man – a man of generous thought. For despite being told her mother's prospect of bearing a son was as likely as a peacock hatching from a duck egg, and knowing a lone girl-child was considered a curse, he came to an amicable settlement in his mind by subtracting his disbelief of the present, from the destiny written on his forehead. It was this clean drop of pragmatism that had unbuckled her from the fate of her sex, if only for a short spell.

And from that moment, she was dispatched to an American missionary school near Tabriz, where they lived, under the strictest instruction to heed not the devotion but the dialect. Trade with the farangis was growing and, it seemed, she was destined to be its biggest proponent. But not for long it appeared.

Remarkably, the future turned out to be less inevitable than any of them had bargained for. Her mother bravely defied predictions by delivering her brother Ali, exactly one day after a great economic depression swallowed their enterprise.

And overnight their feathered nest was plucked.

How it had injured her father! Took away his conviction. And the staircase he was climbing began to crumble beneath his feet. It was where it all both ended and began.

The heaving capital sucked in their small family and handed to them a new set of instructions they did not understand. Meanwhile, her mother defied predictions once more by delivering her sister, Soraya. And her father set about rebuilding his enterprise, from a small carpet stall in the Grand Bazaar.

Nowadays, Parissa spent her time weaving her desires into woollen saddlebags, Kilims and carpets. And though not fully formed, her aspirations were beginning to take shape. Having been neither here nor there during her early life. And having been infected with an early puff of intellect. And having evaded for a while the stamp of her gender. And having escaped the confines of her father's eye. She felt her opinions peeling away from tradition. Was it only she who saw the growth of a spirited confidence amongst her progressive sisters? This was where she wished to be. And where she was not.

In the capital, women who had discarded the veil completely and wore the European garb seemed enhanced with a sort of graceful courage. If only she could immerse herself in that bold adventure. But surely it would be impossible. And if her father had the ability to pry into her mind he would express great horror.

"Young people today have been enticed by the fancy that extrinsic beauty is more valuable than that which lives in the soul," was his repeated phrase.

"But father, de-veiling is surely about progress, rather than beauty?" she had insisted knowing that, with each utterance, she injured her mother's memory. "I have heard many stories of women who were allowed to join the Soviet army to defend their country in the Great Patriotic War against Germany. And only yesterday my friend was telling me of a celebrated woman aviator who was a navigator in the Soviet airforce."

He did not like this kind of talk.

"Their fathers are fools. All of them! They will not thank themselves later when there is no one to give birth to the children of the nation!" he said.

He was fixed upon the decay which hibernated within the bitter wind of progress. It was not that he opposed change, for he was well practised in crusading for a people's voice. It was the effluence it left behind which he found hard to bear.

One day she was in the workshop above the carpet shop with her sister when her father made his entrance in a most excited manner.

"We have been invited to Mr Dashti's house on Saturday for afternoon tea," said Hajji-Hossein. "His son Karim has some leave from the oil company refinery in Abadan and is coming to visit. Both Dashti and I think he may be a suitable match for you Parissa. Do you have something suitable to wear?"

Parissa was taken aback. She had rarely spoken to her father about marriage and had always taken for granted she would stay at home until the children were grown. Otherwise who would look after them? What would they do without her? Especially Soraya. Ali was now attending one of the new schools in the capital. It was possible he might have to abandon his studies if she was no longer at home.

"But father, I have met Karim. I cannot imagine that he and I will be a suitable match at all!" She attempted to say it in a calm voice.

"Yes, my daughter. But the last you saw of him you were twelve years old. You have both matured since that time. And he has turned into a fine young man by all accounts. He has a respectable job as an oil-worker apprentice at the refinery and his prospects are not bad. You are aware that I did have grander hopes for your marriage but you see our circumstance. We are no longer an affluent family. And you, well – at the age of twenty you are no longer gambolling lamb! You could hardly do better than put yourself in his hands."

"Pari's getting married!" sang Soraya and danced around throwing fragments of wool over her sister.

"Very well father," said Parissa, terminating her sister's flight of fancy with a menacing glance whilst catching hold of her flapping arms. "I would certainly like to meet him and then perhaps we can decide."

"Good. There you are. Go and buy yourself a pretty new headscarf," said he, throwing two tomans in her lap, before departing.

Marriage was something she had been forced to contemplate only once. An old friend of her father had offered to take her off his hands at fifteen. Mr Moshteri, a widower of many years, was pleasant enough but much older than she had ever imagined her future husband to be. He also had a withered arm, which made it difficult for her to envisage touching him.

Fortunately her father's mind was changed when he discovered the man had royalist connections. And the topic of matrimony had been buried alongside other thorny problems, to be dealt with later.

But later was now. And now they were North and South. He wanting to get her off his hands. And she resolute: having stolen a handful of independence whilst he was preoccupied with politics and commerce. Nevertheless her siblings had matured in front of her eyes. They could not be her excuse for much longer. Soraya was yielding about 8000 knots a day, well above the average for her years. Ali, despite his immaturities, was craving more responsibility. Nonetheless, she was fearful at the thought of leaving home. And under such circumstances. This marriage would involve relocation to Abadan. There had been alarming stories about how Iranis were being treated there. And her memories of Karim as a young boy did not fill her heart with gladness. She recalled a small, thin, frame made more unsteady by a stutter.

The following Saturday their family descended upon the Dashti household. The Dashtis were a little less fortunate, living in a small dwelling in the south of the city. Poupak Dashti greeted them with showers of kisses and compliments as her five young children trailed her like a colony of human bees.

"Salaam Aleykom. Befarmayeed! Our home is yours. Please come and sit down. Mahvash, get some shirini for the good people. But before you sit, let me introduce you to my son, Karim. Karim, you remember Parissa? What a wonderful young woman she's grown into! And look, last time you met Soraya she was a baby and now she is a young woman of ten. How pretty she has become! Now, please, all of you. Sit down. Make yourselves comfortable. I will fetch the tea. Please, Hajji-Hossein, help yourself to shirini. Mahvash, take it round to our guests. Please all of you – eat, eat."

They had squeezed themselves into the small visitor room and were sitting on the floor cushions amongst trays of sweetmeats. It was a cold February day and they had a Korsi, a low, blanket-covered table with a pan of hot charcoal underneath – against which they placed their feet for warmth.

Parissa sat next to Karim and both attempted to make cordial conversation, frequently at the same time. Her father was correct. He had changed. He was less shy than before it seemed. She supposed it was the result of his employment and she enquired how he was he enjoying it at the oil refinery.

And as he attempted to explain she watched his lips grasp at syllables perched upon his pillowy lips and felt guilty for the part she played in requesting them. "It is not b-bad," he eventually uttered before appearing to gain more confidence as he continued. "My lodgings in the apprentices' hostel are comfortable but basic."

She asked whether he fraternised with the British workers who had been shipped over to run the oil fields. He shook his head. He sometimes saw the occasional farangi on the street but their quarters at Braime were cordoned off to Irani nationals and the two were discouraged from socialising. Although one of the Irani water tank inspectors, a regular visitor to Braime, had spoken of the superior accommodation provided for the British, who lived in grand houses surrounded by rosebushes and tennis courts.

"All the more reason for change," intercepted her father. He had been listening to their conversation. "If we had control of our own oil we would at least treat our workers with respect. Tell me my boy, are you paid for taking this holiday to see your loving family?"

Karim lowered his head.

"There, you see!" cried her father beckoning fiercely to Jamshid Dashti, Karim's father. "Do you take my point? The Tudeh party were at least campaigning for higher wages and better living conditions. Now they have been outlawed there is no telling what kind of conditions your son will have to endure. I've heard they do not even grace you with running water so that you may do your ablutions for prayer. Is that right my boy? "

"We are allowed access to the pump for a few hours a day," said Karim.

"Well Dashti, this is not really the time for these conversations I have to admit. But if we had Irani members on the oil company board, at least to check the company books, that would be a start. And my final word on the matter is to remind you of the case of the good country of Mexico, who not so long ago declared the expropriation of foreign oil companies on their land. They have won back their sovereignty have they not? That is what we must do with ours."

Her father's diatribe had momentarily disabled the traffic of conversation but Poupak Dashti intercepted with her tray of shirini to lighten the mood. "Upon my soul Hajji-Hossein, you have eaten almost nothing! Please. Let me put some on your plate. Mahvash, get some more tea."

Karim and Parissa talked further of this and that. He complimented her on her carpet weaving skills; they happened to be sitting on one she had woven a number of years ago for the Dashti family. And she attempted to steer the conversation towards practical matters. His lips were full and pink and framed by a feeble, downy moustache. Although not handsome, his eyes had a certain kindness and his square jaw seemed to profess a distinctly dependable quality to his character. She could do worse, she thought.

Alas, fine looks do not testify honourable intentions, her mother had often reminded her. She had married Hajji-Hossein at the age of fourteen with no say in the matter at all.

On departure, Karim asked if he could write to her from Abadan. The postal system, he said, was very poor. But it was possible to get letters out. Parissa agreed, despite her reservations. The meeting had not changed her opinion on the matter. She knew she would find it a difficult marriage. She resolved to discuss it with her father and convince him of her doubts. It was likely to prove a gruelling conversation.

3

Tehran , 1949

In all his born days Mollah Mostafez had never heard anything like it. Even the Holy Imam Hossein, peace be upon him, would surely writhe in his tomb. A baby with multiple genitals was not the work of Allah but the devil himself.

"I suspect…….," suggested Mr Hakim the silversmith, in between lengthy puffs on his ghalyan, "it will be … handed over….. to the authorities." His smoke-ridden words, when they appeared, infringed the space immediately above his skullcap.

"They say the women have been wailing since two o'clock this morning. Their eyes must be as parched as a dried-out, salted fish!" said the teashop owner Mr Shariati, who himself possessed a disobedient squint and so frequently included references to the eyeball in his general phraseology.

Jamshid Dashti, the carpenter with two rusty front teeth, leant towards the middle of the rickety wooden table and bade the assembly to do likewise. It was getting dark outside and the small teahouse in which they were sitting was smeared with a bluish tint from the kerosene lantern hanging somewhere outside the window, in the walkway of the bazaar.

Five dimly lit faces came together in a taut circle around the flickering oil lamp which had newly been put on the table. Its luminary, yellow dance proceeded to flush out a variation of unwitting noses, brows and chins, laced with a multitude of wrinkles.

"I have heard," continued Dashti in a low whisper whilst smoothing down his tunic nonchalantly, "that Yousef Suleymani is refusing to believe he has fathered it!

Apparently he was heard shouting to his wife: is this Allah's work or yours?"

"I wonder if it is a boy or a girl," pondered Abbas Bidandoon, the tea carrier whose slow-wittedness usually astounded his compatriots, and today surprised even himself.

"I think you will find," said Dr Azizi, who had tried to distance himself from the gossip up to now, "a child with genital contradictions will be neither one nor the other."

Bidandoon was having none of it. Quite unusually, a small spell of intellect was travelling around his brain and he intended to grasp at it whilst he was able. His plump lips wriggled and writhed around his sparsely furnished gums, finally settling into a speculative pout, the tension of which forced a number of moustache hairs to stand to attention.

For a while he said nothing, determined to pluck his words carefully from the small selection made available to him on account of his very unfortunate mental circumstance. This state of affairs, so he had been told, had arisen as a consequence of his obscenely protracted birth – itself the result of an unusually large head attempting to exit through an uncommonly small passage. And, when finally delivered after forty-eight hours, so the story goes, baby Bidandoon had drawn no breath, in spite of vigorous pummellings by the midwife. His mouth, nose and ears were duly stuffed with cotton and his body wrapped in a shroud before one of the attendants realised he was moving. Much later, it was discovered that a lack of oxygen to his brain had resulted in a mild mental palsy with which he was destined to wrestle for a lifetime. And which had been improved, only marginally, by sixteen days of schooling in a religious Madreseh. He therefore spoke slowly in order to make sure there was no questioning of his lucidity.

"There must be a measure of proof," he said "within or without," he paused for a short while – and then continued "to provide a clue to the category of this misconceived offspring of nature." His final remarks were spluttered with a momentum not unlike a pregnant goat's final birthing push.

"What kind of clue?" asked the Mollah and immediately wished he hadn't.

Happily, the propeller of Bidandoon's brain had gathered a little speed and he proceeded to deliver a mildly coherent set of theories. "A hidden womb perhaps, a sack of seed, a semblance of female grace or a glimmer of male vigour," he concluded proudly.

Mollah's turban rocked to and fro as he scratched his black and white beard. "Well, I suppose you have a point," he said. "However, an easier way to tell would be this: if it cried solidly for a good few hours after birth it would likely be a girl; a boy if it cried only for a few minutes."

"I declare it to be in the strength of the legs," said Jamshid Dashti. "Vallah, by heaven, a powerful kick is the sign of a male. My boy had the kick of a stallion when he was only three hours old."

"The farangi medical hospitals in the capital are quite advanced these days," observed Dr Azizi. "I suspect they will decide to remove one set of genitals in favour of the other."

At that moment the door to the teashop opened and Hajji-Hossein Forooshi stepped inside, trailed by a light gust of snow. He brushed the remnants of white flakes from his coat and wiped his moustache with a small cloth before removing his hat and beating it on the side of the coal stove to dislodge the snow which had settled in the creases.

"Have you heard the news?" he asked, warming his hands above the stove in the corner, with his back to the assembled company.

"Yes, yes. It's a terrible tragedy," said the Mollah. "We have just been discussing it."

Hajji-Hossein pulled up a chair, poured himself a glass of burgundy-coloured chai from the samovar and leaned over to get the sugar bowl from across the table. Silver veins threading their way through his ebony hair twinkled in the lamplight as he moved.

"It is more than a tragedy," he said at long last, rolling a cube of sugar around his mouth before taking a sip of tea, "It is a setback beyond words. By all that is sacred, we can no longer kneel on our prayer mats and do nothing. We have loitered about the exterior for too long and now we must act before it is too late."

"Are you suggesting we involve ourselves?" asked the Mollah spluttering through a chickpea cake he had just put in his mouth.

"In Ali's name, yes! We have no option but to intervene. Otherwise we allow today's cock of the roost spawn tomorrow's mutant society."

"What kind of intervention do you have in mind exactly?"

"We, my dear men, have a duty to take part in the operation and help sever this diseased canker from within the limbs of humanity. A measure of careful preparation is all that is needed."

"By all accounts your head must be playing with your tail!" exclaimed Mr Dashti, his face a beacon of acute alarm, "Is this deluded sincerity or shallow mockery you ridicule us with?" He was, after all, a mere carpenter. In his most savage imagination he was unable to fancy his skills, or his humble tools, serving in any such gruesome purpose involving miniature genitalia.

"Consider this my friend. A saw, a chisel, and some nails – what better instruments with which to liberate your fellow mortal. And you – you are creative with your hands – you will be able to cobble something together I'm sure. It need not be elaborate of course. Something simple and functional will do the trick," said Hajji-Hossein casually in between mouthfuls of halva.

Mr Dashti was perplexed. "How will this achieve the desired effect, if ever I knew what the desired effect was?"

"The desired effect of course is for our voices to be heard," said Hajji-Hossein irritably. "The farangis and their disciples are endeavouring to wrap our testicals around our ears and we cannot allow it to continue. I have spoken to Mollah Jafari and Hajji Eskandar and they are in agreement. We have been idle for too long. You know that there has been a movement for this sort of thing for a while. And we have always hidden behind our faith, loathed to get involved. Someone handed to me this morning a copy of the Shahad, that leaflet distributed by the Toilers' party. There are plans for a protest outside the palace grounds in a few months. I intend to go and I am asking you all to consider showing your support. Dashti, your skills will be useful in constructing some banners and flags."

Mollah Mostafez scratched his beard for the umpteenth time, and adjusted his white turban. "My belly tells me each of our dialogues is on a pilgrimage to a different location: we are riding different camels; navigating separate ships. I presume you are not referring to the new birth we have recently witnessed," said he.

"If you allude to the birth of yet another dictatorship, I most certainly am."

"Not, then, the devastating defect of the Suleymanis' child who has to choose between being a boy or a girl. "

It was Hajji-Hossein's turn to look confused. Not for the first time, a stray piece of gossip had become entangled in his ruminations about the political system. It was quite tiresome. "No I am not!" he growled. "A thousand defective babies could not overshadow the torment we will be facing if we don't act now. Have you not heard the news?"

His friends shook their heads.

"There has been an assassination attempt on the Shah this afternoon. A state of emergency has been declared and the power is to be reined in."

"I have heard no such thing!" exclaimed the Mollah.

Hajji-Hossein stood and walked towards the counter at the side of the teahouse where he picked up a ghalyan. From the charcoal brazier he lifted a lump of burning coal, placed it on the bowl at the top of the water pipe and returned to the table. He continued: "The shooting took place whilst the Shah was attending an annual commemoration at the city's university. The bullets went into his face and he was injured, but he is alive."

Hajji-Hossein pulled out a small wooden box and a tin from his jacket pocket. From it he selected a mouthpiece which he fixed onto the stem of the water pipe. "The assassin," he continued, "was shot and killed by the king's guards. They say he is a communist sympathiser."

He paused to pull some damp tobacco which had been wrapped around a large piece of peeled cucumber to keep it moist. He pushed the tobacco into the bowl of the water pipe with the charcoal. It sizzled loudly and a thick ribbon of smoke exploded from the incinerating marriage. To his lips he placed the mouthpiece and inhaled deeply, the bubbling water below responding with every inhalation.

"From tonight we are all under martial law. In a few hours' time we will be expected to be off the streets. I tell you this is the beginning of the end. We have barely emerged from *one* absolute rule and now we are already in the arms of another."

Hajji-Hossein Forooshi had lived through three dictatorships, an incalculable number of assassinations, three revolutions, a civil war, a coup and two foreign occupations of his homeland. The last bout of tyranny had left a mighty scar on practising Muslims like himself. His country was still smarting from the enforced westernisation of the nation administered by the previous ruler.

And the modicum of popular rule promised by the current king had not even lasted the length of a pubescent boy's fantasy. Mohammad Reza Shah had clearly reached a point where the inevitable bacillus of absolutism had infected his royal brain. The declaration of martial law was an early symptom. Hajji-Hossein recognised it well, as did many of his circle.

"Take a look at this," said Hajji-Hossein pulling out a crumpled sheet of paper from under his tunic. "The Majlis – whatever its failings – has been usurped once again. We are under curfew, our newspapers have been ordered to close and a constituent assembly has been convened. The Shah has decided to take matters into his own hands, like his father. And the Tudeh party, the only one that might have had our interests at heart, has been outlawed. If we do not protest, our children will be dogged by the shadow of despotism and foreign interference until the last trumpet is blown."

"You know we are not really political animals, Hossein," said Mollah Mostafez. "Better to lie low. It is sure to boil over."

"Yes," said a worried Bidandoon. "Never anger a thirsty camel. The police already patrol the bazaar." He was thinking of his cousin, Habib, who had met a terrible fate under the previous Shah for daring to speak out. He'd been removed from his house in the middle of the night, never to be seen again.

"What do you say then. We are all to be cowards? We've remained aloof for *this* long. Thinking, whatever they do, it won't really affect the way we live and the responsibilities we have toward Allah. Don't you remember how it was? Arrested every day for refusing to wear the western brimmed hats which stopped us from touching our foreheads to the ground in prayer? And our women forced out from behind their veils? Perhaps you prefer to wait until they have eliminated the Sharia altogether and are handing out the crucifix on every street corner."

"Inshallah, it will not come to that," said Dr Azizi. "A tyrant may indeed pluck away a beard by the roots, yet still the jowl is left upon which it grew. You can be sure, the chin of Mohammad will remain forever on the countenance of Persia."

"Yes, but suppose the beard growing from it returns with a *golden* complexion!" squeaked Bidandoon in a troubled voice. "I fear, I have already seen an old man with a golden beard who serves tea at the bazaar!"

"Do not worry," said Dr Azizi. "That's old Mr Nassiri who is betrothed to his pipe. It is the nicotine that has stained his beard yellow."

"Well, it seems, as ever, we have little choice," said Hajji-Hossein. "We are destined to remain a dog with two masters: the tyrant king and the foreigner. And it is impossible to know who is making the rules," said Hajji-Hossein crossly.

"We know who is making the rules," said Mr Shariati. "It's like the Gheimeh puppet show. The farangi is the Morshed who controls the puppet king and forces him to surrender our beloved country's resources," said Shariati.

"You are right Jalal," said Hajji-Hossein "We have only ever wished for a degree of self-determination. And it now seems as inconceivable as plucking a fig from a thistle!" He stood up with gusto and went over to the small steamed-up window. Using a cloth from his pocket he wiped a small transparent circle from which to peer out into the bazaar walkway.

"I have heard talk in some quarters that there is a movement to seize back our oil from the British," said Mr Shariati. "I cannot even imagine what kind of catastrophe would befall us if we did such a thing."

"If we had thought this same way forty years ago, Agha, we would not have had a parliament and a constitution today. You were there, fighting for the cause, I remember," said Hajji-Hossein.

"Yes and how many cousins did I lose for the sake of it? And what purpose has it served? What good is a toothless institution of the people which capitulates in the face of the first corrupt Shah to come across its path."

"If they would simply let us go about our business in the holy keeping of Allah, we could tolerate one-hundred-thousand mouthfuls of insolence and digest a stomach-full of abomination. Why is it that they speak of liberty and freedom of expression on this continent of Europe and yet will not deign to allow us equal freedom to go about our business?"

They were suddenly interrupted.

"Pedar! Father. Come quickly!" The voice of a young boy knocking on the window was muffled from outside.

Hajji-Hossein reached across and opened the rickety teahouse door. His small son, who had been beckoning from the other side of the window, now stuck his head into the teahouse.

"Come quickly they are arresting Mr Mohebi, the wool carder!" he cried.

"Where?" asked Bidandoon.

"Here, in the bazaar. He is trying to resist."

The men put on their coats and followed Hajji-Hossein out of the teashop and down the vaulted passageways – past a line of small stalls. Most bazaaris were packing up for the day. Ali Forooshi led the way with a brisk pace, occasionally looking behind him to make sure his father was keeping up. Mollah Mostafez who was unused to a vigorous pace frequently tripped over his robe and was obliged to keep his hand on his turban for fear of it falling off. It was a cold February evening and their hot breath trailed behind as they ran. An angry snow attempted to penetrate each little opening amongst the bazaar architraves.

A little further on shouting could be heard and on their approach it grew louder, emanating from the outside corner of one of the enclaves. The scene was a crowd of people in the centre of which two military policemen, with peaked hats and guns, were searching one of the tradesmen's stalls, which he had started to pack up. Balls of brightly coloured wool lay in the snow on the ground, wet and muddy. As one official rummaged through Parvis Mohebi's belongings another held him tightly by the arm. He struggled and shouted.

"In the name of Allah, by my own soul, by the head of my father, let me rest in peace. I have no communist connections. I hate the vixens. I'm just a poor wool trader. Let me go. Find your reward in heaven before it's too late!"

"Let him go you hell-burning, father of a dog!" cried a man in the crowd.

Hajji-Hossein pushed through the throng. "My dear Agha, why are you arresting this poor servant who has done nothing wrong other than to serve his community and his God?" he said.

"Hajji Forooshi, thank god you are here!" exclaimed the prisoner, struggling to kiss his hand. "Tell them I have done nothing. I have a family and six children. They will all be condemned if I am!"

"Who are *you*?" asked one of the military.

"I am Hajji-Hossein Forooshi, carpet seller and member of the guild of carpet makers. I work in the bazaar every day – we are a peaceful crowd. We don't want any trouble. We are here to make a livelihood." (The crowd was getting bigger). "Why are you arresting this man?"

"We are under orders to arrest communist sympathisers and members of the Tudeh party. This man has been leading protests and inciting anti-Shah propaganda."

"It's all lies!" shouted Mr Mohebi and fought to get away. One of the officers smacked the side of his face with the butt of a gun. Mohebi's ear began to bleed. Trickles of blood ran down his cheek and dripped onto a patch of snow directly below.

"Someone fetch his wife!" shouted one of the stall holders.

"I'm sure you have mistaken this man for someone else," said Hajji-Hossein attempting a morsel of diplomacy. "Can we not come to an agreement?"

It was getting dark and one of the officers shone a torch up and down Hajji-Hossein's face, inspecting it carefully.

"Hey old man, perhaps you have not heard that your king has been shot and injured in an attempted assassination?"

He took a strand of Hajji-Hossein's black moustache and twisted it repeatedly so that the skin underneath became taut. "Perhaps you do not even care. Is that it?"

Hajji-Hossein attempted to speak. "I hope the Shah libs a long and frosferous life. Vut you will not hind his enemies here."

The officer pulled Hossein's face close-up to his own, using his moustache.

"Are you sure about that?" he asked baring his yellow teeth. Hossein did not reply. The officer pushed him away.

"Bring the wool merchant!" said the officer to his underling. And turning to survey the hushed crowd he growled in a low voice, "We will be watching you."

A woman pushed her way to the front of the mass. She was clutching a baby under one arm and attempted to hold her floor-length veil around her head with the other.

"In god's name, let him go. He has done nothing!" she cried, squeezing the officer's arm. "I am the mother of his children. We are poor people, if he goes we will have no food. We will wither and die. Look, I am a nursing mother!" She thrust her baby into the officer's face. "Do you want me to dry up? Do you want my baby to suffer?"

The officer looked at her coldly. "Take off that chador so that I can see your face woman," he ordered.

She let her long veil slip off her head and onto her shoulders. The officer pulled it off her shoulders roughly. "Look at yourself, mother," he said. "You are not even able to keep up with the times! You and all your kind, hiding behind these pieces of filthy rag!" He ripped the chador it in half. "Don't you know your fellow sisters have given this up long ago? Go get yourself a nice coat from the high street. Show a bit of leg for a change!"

The other official sniggered and there was a rustle in the crowd as the women pulled off their veils.

"Bring the man!" the officer ordered, "And all of you get into your houses or I will arrest you all for breaking the curfew!"

Mr Mohebi's wife clutched at her husband, crying.

"Go home woman," he whispered. "I will be back shortly."

"Ay vay, what am I to do without you!" she sobbed.

"Allah will look after me, don't worry," said he. And before long they were all gone.

The only trace of the incident was a small pool of blood in the snow, seeping outwards to form a pretty pattern, quite unrepresentative of the ugly scene which spawned it. Mahvash Mohebi was on the ground, sobbing, shivering and attempting pick up the leftovers of the wool strewn all about.

Dr Azizi pulled her up gently. "Come, I will take you home," he said.

The crowd of people started to disperse, talking amongst themselves. "That's what happens when a king has too much power!" shouted one man. "Are we ever to be left alone to live our lives?"

Hajji-Hossein, his lip still smarting from the incident, called his son over. "Let's get home," he said.

"Pedar, what is happening?" asked Ali. "Why have they arrested Mr Mohebi? Has he done something wrong?"

"I don't know my son. But do not worry yourself. You're too young to be worried."

"I am twelve. That is almost old enough to run a business!" exclaimed Ali Forooshi.

"Yes, you're right pessaram. You're very right. One day soon I'll explain."

"Can't you explain now? It's to do with the Shah isn't it? Is he a very bad man?"

"No, he is not a bad man. He is simply misguided and out of touch with his people."

"Parissa says his people are out of touch with him," suggested Ali.

"You know your sister has a very odd mind like that! You are not to listen to what she says, do you hear me? Now let us go home. It's freezing and they say it's going to snow again tomorrow."

****

On returning home Ali was bursting with news of the assassination attempt on the Shah, and Mr Mohebi's arrest.

"Do you know what Parissa? They think he is a traitor!" he said as his sister laid the sofreh for some food.

They sat on the floor to eat.

"What's a traitor?" asked her sister Soraya

"Someone who works for the Tudeh party of course!" Ali replied.

"Well, father sometimes goes to their meetings, don't you father? I have heard you say so. Does that mean you are a traitor too?" asked Soraya.

"Of course not!" interrupted Ali, "Everyone knows you are only a traitor once you are arrested. Father hasn't been arrested, so he is not."

"Eat please," said Hajji-Hossein sternly as Parissa ladled Abgoosht into their bowls. He detected the continuance of their conversation, under their various breaths and behind their small hands.

When the meal was cleared, Hajji-Hossein reached for his opium box. He knew Parissa did not like him smoking this duplicitous remedy. She was right to question it. His flesh became unholy and his reasoning crippled. But it had been his succour since the death of his wife: the only ease for his troubled mind. And he frequently had to endure his daughter's idle talk, straight from the bathhouse, about the strictest of characters whose lives had been ruined by opiates. Last week it was Mr Sardari, the potter, who had been found by the authorities in urine-soaked clothes after having lain in a stupefied state for the whole summer.

With a penknife, Hajji-Hossein pinched off a small nugget from the dark brown bar which he had taken out of the wooden box. After weighing it on a miniature pair of scales he placed the lump on the bowl of his water pipe. From the stem of the mouthpiece he inhaled the corrupt and caramelised smoke. Closing his eyelids with sluggish relief, his habitually proud torso melted into a buttery corpse over the cushions. To this day, the speed at which he became caught in its delusionary current amazed him still

Before long he had drifted into a state of snoring wakefulness, where his mind shuffled vividly through the detail of the day. An unpopular king – shot in the mouth. Students chanting in the streets for the return of his country's black gold. And the strange case of a child born with multiple genitals. These were indeed distorted times. And as his mind was carried away he heard his mouth, independent of his will, mutter a line from the Bostan of Saadi: "The king may be as the tree; but the people are as the root. And it is from the root which the tree acquires strength."

4

London, 2003

The final conclusion came during an editorial meeting: at the exact moment when Greg Hardy, in his bird-like tone, pitched the idea of how to boil the perfect potato. To be more precise – it actually took place post-utterance. Yes: post utterance and immediately after that moment of silence, during which the assembled company considered Greg's 'creative' proposal. It was at some point during the subsequent avalanche of totally disproportionate applause that Manu Zand resolved to burn a few bridges.

In future conversations with his children he would need to justify where those bridges went. He couldn't blame it on Greg. The boiled potato incident was merely a catalyst. Those kinds of excuses wouldn't wash with kids. They had wits about them. He knew that from Alice's three year old niece. She had spotted him flicking five South African Rand to a busker in Camden, and with one barefaced toddler question had subsequently reduced him to a complete charlatan.

Surely it couldn't be difficult. Lawyers did it all the time – and for more preposterous reasons.

In defence of the abandonment of a successful career as a food critic.

Number one. Lack of tools to do the job – aka no sense of taste or smell. Clearly, that was a no-brainer. What about the less convincing grounds: the burden of mealtime responsibility. It was as hard to explain as finding the source of an unscratchable itch. Simply put: there was a yearning to eat a delicious meal without obligations. Without the need to assess. To evaluate. Measure each tang. Weigh up every flavour. There was no guarantee that would ever be possible, but he needed to experience it.

And finally, there was a real sense that some global life-sifting was called for. Instigated mainly by that glorious work of art now positioned across his oak floorboards. He felt it to be more magnificent and prophetic with each additional day it remained in his possession. But equally it was beginning to disorientate him to the point of paranoia.

It was an explosion of colour in his black-and-white life. And it prompted recognition of how stark his existence had been up to the present point. Every time he glanced at the spidery Anglo-Saxon characters embedded in the multicoloured geometric patterns it threw out more meaning. Of the fateful clash of civilisations. Of the richness of time. Of the interlocking between harmony and distress. And the message, it seemed, was for him. He needed only to decipher it.

Although superstition had never been part of Manu's constitution, he felt its authority now. It implied that a part of him had been left fallow. The time for ploughing was henceforth.

So when he broached the subject of his resignation to his editor her head jerked back, as though he had pierced her forehead with an arrow, and she blinked, wide-eyed.

Manu was leaning against the rim of a beech-effect sideboard having an after-shock moment, as he realised there was no return from whence he came.

Jan Jackson, a masculine-looking woman wearing a colourful flowery dress that clashed equally with face and body, was banging her pen against her teeth as she sat behind her desk. "Well, that's a little drastic don't you think?" she said.

"I need to take substantial time off and this seems the best way," explained Manu, attempting to drown out the protesting voices in his conscience.

"And anyway – I'm not really much use to you in this state."

She searched his face, now tapping her pen on the table.

"I think it's rather reckless. And I can't let you do it. For God's sake, take a month off. If you still feel the same way at the end of the month, come back; I'll fire you myself!"

She yanked her muscular torso out of the chair, strode across to the centre of the room and heaved her well-toned rump onto a high square table in front of him. "What do you say to that?" asked the rugby player in drag, as she swung her legs from side to side, like a flirtatious adolescent.

"Only if you're sure?" said Manu, purposely resisting the feminine call-to-action emanating from her stockinged calves, which concluded in a pair of red court shoes.

"Yes that should be fine. We've got a new journo starting this week. He's not as experienced as you. But I can put him on food and Sarah will just have to hold the fort whilst you're away."

He was relieved and pleased at the outcome and spent the rest of the morning excitedly clearing his desk. The array of choices in front of him made him feel exhilarated and debilitated in equal measure. Is this what people felt like when they were told they had a month to live? Lists of things he had always wanted to accomplish poured into his woolly head.

Before he left he made a phone call from his desk.

"Cy. It's Manu. Just wondered if you were around at lunchtime. Can we meet up at Laure's café?" He raised his hand to another colleague who was waving to him from across the room. "No. Nothing in particular. Well, a little Persian history maybe. Actually I've just been given a month off so I'm celebrating. I'll tell you about it when I see you. And if you have a copy of Omar Khayyam's Rubaiyat in Farsi can you bring it with you."

At the Finchley Road end of London, Laure Doucette let herself into her small café peaked with a candy-striped awning. Inside it was grey and cold. She went to the boiler in the cupboard behind the counter to turn on the heating. Her large mass of caramel-coloured hair was squeezed into a blue cap. A solitary curl had wriggled out and as she turned on the little electric blower on the floor in the corner of the room it began to perform the samba around her face. She opened the blinds and the bright sun erupted through the window panes tossing yellow squares across the wooden floor.

As she was taking off her coat the little bell on the door pinged and a short, plump little woman in a pink headscarf marched in with the purposeful stride of an award-winning businesswoman. She quickly unbuttoned her exceptionally tight fitting mackintosh, which had the unenviable responsibility of clenching together all manner of wayward bodily parts from the knees upwards.

Phyllis Sotheby, aged 65, had been busy-bodying herself at Soupcon Café since its opening. Her impenetrable small talk had fortified the very foundations of the business. She'd been taken on as part of a job lot when the previous venture, a charity shop for the deaf, had folded. Having worked in an environment where her discourse had gone unheard for thirteen years, Phyllis Sotheby had since made up for lost time. She often squeezed so many words into a phrase that Laure would hold her breath in tandem, fearing the poor woman would expire.

Phyllis untied her headscarf, pushed back her fluffy grey hair and peeled off the last sleeve of her coat with a mighty yank. She had come on the bus. And what a bleedin' journey it was. Best part of an hour. That Mayor had a lot to answer for, talking of which… wasn't he caught drunk at some do or other? That reminded her of a lovely glass of wine she had the other day, Cabinet Sobinon. Sobinon or Sobingong? French, or was it German? Actually, no, it was French…..

Her words lost their momentum as she gasped to take a much needed breath.

Laure interrupted before she could continue. "Let's put on the kettle and sort the vegetables. I've got today's menu here: Smoked Carrot; Lamb and Barley Broth; Potage of Leek and Brie; Mexican Tomato and Chicken Consommé with sage. Samantha is coming in earlier today so she can help with the peeling."

Phyllis took the cue and scuttled off to the kitchen. They spent the morning peeling and boiling, for that was mostly what was involved in a soup café. And by noon the place was already three-quarters full. A lanky man, totally grey except for a ginger cactus beard, sipped his soup whilst reading Don Quixote. The leaky eyes of a white poodle, sitting under the next table, followed the journey of his spoon from bowl to mouth, and back to bowl. In another corner three young mothers surrounded by babies and prams exchanged views on nappy creams, male bonding and George Clooney.

Manu arrived at the café just as his stomach began give voice to its hunger. He had not been in contact with Laure for a few weeks. And she hadn't been in touch either, which was unusual. They were close friends after all. Especially since John deserted her a few years ago for a waitress who worked in their Soho restaurant. Last he heard, John Laird had returned to Scotland to play personal chef to a Scottish Earl. Laure had been better off without him. He was one of those overweening characters with a frustratingly good looking face, and an irritatingly sharp intellect. No wonder it had taken her a good few years to get over it.

Even the flittingly brief explosion of an affair she had with Manu, after the break-up, had not been enough to divert her attention. That episode had frightened them both: Laure because she was still smarting and confused, and Manu because it had been the most passionate relationship of his lifetime. He'd locked the incident away. Even the therapist hound had been unable to expose that little trauma, which made him feel quite smug.

Phyllis greeted him at the counter with a torrent of ceremonial words. How nice it was to see him. Was it true he wasn't well? A friend of hers had lost her sense of smell once. Or was it her balance? It might have been her balance because… yes, they'd given her a walking stick….

"Nice to see you Phyllis," Manu responded. "I have been under the weather but nothing that a bowl of broth can't fix."

She handed him a small handwritten menu from which he chose his favourite: Potage of Leek and Brie. Sticking to the familiar, he reasoned, may lead to tasting by recollection, if nothing else.

Laure appeared from the kitchen her cheeks flushed, wiping her hands on her apron. "You have been avoiding me," she said, offering her cheek to him over the counter before following him to the table at the window.

"How are you feeling?" she asked as they sat down. "Have you recovered?"

"No," said Manu. "I still can't smell or taste anything, although I feel alright in myself – perhaps a bit light-headed maybe. The blood tests haven't picked anything up. What about you. You look a bit rushed off your feet."

"Yes. Well it's always like that in the winter. But I've been extremely busy, more than usual. Seems like the whole world has cottoned on to soup!"

Her usually dark blue eyes looked rather flat and despite the flush in her cheeks she looked weary.

"Why don't *you* take some time off for a while?" he asked

"We'll see. My father is still unwell so I shall pop over and visit him soon. Actually, I wonder if you could source me a trainee chef or someone who could take over for a week or so."

"I'll ask around," said Manu as he took the bowl of soup which had arrived. "I'm having a few weeks off myself. I think it's best. Might even spend quality time with Alice."

"Still not going well then?" she asked.

Manu scowled and shook his head.

"Talk to her, Manu." she said. "The children thing, you know."

He grunted. "I suppose. I'm just not sure what I want these days."

"I can tell you what you *need*!" a bellow from behind him made him jump. "Take the advice of Dr Jamshidi. You need to loosen up; confront your demons!"

Cyrus Jamshidi threw onto the table in front of Manu a book of poetry by Omar Khayyam, before parachuting his hands onto Laure's shoulders. "Hello gorgeous!" he whispered, picking up her hand and obliging it to accept his kiss.

"You look radiant today. Good enough to eat! Etes-vous a la carte?"

Manu rolled his eyes. Despite being close friends, everything about Cyrus was the converse of himself. Their complexion was similar it was true. But Cyrus's blue, unshaven stubble was sexy, his greasy hair appeared sleek, and his indifferent sense of fashion was chic. Today he was wearing tight jeans and a windcheater. His hairy hand, (parading an overweight silver identity bracelet with an inscription in Farsi) pulled up a chair and turned it backwards. He sat with the back of the chair pressed against his chest like a shield. The protruding hairs from his unbuttoned shirt fought to be seen above the wooden breastplate. It was all terribly clichéd, but it worked like a dream.

Cyrus then proceeded to run through the usual rituals: the tucking of the black hair behind the ears after every minor repartee; the huge glinty-eye grin; the flashing of the immaculate white teeth; with a finale of the suggestive wink, followed by a 'naughty little boy' pout, which (for some reason quite beyond comprehension) charmed the pants off whatever sex he was fraternising with. Now he was holding onto Laure's hand like a sick puppy. He was gazing into her eyes whilst firing jokes to disarm her. She was even blushing. Blushing for goodness sake. Surely Laure wouldn't fall for that.

Although his command of English was technically immaculate, he had an Iranian accent, glazed with an American twang. His Ts had a shrill but clipped reverberation and his Rs were coated in a deep throaty growl. It sounded engaging and exotic no doubt. There it was again, she was definitely blushing. A gust of irritation seethed through Manu's body. Did Cyrus seriously think she would be interested?

"I'll have a burger with chips," said his friend to the young girl who offered to serve him. "Oh I forgot. You only do healthy food here!" he winked to stop the waitress panicking. "Gimme the tomato."

Laughing, Laure stood up to return to the kitchen.

"Hey babe. You're not going?" lamented Cyrus in a Peter Pan kind of voice.

"Sorry. I must get back," said Laure. "Oh Manu, say good bye before you go?"

"So, what's this thing you wanted to talk to me about then?" said Cyrus, pinching a piece of bread from Manu's plate.

"Thing?"

"Persian history? You said on the phone?" said Cyrus, as he took the bowl of tomato soup from the waitress.

"Well, not Persian history as such. It's just this rug I have from my old neighbour back in Tehran."

Manu ran through the story of the carpet as Cyrus supped his soup.

At the appropriate point, Cyrus raised one eyebrow and looked up from his bowl, his spoon poised by his mouth. "And it's in English?"

"Yes."

"What, actually *woven* in English?"

"Yeah."

"I don't understand."

"There's a translation of The Rubaiyat by..."

"Yes, Edward Fitzgerald. I know."

"There you go then. A line from his translation."

"And it's actually in *English* as opposed to Farsi?"

"Oh for goodness sake!"

"Okay, Okay. What's the line?"

Manu recited the passage from his mother's book. Cyrus picked up his own book of poetry on the table and flicked through it. "Here we are. The forty-seventh quatrain," he said.

The man was well versed in Iranian literature, having studied it at university in Paris, and he demonstrated it by reading the lines loudly in Farsi with added dramatic resonance.

People in the café began to look round to see what all the commotion was about.

"Keep your voice down. People are looking!" said Manu under his breath.

"Hey *baradar*, relax," said Cyrus. "No one's going to *arrest* us."

"Okay fine. But it's embarrassing. Anyway, why would a carpet weaver in Iran, with no likely knowledge of English, weave into a rug an *English* version of a Persian poem? It just doesn't make sense. And what does the actual translation you've just read mean?"

"Well it's not sinister if that's what you are implying. It speaks of being grateful for wine and love, because once you die it's an empty space. So basically it tells you to enjoy yourself before you kick the bucket! Or something like that."

"Oh, right. Not what I was expecting," said Manu.

"No it doesn't make much sense. Did you say the old lady got the carpet in 1951?"

"Yes."

"And there's a reference to Abadan on the back?"

"Yes."

"Well that may be a clue because, if I'm not mistaken my dear Watson, that was the year the Anglo Iranian Oil Company was nationalised."

"Of course," said Manu, in an attempt to conceal a total blank. It was official. He knew nothing about his country's history. (Wasn't the Shah like a benevolent leader? Hadn't he handed back property to the poor?)

"And Abadan, of course, is where the oil refinery was based," continued Cyrus authoritatively.

"Right, yes," said Manu fumbling with his spoon.

"There must have been loads of English personnel living there at the time. But if this was commissioned as some kind of souvenir, you'd think they'd want the script in Farsi, not English. Maybe it's political, who knows?"

"Yes, maybe. Do you want a coffee?" said Manu.

There was a level of ignorance beyond which he was incapable of confessing.

"No, I've got to go. Got some editing on this documentary, you know, about protests over Iraq?" said Cyrus standing up to go. "Anyway, it's interesting. If there's a sinister story attached I'd be up for investigating. Perhaps it's a clandestine message, from a secret agent! Let me know if you come up with anything."

"Yeah , yeah. Okay."

"Do you want to borrow this book of the Rubaiyat?" said Cyrus.

"Not sure if there's much point. My Farsi is equivalent to a ten year old's," said Manu, glumly.

"Never too late!" Cyrus flashed a smile as he dropped some money on the table before he left.

Chastened by his ignorance, on his way home Manu stopped off at George's Bookshop and picked up a few digested accounts of Iranian post-war history, which he spent the afternoon reading.

His knowledge of the country's political history was about as comprehensive as a Ladybird book. The revolution, which had forced his family to flee Iran when he was a teenager, was a distant story, decoupled from own autobiography. It had never been of any interest to him. Why? Because he had lived through a childhood of comfortable pottering, in a cocoon woven by loving parents with no particular interest in religion or politics. The cocoon had the luxury of a servant and a swimming pool. Inside the cocoon dinner parties, social events and extravagant seaside holidays took place, to which children were always invited. Manu had only left the comfort of the cocoon twice: once after the death of his brother; the other time on a visit to Pashti's home.

A small, frail looking old lady, Pashti appeared every day at six in the morning and departed after serving the evening meal. It was like having someone else's grandmother on a perpetual visit. If she was ill her daughter would appear. She had no grasp of the English language except for the word 'milk'. Her version sounded like the cry of a cat, with a 'k' at the end.

One night his parents had an important function and due to last minute arrangements were unable to get a babysitter. They asked Pashti to take Manu and his brother to her house for the night. Would they have allowed this had they known where she lived? Probably not. Her home was a small, square, mud hut on a piece of wasteland, next to mounds of stinking rubbish and narrow channels of effluent. The whole extended family had squeezed their life into one room which led off a small courtyard, offering a tap for ablutions and a concealed pit for excretions.

In the corner of the room languished a headless, old, rocking-horse. Manu recognised it as one his mother had discarded the previous year. And the bulk of tight space was dressed from head to toe in Zand family leftovers. Nooks and crannies were punctuated by battered toys Manu had not seen since his younger days. A small sideboard, once in a Zand corridor, now stood battle-scarred against the mud wall: its missing leg replaced with a glass bottle. Even the clothes worn by Pashti's grandchildren were distorted variations of Manu's castoffs. The scene was a complete inversion of the Zand family bubble: its alter ego. It was the Mr Hyde to all things Jekyll in Zand's life. And it was the first indication that the Zand family cocoon was suspended somewhere between ignorance and complete fantasy. The incident had remained a small scar on his conscience.

Now, Manu sat disconsolately on his new Persian rug, feeling the raw air aftermath of a burst bubble. Scattered around him, in historical volumes, was an abundance of bookish truths. Having tiptoed through its vast narrative and become tangled in the cause and effect of it all, he had gained a perspective which had been lost on him previously. By five thirty in the afternoon a series of illusions had been well and truly shattered. 1) His boyhood benign dictator –

was no less than a ruthless sidekick of the occident. 2) The country that had taken him in and which he had grown to admire had taken advantage of a vulnerable nation, fortified totalitarianism, and suppressed fledgling democratic rule. And 3) The BP petrol station at the end of his road, where he often filled his tank, owed its prosperity to aggressive profiteering from Persian oil.

Manu went to the fridge. It was empty except for a three grumpy looking tomatoes and a resigned looking carton of orange juice. Since the onset of his condition he had refrained from stocking cupboards or the fridge. Even now, there lingered a kind of futility to it all. He picked up the tomato and sniffed around the skin. It was barren.

If ever there was both occasion and reason to surrender to one's constant cravings, it was now. Surely there was a legitimacy in indulging to your heart's content when saddled with an impotent palate. Even the dietary dictator would 'get it', wouldn't he? For years Manu had resisted the temptation to confront this tyrant which had established a permanent residency inside his head. It was a despotic commander-in-chief, a sort of Mussolini of the Mind, in skin-tight lycra shorts and trainers. MoM regularly quashed any gastro-cravings with regimental force and had insisted on manacling all gluttonous behaviour to Manu's increasingly overweight imagination. 'Real life,' insisted MoM, should be commandeered by a series of regulations, of which *No-Second-Helpings* was one and *No-Snacking* a significant other. Otherwise, how would a foodie who eats for a living get by?

Long before 'the event', there had been consistent rumblings from the digestive department, signalling rebellion in the ranks. MoM's autocratic regime had been loosening its grip and members of the organ community were showing collective discontent. For a long time they had been petitioning Manu to review his lifestyle and cut them a trifle of slack. Why was it that every other entity on the planet was allowed to partake in guiltless piggery?

Despite the brewing of this internal mayhem, Manu's conscience had been loath to get involved. *Better the dictator you know* had always been the overriding motto of the moment. However desirous regime change was, it could be risky. And the consequences could prove to be a weighty burden, with all the personifications of a mature Orson Welles. And thus far, a mid-life banquet, though tempting, had remained a utopian carvery beyond immediate reach.

Now though, faced with a vacuum where taste, smell and career were concerned, it could well be time for the gorging to begin!

5

London, 2003

"Come to Iran? What do you mean exactly?"

Manu was leaning against the bar in The Flask with a quizzical look.

"Er, for a holiday?" said Cyrus, a ripple of condescension working its way across his face and stopping short of a smirk. "You know. That thing? That thing people take occasionally when they need a break?"

He leaned forward to stub out his cigarette in the ashtray next to Manu's elbow.

"Why would I do that? It's the very place I'm trying to erase from my mind," said Manu.

"What is it with you? What's the big deal?" said Cyrus trying to catch the attention of the barman in the background.

"That's just it. It's not a big deal. Why would I *want* to go back? I have no interest in the place."

Cyrus pointed a finger towards his friend's face. "Let's see. You have a month off work. You have nothing better to do. You want to find out about this carpet and where it came from. I'm planning to see my family for No-Ruz. You could come with me."

"You're going back home for the New Year?" said Manu.

"That's the idea, yes. Although I'm a little broke – so still considering it."

"Instead of coming with you, how about I pay you to do some research while you are there?"

"You're going to *pay* me to research? Research what? Deevaneh hasti?"

"No, I'm not crazy," said Manu. "And can we keep it in English, please?"

Cyrus's face broke into a syrupy grin. "When are you going to face your fears, agha jahn?" he said putting his arm around Manu.

Manu looked around the room and shook it off with half a smile. He then beckoned his friend towards a free table.

"What fears do you think I need to face?" he asked as they sat down.

"You are denying your roots, man. It's crazy. Look at me. I am happy with myself. I don't have to pretend I'm English. See over there: those gorgeous girls looking over at us?"

"What about them?"

"They don't care that we are not natives. They think it's quite sexy. Look. The blonde one's smiling at me right now." He nodded towards the far table and raised his glass to them with a suggestive wink. The girls looked at each other and erupted.

"Stop that, for God's sake! Anyway they almost certainly think we're Italian or something. If they knew we were from the Middle East they would run a mile."

"You have to do something about this enormous chip on top of your shoulder," said Cyrus.

"There is no chip," said Manu gruffly tearing open his third packet of crisps that evening. He stuffed a few in his mouth. Actually, the 'chip's' existence had already been confirmed. Confirmed by Mrs Friedlander, one-time therapist with confrontational breasts and a cajoling voice. Verification had come following a short rifle (by her) through his emotional baggage, using a range of analytical tools with dubious origins and horrible sounding names. It was an unpleasant experience and one in which a series of suppressed ghosts had exposed themselves crudely. He would have been quite content to thrust them back into his box of psychoses, but she insisted on withdrawing each raw and tormented knot into the present, for inspection right under his nose.

Ah, this looked interesting: the death of a younger brother, drowned at the age of four. How did he feel? What was it like?

Tragic. Naturally. He had fallen into the pool. Manu was so busy playing that he had not raised the alarm soon enough. Or that was his recollection. It was alright, his parents had never really reproached him.

Had he felt just a little accountable? Possibly a little. Okay, okay. There *was* the small galaxy of guilt. What now?

Perhaps this had shaped his reaction to responsibility and relationships: the disciplinarian quest for remaining in control; his fear of forming close attachments? They all fitted rather snugly into Mrs Friedlander's chest of apocalyptic psychoanalyses.

Unhappily, the chest (however full) never appeared to be full enough. Friedlander's hounding instincts, having had a whiff, were now lured by the scent of tortured soul. What was this. A bout of cultural schizophrenia perhaps? He remembered her face lighting up as though she had unearthed the very root of his troubled mind.

A vigorous game of conversational tennis had ensued.

What difficulties had he faced as a teenager settling in London after growing up in Iran?

Social exclusion, misinterpretation, prejudice, tasteless food and cold weather.

How had he dealt with that?

Suppression of his Middle Eastern identity.

How?

Self-denial. Repression. Isolation. Secrecy.

Had he ever wished to return to his country of birth?

No.

Why not?

Because the religious revolution had closed the door.

Was he not a Muslim himself?

No.

Had he made an effort to understand it?

No.

He had not returned to Mrs Friedlander's bosom thereafter. As he perceived it, the experience had been more of an agitation than an awakening. There was no pot of gold, no revelation and, without question, no exit from the wilderness.

"Let's invite them over and find out," said Cyrus.

“Invite who over?”

“The girls. Let’s invite them over and find out.”

“Find what out?”

“Find out if they think we’re Italian.”

“Definitely not!” said Manu. It was a typical example of Cyrus’ thick skin. Unlike himself, the man presented an intact and unambiguous identity, whatever part of the world he happened to find himself in.

“Anyway. You haven’t told me what you think of idea,” said Cyrus.

“I *have* told you. I’m not interested.”

Manu looked at his watch. Where was Alice? She was supposed to have joined them.

“You can stay with my parents. They have a spare room. They would be so happy to meet you. And I could show you around.”

“Perhaps she’s had to work late,” said Manu.

“Who?”

“Alice.”

“Just say you’ll think about it.”

“I’ll give her a ring,” said Manu and stood up to go to the bar.

An hour later, Manu was in his flat, preparing a meal. Marengo Chicken wasn’t a particular favourite, but the three grumpy tomatoes had persuaded him to put them out of their misery. The other important ingredient, a slosh of cognac, gave him an excuse to keep the bottle in close proximity for medicinal purposes.

It was a relief to progress to real food. Over the past few days the take-away had furtively worked its way to the top of his daily menu. There it sat, with its artificial smirk and extravagant twang. Manu had found himself yielding to its convenience and was dismayed. But there was no point in spending money on exquisite ingredients that tasted of nothing. This was the first time he had attempted to cook a proper meal since the bereavement. He considered it a bereavement now. Where previously they were ‘missing’; now they were ‘missing, presumed dead’.

He set about frying the chicken pieces in some olive oil, crushed garlic, and cognac. Despite having prepared the dish a number of times, until now he hadn't contemplated the essential role played by the unassuming taste bud in its formation. That he remembered all the ingredients and the approximate weights and measures was immaterial. Without sampling along the way he simply couldn't judge. All freeform cookery skills (first savour then flavour) had become redundant. It was a sort of culinary blindness. For which the only cure was a recipe book. A recipe book! That was something which had always been for amateurs. Now he was one of them.

Pierre Dumont, good friend and Michelin Star chef at La Maison de Bonheur, in Mayfair, had taunted him recently with descriptions of his new à-la-carte menu. "There is something on there that will cut through your incapabilities like a knife my friend," he had suggested. "I challenge you to try it and say you can't taste it."

He wasn't sure he could go through the trauma again.

Alice arrived as he was putting his concoction in the oven. She looked tired and slumped onto the leather sofa, kicking off her shoes.

"My god, it's hot in here! What's for dinner? I'm starving."

Chicken Marengo turned out to be chicken disaster. Too much salt, not enough garlic – all reviews provided by Alice. This was really starting to get him down.

They settled down on the couch to watch TV and Alice fell asleep almost straight away.

The truth about their partnership was this: it had settled into mediocrity, sidled into the middle-lane, sat on the fence. In a nutshell, they had averaged themselves out.

Worse still, at certain points where their aspirations did coincide, these were the very points of least usefulness and most irrelevance. She loved black coffee, as he did. He despised Hip-Hop, as did she. This was as synergic as it got these days. Subtract the sex and you were left with the bare minimum necessary to sustain a relationship.

But at least this relationship had been the longest. Many of his Affaires de Coeur had been short and sweet – the majority only short. Being schooled largely in the private, single-sex, arena had meant a belated entrance to the institution of lovemaking. Once admitted, Manu had experimented (with extreme vigour) a variety of positions ranging from Cadet to Casanova and found all of them equally unsatisfying. Put simply: he could not master the sexual intricacies; failed to understand the purpose; and seldom grasped the rationale. Friendship from a friend. Sex from a lover. What more was necessary? He had dabbled with fiery passion only once. The absolute intensity had terrified him and sent him scurrying back to the sanctuary of muffled affection.

He looked at Alice's sleeping face. A tiny blue vein was throbbing through the leftover, blue eye shadow on her tissue-paper eyelid. It wasn't all her fault. After all, exactly what kind of excitement was left to be had at his age? Thirty-nine was practically the end of the road.

He began to doze with these sentiments fluttering around his mind and soon they evolved into hundreds of white doves swooping over a large cast-iron gate which shimmered into sight. On the other side of the gate was a patchwork of colours: like the pixelated adult channels he was too miserly to pay for in hotel rooms. Through the blur he could decipher a collage of trees – in a variety of autumnal shades – surrounding what appeared to be a large lake. The movement and silhouettes suggested communities of beautiful (mostly naked) people undertaking a variety of leisure pursuits. Guarding the gate was an intimidating looking figure of a man – possibly the gatekeeper of thrills and fancies. There was a mean looking Kalashnikov hanging behind his back. *Can I help you sir?*

"Just wondered what was past that gate," said Manu.

The Gatekeeper, who Manu recognised as a distorted version of himself, laughed loudly. A*h, you won't want to go there sonny! Not in your state. Anyway, there's a fee, and it's not cheap either.*

“I simply want to have a look,” said Manu. “To see what’s on the other side.”

The Gatekeeper was having none of it. *That’s what you all say! You’re all the same you common-placers: just want a little taste. Well, to be quite frank, I’m sick of it! What’s out there is what’s out there. You either pay the necessaries and take your chances, or you make do with run-of-the-mill. And before you ask – yes the grass is greener. A lot.*

“But if the price is high I’d like to see what I’m getting.”

The Gatekeeper was rather bewildered at this line of argument. *OK, sonny. It’s more than my job’s worth, but if you’re a serious contender I suppose I could let you have a little glimpse.* He picked out a large key from a variety hanging off his belt and began to unlock the tall gate behind him.

Manu felt a surge of excitement emanate from his gut. Secretly he knew there was something distinctly more exciting out there. Something more meaningful and worthwhile. Had he become so retentive he had turned into a human dam struggling to contain a variety of wayward tendencies? He had suspected it for a while. The floodgates needed opening to prevent a serious rupture of his personality. And now he was about to let loose and find out what he had been missing all this time.

“What did you say?”

Both his dream and the answer were snatched away by Alice who had woken from her sleep with a start. “Did you say something?” she repeated with a yawn.

“No,” said Manu. “If you’re tired shall we go to bed?” he whispered kissing her ear.

The opportunity was lost but in its wake were crystals of clarity. He had spent his life mechanically preserving a childhood bubble where truth and reality were denied entry. Thus, the very essence of life was passing him by. The absence of pulse and grit in his daily existence had turned him into Mr Moderate. Only one choice presented itself: *march towards the gunfire*.

6

Tehran Iran – 1950

Amid the juiceless August heat of Tehran city, where a sliver of shade is more valuable than a gem in the Peacock throne, the occasional pocket of relief could be found amongst the corridors of the Grand Bazaar.

This living edifice was a giant brick heart responsible for the sustenance of the city. And yet it was itself a city. A metropolis, where the peculiar coalition of commerce and religion clung together with equal fear, for each dreaded the heavy price of modernisation by diktat. Nonetheless, even the most trivial liberal transaction represented a small triumph over absolutism.

It was hard to tell at what point kings upon kings had elected to sweep away the very opportunity which had cultivated their own royal rule. But sweep it away they had. And if ever it had been the case that the sweat and the destiny of the common people languished on the mind of any majesty, it certainly was no longer so. Even the golden bond which once existed between merchant and monarch had been blown off course by the strong seductive gust from the West. The imperial ear had, long ago, grown deaf to the itinerant bartering cries – now here, now there, bouncing off the walls of the bazaar corridors. But, deep inside the vein of this shelved population lingered a coursing hot blood. And languishing in its throat was a collective growl. It was thickening with every disregard of its voice. In exactly twenty-eight years it would demand the right to be heard.

Though he didn't know it now, Doctor Ahmad Azizi would be part of that demand. He would be a mere speck in the crowd of thousands outside Shahyad Square, chanting for an Islamic Republic to loosen the tyrannical grip from around the country's neck.

For the time being, Doctor Azizi snapped shut his leather bag and began to wash his hands in a bowl of water, at the corner of a room in a lodgings on the west side of the bazaar. A fly buzzed noisily around the basin, stopped and buzzed around his face. Then it landed on his nose. He swiped it away with his forearm and dried his hands on a small towel.

"Well Suleymani, the wound seems to be healing very nicely," he said, peering into a wooden box and tickling a baby which was squashed within it. "My advice to you is to clean it with salt water and alcohol rinses three times a day. And try and keep the flies out, or they will be feeding off it."

"A thousands blessings to you," said the portly jeweller who was now the proud owner of a baby boy instead of a baby girl, thanks to a pioneering operation which had eradicated all outwardly protruding female genitalia. It had been an expensive procedure and one that had cost him a good many export orders, as well as a number of bangles and rings, now adorning fingers of the wives of surgeons and medical officials at the American Hospital in the east of the city.

"The hospital has said we simply need to observe his urination capabilities," said Dr Azizi. "You must keep him uncovered so that he may urinate into the air. Then you will be able to tell that he is passing water in an acceptable manner."

Just then, as if for illustrative purposes, a little fountain of bright yellow urine spurted upwards from the baby's newly fashioned penis, which happened to look more like a withered purple grape than anything resembling a male organ. Shabnaz Suleymani, the boy's mother, clapped her hands. "You see my husband, it works perfectly!" she squealed.

Mr Suleymani slapped Dr Azizi on the back. "I cannot believe we have a boy at last, Ahmad!" he said leading Azizi to the door. "You know as well as I – a house full of women may indeed be good for the appetite and the constitution, *but never for the fortune*."

At least he had not cast the woman out of the house, thought Dr Azizi as the new father chattered away in the twilight of his consciousness, making more references to his female household. It was true, until the latest debacle, every one of Suleymani's prayers had been answered with a girl, to a total of four.

"And what happens?" Suleymani's voice penetrated his thoughts. "You know I am a God fearing Muslim, Ahmad. A God fearing Muslim. And every prayer I finish off with a petition for a boy. Then what happens? I get a mutant!"

Whom you refused to believe had come from your own loins, thought Azizi.

The birth of the poor baby, now called Arvin, had sparked a furious debate about his parentage. Luckily this had been resolved soon after when it was noticed that a tiny red dot just below the baby's eye was growing bigger by the day. At this point it had assumed the shape of Syria. Azizi looked at Suleymani's chattering face and, specifically, at the large red birthmark beneath his left eye which looked like a yawning fish. Yes, that birthmark had been a blessing for all concerned, he thought.

"I will return to see him next month. In the meantime, you know where I am if there are any problems," said Azizi.

"Incidentally," said Suleymani, "I will see you at the meeting at the mosque this evening. I hear the Pish Namaz will be rallying the crowd in favour of action."

"Yes – he is, and you will," said Azizi as he left the house.

An undecided hot breeze flapped his linen jacket and caressed his greying hair as he walked along the road and up to the green square. Here several youths were splashing each other in the fountain and whistling at pristine young women who trotted by, their thick black hair twisted in the latest chignon style from Europe.

"Hey, you wanna do a party?" called one of them, in broken American, to a young girl in culottes who was cycling past. Azizi hissed under his breath and shook his head. A growing lack of respect and honour was seeping steadily into today's society which he found hard to bear. The rape of a young woman outside the telegraph office recently had caused great distress to the community. When he was a young man courtesy and integrity were securely nailed to the framework of human behaviour. Now corrosion had set in and Azizi knew exactly what was causing it. The sugary and caustic component of western capitalism was responsible for this disintegration. It was no wonder that many people felt communism had something to offer.

Azizi continued to the mosque where he removed his shoes. It was twelve o'clock and time for prayers. After washing his hands face and feet at the fountain he found a space amongst the crowd of other worshippers and spread out his prayer mat which he had removed from his bag. A girdle of chanting fastened him to the spot. As the ground came up to meet his forehead a comforting absolution came rushing in to a hollow place in his heart.

When prayers were over, he made his way through the back entrance of the mosque into the bazaar. Its complex network of passages wove together every discrete little fragment of Persia under one roof. Competing with each other to overpower his senses were the recurring musical cry of the walnut seller, the sweet perfume of saffron and the sharp odour of silver polish. And as he progressed through the main walkway, he was sprayed with pustules of sunlight from the tiny punctured holes in the domed ceiling.

He loved the intensity and autonomy of this place. The population of merchants, peddlers and artisans was as enduring (and sometimes seemed as ancient) as the walls which embraced it. All amenities known to man were situated in it, or around it. All crafts were practised there. All commodities were hawked there. Any ablution necessary for body or soul was catered for. Every legal (and the odd not so legal) method of social interaction was conducted there.

It was the nucleus of a multitude of endeavours. Wives and mothers kept house at various sides of it. Little sons (and sometimes daughters) went to school next to it. Young men worked in the midst of it. Grandfathers loitered in teahouses punctuating it.

"Will you be coming to see Somail later, Ahmad?" a voice called from one of the stalls.

“As sure as I’m alive Ebrahim!” called Azizi waving to his uncle’s cousin who had made himself comfortable in a wheelbarrow at the side of his shop. His son’s leg had become infected after being bitten by a snake.

“Wonderful. Your auntie has made you some baghlavah to fatten you up!”

A closer-knit community than the bazaaris was difficult to find. In any particular corridor the goldsmith was the father of the silversmith, who was the son-in-law of the grocer, who was the cousin of the potter, whose wife was the daughter of the hatter and so on. Everybody knew everybody else’s business and everybody’s business was the subject of discussion.

Dr Azizi pushed through the tourists and shoppers haggling over the smallest savings. The bazaar was particularly hectic today and the heat clawed at his skin as he pushed through the seizing hands and coveting faces. It all began to devour away his serenity. He felt himself searching for the smallest of breaths. Then his soul sank to the bottom of his shoes.

What began as an intelligible comment from a fellow passing merchant dissolved into a babbling blur. What originated as a crisp depiction of faces in vigorous conversation turned into a mirage of lips and eyebrows, all oscillating and merging into one big jelly of a scene. Then nothing.

“My dear sir. Sir!”

“Wake up!”

“He’s lost consciousness. Get him some water.”

“Someone told me his brother has…. ”

“Sir, can you hear me?”

A blue mess and a red mess appeared before his eyes. They were joined by a number of black smudges here and there. Were his eyes open? He couldn’t tell. Then a smell of unbearable putridness. Clarification. He needed clarification. It was not long before he received it.

“He’s opening his eyes,” someone said. The sentence was imparted from what appeared to be a pair of vivid red lips. A lady in a bright blue dress emerged into something resembling a definition. A number of other faces surrounded her. She was peering into his nostrils. Then he realised he was lying prostrate on the ground. Someone was holding smelling salts near his nose. He pushed it away.

"What's your name, sir," said the lady in the blue dress. She smelt of rosewater and cigarettes.

"Azizi. Doctor," he said through his dry mouth. She had a glass of water in her hand and she pushed it to his lips whilst supporting his head with her other hand. He took a sip.

"You fainted."

"It must be the heat," muttered Azizi, attempting to sit up.

Her face turned a full ninety degrees and he saw it right side up. She had jet black hair, bright red lips and black marble eyes outlined in yet more black. She was surrounded by two or three other tourists and craftsmen.

"Can I fetch someone for you?" asked one of the men.

"No. I'm fine. Thank you, the South Suq. Where is the South Suq?" said Azizi trying to locate his bearings.

"Just behind you."

He raised himself up gingerly. His legs felt a little shaky but he managed to stand and began walking towards his destination, at which point the crowd dispersed. He had only gone a few yards when he felt unsteady once again and leaned against the wall.

"Where are you going?"

It was the voice of the woman in the blue dress who had followed him a little way.

"Shariati's teahouse," he pointed in the general direction.

"Let me take you."

"No. No. I shall be fine," he said as he started towards the South Suq.

"I'm walking with you. You're still unsteady," the woman said firmly, putting her hand under his elbow.

They walked in silence for a short while, Azizi having to stop every so often to take a sip from the glass of water she proffered.

"Do you live locally?" she asked.

"Not too far," said he, ungenerous in his conversation.

"I can go and fetch your wife if you like."

"I don't have a wife," he said.

"Perhaps you would like something to eat," she said, taking from her handbag a bag of salted greengages.

"No thank you," he said, surveying her face. She was a beautiful woman, made more beautiful by paintbrush. Her black hair was styled into a chignon at the back of her head, like the movie stars he had seen in newspaper pictures. A figure-hugging blue flowery dress advertised her full hips and plentiful bosom. Azizi blushed when he realised she was watching him focus on these aspects of her figure.

"I can manage from here," he said.

"No I insist on making sure you arrive there alright," she said as they walked.

He assessed her in thirty seconds: westernised Iranian; a royalist most likely; definitely a career woman. Exactly the type of woman Azizi usually had nothing to do with.

"I work at the university," she said, as if reading his thoughts. "A lecturer. In literature."

Ah, thought Azizi. Well, in that case definitely one of the women's rights people.

"And you. You're a doctor you say. A doctor of what?"

"Medicine, naturally," he growled.

"Medicine. Yes medicine. That's good. Do you work at the hospital?"

"No. A practitioner."

"My name is Nargess," she offered her hand, presumably for a handshake. Azizi took the cue and shook it quickly.

As they neared the teahouse he said "We are here. Thank you for your concern. I shall be fine now."

She looked a little dejected and Azizi felt embarrassed about his treatment of her.

"Thank you for your help. My friends can assist me now," he said gently, pointing to the teahouse.

"Nargess Shabi," she said "if you ever find yourself in the vicinity of the university that is."

He nodded with a forced smile and went inside. Was she making advances he wondered? He had heard that some women even made the first move these days. She was not young, as he wasn't. Azizi put her at early thirties. How did a woman of that age find the effrontery to be so forward? Perhaps she had been educated abroad. Yes, that was the most likely scenario. In Azizi's mind the Persian population fell into two main categories. There were the traditional Muslims, some (like himself) well-educated and moderately wealthy, who supported a republic or (at the very least) a reduction in the king's power. And there were the royalists who were happy to endure anything as long as they could emulate the Western nations. Where did Nargess Shabi fit in, he wondered? Was she of this latter persuasion? But surely an educated woman of her calibre would have more principles than this? If not, it seemed a pity and a waste. He had a cousin who worked at the university, perhaps he would make some enquiries. But then he quickly banished the thought as he entered the teashop.

Inside, Hajji-Hossein was doing his books and calculating his earnings. Azizi slunk into a chair next to him. "This heat is stifling isn't it?" he said wiping his brow with a cloth.

"As stifling as the fires from hell," said Hajji-Hossein – a pencil in his mouth and in between calculations.

Shariati, the teashop owner, came over with some tea.

"Are you going to the meeting at the mosque tonight?" said Hajji-Hossein as he flicked the beads on his abacus backwards and forwards and wrote in his book.

"Yes," said Azizi. "I think the subject of discussion is this supplemental agreement they are trying to force through the Parliament. Do you know anything about it?"

"Only what I have read in the newspapers," said Hajji-Hossein. "The British are fearful of losing control of the oil company so have offered this paltry concession which the Shah is attempting to get his cabinet to accept – even though it barely addresses our objections."

"Our only hope is that the upcoming elections change the orchestration of the Parliament – and maybe give it some backbone for once," said Azizi as he picked up a copy of the Bakhtar-e Emrooz newspaper and began to read. He shook his head seriously. "This election campaign is turning out to be a monkey's tea party. The Shah, who has just returned from a visit to Britain, is once again trying to force through his own pro-British candidates by convening a self-appointed senate which tramples all over the lower house. It's outrageous."

Hajji-Hossein sighed miserably as he rose from his table and packed his books and abacus away. They both knew full well that following each of the king's visits to the West, the selfish hand of capitalism tightened its grip around the throat of the community.

"Where are you going now?" asked Azizi

Hajji-Hossein laughed. "I tell you where I'm going. I'm going to the oil company headquarters in Sepah Avenue. Apparently a letter has arrived from Karim Dashti, you know, Dashti's son who works at the refinery? The letter is for Parissa. I am going to fetch it."

"Do you think it a wise manoeuvre to get her betrothed to an oil company worker, at this stage of the proceedings?" asked Azizi.

"Well, he is Dashti's son and a fine match I think. You know she's not getting any younger Ahmad, and I do not want her on my hands forever! But more to the point, my view is this: once the oil company is nationalised, Karim Dashti will be in a suitable position and his prospects will be good. He will probably rise through the ranks very quickly. And… well you know the rest. It's a good gamble."

"I have heard she's not too taken with him," called Bidandoon from the other side of the shop as he went about collecting the empty tea glasses from the tables.

"She's like any young girl, my man. She does not know her own mind. I have agreed that she can take her time getting to know him, after all he is still in training. But once his training is finished you can be sure she will have changed her mind."

Shortly after, Hajji-Hossein left the teashop and made his way through the stifling bazaar to the north of the city. He walked up the main, tree-lined boulevard with the hot sun hitting his back and past the Shah's Golestan palace, where tourists lingered around the entrance to the crown jewels. Then he deviated through the narrow streets and around the back of the imposing police headquarters. It was here where, he imagined, individual upon individual to be incarcerated whenever there was disagreement over any aspect of the Shah's policy. Upon turning the corner he stooped to re-tie his shoelace which had become entangled in the side of his sock. Next he took the opportunity to clean his shoe of the dust which had gathered on it from the road. And as he was doing so he his attention was suddenly captured by a hissing noise. He looked around and could see nothing but brick walls. He carried on cleaning his shoe regardless. It happened again, this time a whisper. He thought he heard his name. How could it be possible? There was not a soul on the street or in the alley. He spoke out loud. "Who is it!"

A faint voice continued "Hajji, Hajji. Look down behind you."

He turned around and examined the pavement behind him. There was nothing but a very small grill in the ground. Suddenly a man's finger protruded through the bars of the grill. Hajji-Hossein jumped. "Who is this!" he said angrily, crouching down to look through the grill. He could see only blackness and smelled only mustiness.

"It's me. Mohebi. Can you hear me?"

"Parvis. Is that you? What in god's name are you doing down there? Have they had you cleaning the sewers for a year? That is the last we saw of you. We thought you were dead!"

"I have been imprisoned all this time," said the voice. "They have put me in a zeerzamin chamber, under the ground."

"And how did you tell it was me?" said Hajji-Hossein, curious.

"When they put me in here I managed to keep hold of a little mirror I carry in my shoe. If I hear someone walking past I put the mirror up through the holes, like this." A small mirror appeared through the grill. "Then I can see who is going past," said Mohebi.

Hajji-Hossein looked about himself. "If they catch you, you will be beaten," he said gravely.

"Could you get a message to my wife and tell her I am alive?" he pleaded.

"Of course. Of course."

"And how is she. Is she coping well?"

"I believe so. The other wives have rallied round and are ensuring her well being. Tell me, what sign is there of your release?"

"None at present. I am locked up, with upwards of twenty people in this small cell. The guards have not given any indication."

"Well I cannot understand it. For they have caught and beaten to death the man who attempted the assassination. He was a lone operator by all accounts. They must surely release you soon. Are they treating you with respect?"

"We are left alone most of the time now. When I first arrived they tortured a few of us to try and extricate a confession. Things have settled down somewhat since then. But I need to warn you, I heard some of the guards discussing a raid yesterday. Is there to be a meeting at the mosque tonight?"

"Yes a rally to discuss the topic of oil and the election rigging which is taking place."

"Be warned. I believe that they intend to raid it," said Mohebi.

"Have you heard anything else?" asked Hajji-Hossein with interest.

"Not really. Most of the guards and officials here are lazy and indifferent. Before I arrived I believed they were motivated by a particular belief, or a type of creed. Why else would they want to arrest and torture their own kind? But they are motivated only by greed and money. If the Shah knew they spent their time gambling and drinking he would not want to pay them a day's wage."

"I wonder how they knew there was a gathering in the mosque tonight," said Hajji-Hossein.

"I think the son of a guard has infiltrated the wider protest group. You can trust no one Hajji-Hossein, believe me."

Hajji-Hossein noticed a figure approaching at the end of the road. "Someone is coming. I will have to go," he said. "I will return regularly to see how you are."

They said their farewells and Hajji-Hossein carried on his way. Mohebi's wife would be pleased to know he was still alive. The authorities undoubtedly had no evidence to link the poor man to the Shah's attempted assassination. But when had that made any difference? Everyone knew, even a good alibi was a worthless currency in the eyes of the secret police. The man was fortunate to have kept his life. If they really intended to raid the mosque that night, trouble would ensue. Even the king's men knew it was foolish. An unwritten agreement had always existed where the inside of the mosque was concerned. It was long considered sacred and sanctuary could be sought there. The religious leaders wouldn't tolerate it. Still, with things as they were at the moment anything was possible. There was no telling what the Shah might order. After all, he was his father's son.

Shortly after, Hajji-Hossein arrived at the Anglo Iranian Oil Company Headquarters.

A native young man was sitting behind the front desk writing in a book. He looked up when Hajji-Hossein appeared.

"Can I help you?" he said in an officious manner.

Hajji-Hossein did not recognise him. Normally when he came to fetch Parissa's letters there was a young Iranian woman at the front of the office. But today she was not there.

"I have come to pick up a letter for my daughter," said Hajji-Hossein.

"Name," said the receptionist

"Parissa Forooshi."

The young man stood up and walked to a tray at the back of the office where he began to rummage. Hajji-Hossein noticed some new framed photographs hanging on the wall. A series of depictions of BP service stations in different parts of the world boasted of successful foreign markets. Other pictures showed middle-aged men in suits. Directors, Hajji-Hossein supposed. And everywhere there were pictures of western workers standing in a rows holding awards, or waiting to be introduced to the Shah on some visit or other. Not a sign of the backbone of the company: native labourers who toiled in unbearable conditions to extract every drop of black gold.

"Excuse me one moment," interrupted the receptionist, and disappeared into a room at the rear. A short while later he returned with another young man. A foreigner, with sandy-coloured hair. Probably English.

"Could you tell me when the letter was sent, Mr Forooshi?" the young man asked.

For a moment Hajji-Hossein was thrown off guard for the young man was speaking in Farsi.

"Mr Forooshi?" the young man enquired again – looking into his eyes.

"Yes. Apologies," said Hajji-Hossein "I was thrown by your excellent Farsi."

The young man smiled knowingly. It was obviously a frequent reaction from the indigenous population.

"I have been living in your beautiful country for six years," said the man.

It was very rare for foreigners to be able to speak the language and Hajji-Hossein stood for a moment assessing the figure in front of him. He had golden hair, slightly wavy, and light blue eyes which were contaminated with specks of yellowy green. Above these were a pair of almost-white eyebrows, bleached by the sun. Although he looked quite young there was a maturity in his face, which was characterized by a few creases. And he had a small dimple in his chin.

The young man spoke again. "If you could tell me when the letter was sent that would be helpful. There has been a problem with the post recently, and some mail has been delayed along the way. It might be that your letter is amongst those."

"Yes. The letter is sent each Saturday. And I usually pick it up every Thursday," said Hajji-Hossein.

The English man asked the receptionist to show him the list of deliveries, which he did at the back of the office. After some consultation the English man returned to the front desk.

"I'm afraid it appears that the Saturday mail is one of the consignments which has been delayed. We are expecting it to be delivered in the next day or so," he said, and apologised for Hajji-Hossein's wasted trip.

"Where are you situated, Mr Forooshi? Perhaps I can get one of my workers to deliver it to you when it arrives."

Hajji Hossein obliged with the exact destination address and left the quarters pondering this strange meeting.

He walked back to the bazaar where stallholders were packing away their stalls in time for mid evening prayers. The bent and stretched musical words of the muezzin floated out of the minaret in the mosque adjoining the bazaar. After picking up his son from the carpet stall, they joined an already large crowd in the great hall for prayer. After prayers a leading Mujtahid went over to the marble Mihrab where he mounted the raised pulpit to speak to the crowd.

"In the name of Allah, the almighty. We are gathered here to pray for our country. You know that one of our brothers, Sayid Abu Al-Qasim Kashani, has been exiled to Lebanon by our leaders, as part of the purge to stop demands from our people to have a say in running our country. We cannot allow this to continue. Like us, he wishes only for free and fair elections. Like us, he demands possession of our own oil. And we, like him, ache for the freedom to live under our own laws – instead of the laws of those who have nothing to do with us.

"You. People of the bazaar. I urge you all to show your support for the National Front – lead by Mohammad Mossadegh, in the October elections. They are fighting – like us – for a free press, better economic conditions, honest elections and control of our own oil. Let us end this brutal rule once and for all!"

"And you religious teachers and leaders. We are told by our high authority we should not get involved in political things. But how much longer can we sit on the side and ignore it. Islam teaches us: those who concern themselves not with the affairs of Muslims is not *himself* a Muslim!"

The crowd bayed and shouted. Their response echoed against the tiled walls. Hajji-Hossein noticed a military policeman standing, motionless, at the back of the mosque. He seemed to be talking into a machine. Suddenly a loudspeaker hailed from outside. "In the name of your country abandon your treachery and go to your homes! Abandon your treachery and go to your homes now, before we are forced to enter!" The words bounced from wall to wall.

The Mujtahid stopped speaking. There was a silence in the mosque. Only the trickling of the fountain could be heard.

Then he resumed. His voice was louder and stronger. "Shall we allow them to make us cowards in our own Masjid!?" he shouted.

"They have Allah to answer to if they enter!" shouted another man in the crowd.

Ali tugged at Hajji-Hossein's jacket. "Father, let us leave. I am frightened," he squeaked.

"Do not worry my son. They will not enter. This is a sacred place," said Hajji-Hossein, "Even the Shah's men know that."

"I will repeat myself. Abandon your words and leave the mosque now if you do not want to be arrested for causing a disturbance!" said the loudspeaker from outside.

"Tell them to go to hell!" shouted another man. The crowd chanted in response.

Suddenly from outside came the sound of heavy running boots. Then, between fifteen and twenty military policemen burst open the doors and poised their rifles at the congregation. Their faces were fired with meaning and purpose.

"Leave peacefully and go to your homes!" shouted the loudspeaker from outside.

"This is a sacred place! "shouted the speaker waving an extended arm around towards the military police. "Remove yourself from the entrance!"

The police did not respond to this request.

"Do as he says my people," said the speaker. "We are not fighting men. They will not harm us if we do not resist."

The police moved aside and the panicked crowd began to head towards the two exits, which were too small to handle the urgency of their intent. Hajji-Hossein held his son's hand tightly as they were forced through the human sieve and catapulted outside into the evening sun. A young man who had been hurled out ran back towards the door of the mosque to re-enter. "You despotic dogs! It is you who are betraying your god! May heaven send you misfortunes!" he cried.

One of the officers waiting by the door hit the man's skull with his truncheon. The sound of the crack reverberated off the pavement. The immediate crowd reacted with collective rage.

The police fired into the air with their rifles and the loudspeaker went again "Do not try to fight us we have guns and we will use them!" The guns were fired into the air again and people scattered in all directions as they ran for their lives.

Hajji-Hossein clutched his son's hand and forced his way through the chanting crowd. In the rush to get out of the incensed throng, he fell and cut his face on a stone. Ali helped him up. And they began to run down the high street towards their house.

The turquoise metal tip of the mosque's dome pierced through a hovering halo of golden light generated by the weakening rays of the setting sun. Beneath it, little dots of motor cars and shoppers on the surrounding streets went about their daily business as though nothing had happened. To them nothing had.

7

Tehran 1950

Three days after the mosque incident, Hajji-Hossein sat on a rolled up carpet in his shop in the bazaar. His head felt as woollen as the very rugs which hung around him, for he had been rather excessive with the opium the night before.

It was early in the morning and the shoppers had scarcely begun to trickle through the walkways. A few doors away, the sound of Dashti the carpenter's methodical sawing attached itself firmly to the pulsating headache, which had taken root inside his skull.

Without warning the jabbering shriek of a rose-ringed parakeet sliced painfully though his delicate constitution. "PRODUCING THE FINEST KNOTS!" it squawked with a piercing voice.

Hajji-Hossein groaned loudly. "Quiet! Or I'll sell you to the nearest bidder!"

"NEAREST BIDDER!" mimicked the bright green bird parading backwards and forwards across the small table outside the shop.

Hajji-Hossein stood up gingerly and found his way to the entrance. "Come here you feathered rat," he growled between his teeth, attempting to grasp the parrot by its beak. The bird squawked loudly and flapped its wings in a panic, breaking free and fluttering into a nearby cage hanging above the table. His master clamped the door of the cage shut with a grunt and went back to his glass of tea.

He was in no mood for work today. Even though it was early, the stifling heat had already infiltrated the bazaar chambers. The heavy woven gilims, matted wool namads, and large Kashan rugs hanging from the walls of the chamber, simply inflamed the stuffiness. "What fool needs carpets on a day like this?" muttered Hajji-Hossein as he finished his tea and rested his head on a low-hanging carpet bag behind his neck. "And, what fool would enter the trade of carpet selling?" he asked himself, miserably surveying his stock from where he sat. Most of it came from outside of the city, having been woven by his contacts in Tabriz where he used to live. He would take a delivery from them every month. Some were left over from his days as a carpet merchant, and a few were woven by his daughter.

Even though trade had been improving since the war, competition was still severe. His business contacts from Germany had trailed off since the country's defeat and the market amongst locals was small. What a strange irony it was that the only lucrative gains to be made were with the very foreigners he was attempting to cast out. Was this a time honoured dilemma he wondered? Surely not. There was a world of difference between meddling and merchandising. An economic transaction symbolised a deed of honour and trust. Misappropriation of a country's natural resources was a different matter altogether.

There was no denying it, the desire for his country's isolation was sure to affect commerce. After all, who would want to procure goods from a place that had demonstrated its intolerance of foreigners? It was a sticky issue and one that Hajji-Hossein had still not resolved in his own mind.

But one thing was certain: as long as royalty insisted on furnishing its own pockets and being led by the nose ring of western intentions, the country would never find its own feet.

He often bemoaned his homeland's long-suffering population. It had learned to forever endure the plotting and plundering of this or that king who had been thrust into the country's bosom as result of this or that tribal war, and concocted this or that rule for this and that reason. Happily, his country-folk had been showered with occasional relief when dynasties and their corresponding edicts had ceased to exist. But, if truth be known, even the pernicious summer hurricane of Sadobistrooz which annually tore through eastern provinces, sandblasting homes and uprooting villages, had shown them greater benevolence.

"Good morning to you. It's Mr Forooshi isn't it?" His train of thought was interrupted by a male voice. He looked up.

Standing at the entrance to the shop chamber was the young gentleman of a few days ago, whom he had met at the Anglo Iranian Oil Headquarters in the centre of the city.

Hajji-Hossein leapt to his feet. "Welcome to my chamber," he said. "Please come inside."

The English gentleman squeezed his way past the stacks of rugs and carpets and came into the small shop.

"I was passing through the bazaar and I thought that I would stop by to deliver the letter for your daughter that arrived this morning," said the man, holding out a letter for Hajji-Hossein.

"A thousand thanks to you," said Hajji-Hossein taking the letter. "She will be most pleased. Please sit for a few minutes. Take the weight off your feet."

He did so, on the wooden chair at the side of the shop. "You have had an accident it seems?" said the young man pointing to Hajji-Hossein's black eye and the scar above his brow which he had sustained from his trip outside the mosque.

"It's nothing. I fell the other day. But thank you for enquiring."

"Incidentally, let me introduce myself. Alec Conroy," said the man holding out his hand. Hajji-Hossein shook it hesitantly. The young man looked around. "You have a most impressive array of carpets here," he said.

"Yes, most of them are from the regions of Qazvin, and Tabriz. All hand knotted. Some from Kermanshah and Shiraz, like this one." He pulled over a large pale blue and grey carpet and folded it over so that the English man could see the intricacy of the knots at the back of the carpet.

"This is beautiful," said Alec Conroy, running his fingers over it.

"Are you interested in carpets sir?" asked Hajji-Hossein.

"Oh yes, very. I have a few already in my house. I bought them mainly from Mashad and Hamadan."

"Well, you must try one from Tabriz! This is my home city and we produce simply the best carpets there. I used to have a large number of carpet workshops myself in the old days before I moved to Tehran. And the girls in Tabriz, they have the most delicate fingers, producing the finest knots."

"PRODUCING THE FINEST KNOTS!" screeched the parakeet from his cage. Hajji-Hossein ignored it. "You see this one here, this was woven by my daughter. She has shown an extraordinary talent in this field." He pulled across a small red and black carpet with jewels of yellow and green.

Alec Conroy smiled and nodded. "This is certainly one of the finest examples I have seen," he said.

"My daughter is very talented. She mainly works now for private buyers. You know: they commission a piece of work and she obliges. She is an expert in the Ghiordian Knot which is the tightest knot you will find. Her carpets will last for hundreds of years. Unlike these western ones which unravel in the blink of a bird's eye. You have heard of the famous Greek tale have you not?"

"No, I am afraid I haven't"

Hajji-Hossein proceeded to tell the story of King Gordius' challenge: that whoever untied the knots on his oxcart would rule all of Asia. Even Alexander the Great was thwarted and in his frustration was reduced to drawing his sword to sever the knot with a powerful stroke.

Alec Conroy laughed. "What a wonderful story!" he said, walking around the shop looking and feeling the various rugs.

"So you have been in this country many years?" said Hajji-Hossein, following behind him with interest.

"Yes, I came over after I finished university in England. For a time I was working for the British legation and then I began work at the AIOC. I love it in this country. The people, the culture, the arts."

"Perhaps you have a drop of Middle Eastern blood in you, sir!" said Hajji-Hossein jovially.

Alec Conroy laughed. "Yes, I sometimes wonder myself," he said. "Although the hair," he lifted up one of his locks, "the hair says it is unlikely."

"Well, history shows our people were once golden, before the invasion of the Arabs! You will occasionally see blue eyes in the nooks and crannies of our land," said Hajji-Hossein. "But, in all seriousness, I have scarcely heard a better Farsi accent on a….." he stopped.

"A farangi?" Conroy finished the sentence for him with a laugh. Hajji-Hossein was a little embarrassed. He had been looking for a term – he did not know what – but the only word which flew into his head was the one used to describe foreigners.

"Well, my English friend," said Hajji-Hossein hastily "you must come through to the workshop, where I will introduce you to my daughter. Perhaps I might even persuade you to have a carpet made to your liking! Do you drink tea?"

Conroy nodded.

Hajji-Hossein hurried into the corridor, stopped a tea seller with a tray on his head and purchased two cups of tea.

He handed one to Conroy. "Follow me."

He opened a small door at the back of his shop at the foot of which were two or three stone stairs leading up to a darkened landing with another door. He opened it and beckoned the man into a small workshop, covered in carpets of all sizes. Against its walls, from floor to ceiling, were stacked giant reels of wool in an unimaginable number of colours.

"Stop your work for a minute my daughters. Parissa, this English gentleman has kindly delivered your letter from Abadan. And I have told him about your carpet making skills."

Parissa and her sister Soraya were sitting on a wooden bench at the far end of the room, in front of an imposing vertical loom. From the top of the loom a mass of wefts rained down to form a half-finished scene: a gold-coloured deer running through a forest of surreal red leaves, his bright yellow chest headed towards a man with a bow an arrow.

Parissa stood up from her loom and came round to the front of the bench, into a strand of sunlight which penetrated the room from the window at the side. The ridges in her black trousers and cream coloured tunic shimmered in the light. Her hands were clutched together in front and her scarfed head was lowered. A strand of her long dark hair had worked loose from her headscarf. She proceeded to tuck it back in.

"That's beautiful! And unusual too," said Alec in Farsi, pointing to the unfinished carpet with a questioning look.

Parissa's eyes widened in amazement when she heard him speak. She looked up directly into Conroy's face for a few seconds. A subtle blush worked its way inwards from her cheeks and stopped short of her well defined lips. Soraya who was standing behind her sister's back, peered around it to examine the stranger closely.

"The deer is running towards the arrow," said Parissa intuitively.

"Yes," said Alec slowly. "Why?"

"He runs towards his destiny," she explained.

"And there you have it," interrupted Hajji-Hossein. "This is my daughter Parissa, whose head is full of wild stories! Please, sit down Mr Conroy. Soraya fetch the cushions," said Hajji-Hossein pointing to the corner of the room where a small stool and table were situated upon another brightly coloured carpet. Soraya fetched a large cushion which she quickly threw down and ran back to the safety of Parissa's back.

"Tell me, Mr Conroy surely you would like to have a lovely carpet made? I will offer you a very good price," said Hajji-Hossein as he beckoned him to sit down in the only spacious corner of the room.

The workshop was stuffy and hot, made worse by the small window at the back of the room through which a shaft of concentrated afternoon sun was pouring. Alec sat gingerly upon a cushion against the wall. Hajji-Hossein sat next to him. A sweet fragrance of rosewater lingered momentarily in the pocket of air around his face, as Parissa crouched forward to arrange the cushions behind her father's back.

In response to her father's request Parissa went in search of a hand fan amongst the wooden boxes under the window. Alec watched her slight figure as it dipped in and out of the bright beams, unwittingly betraying the black silhouette of her body through the somewhat shapeless tunic. She located the fan and brought it to her father before kneeling down politely in front of them.

Hajji-Hossein quickly took control of the conversation by offering Alec Conroy a description of the minutiae of his daughter's carpet weaving skills, taking appropriate opportunities to applaud her talents during noticeable points of the Englishman susceptibility. Next to him was a farangi who undoubtedly appreciated the beauty of Persian culture and art. Hajji-Hossein had no intention of letting slip the prospect of a wider patronage.

Coincidentally with every verbal illustration of his daughter's aptitude, her cheeks would redden and she would lower her eyes modestly. One of her ears had worked its way out of her white headscarf and looked uncomfortably aglow.

"I do have a bare guest room in my house. A carpet for that would be ideal," said Alec Conroy.

"There, you see? Now, you must tell Parissa what you want and she will do exactly as you bid. She will show you colours and yarns. Silk is, of course, the best, but you must choose. Perhaps a combination? And the size?"

"I will need to return with some measurements," said Mr Conroy.

"Of course. Return soon and we will discuss the details. I will calculate a good price," said Hajji-Hossein.

"Do you enjoy weaving?" Alec asked Parissa directly.

She nodded shyly "I weave most days but sometimes I stay at home to cook and read."

"She is an avid reader," said Hajji-Hossein. "My fault of course, for sending her to school!" he laughed.

“My Farsi is not good enough to read complicated works but I am very fond of some current authors and poets,” said Alec Conroy.

“In any case,” said Hajji-Hossein rising from his seat and steering the conversation to a close. “Please return with details of your liking and Parissa will start on the rug immediately.”

Hajji-Hossein showed the Englishman to the door, down the steps and back into the shop. “I will come with you up to the end of the Suq, as I need to see a fellow bazaari,” he said.

On their exit, Hajji-Hossein beckoned a bazaar colleague to look after his shop whilst he was gone. And as the two men proceeded up the bazaar corridor Hajji-Hossein nodded variously here and there to compatriots in his little empire. “So tell me, have you a view about this move to nationalise the oil industry?” he asked.

Alec Conroy looked at him, surprised. He had never been asked his view on the matter by an Iranian. He hesitated before responding. “What view do you require? Mine or the official one?” he returned with a half smile.

“Is there a difference?” said Hajji-Hossein.

Alec Conroy laughed “There happens to be in this case,” he said.

“Aha. Well then. Let us – let us hear your view.”

“I do think – believe – nationalisation is justified.”

“You are saying this to satisfy me my friend!” said Hajji-Hossein, patting the young gentleman on the back.

“On the contrary.”

“But how can you say such a thing when it is *your* country that will be denied the riches of such a venture. And when the results may even mean the loss of your position?”

“If the results cost me my position then, yes. For me it will be a great loss. For I love this country as if it were my own.”

Hajji-Hossein looked a little confused, and slightly disbelieving. He couldn’t imagine such a state of affairs.

"As for my country," continued Conroy, "although I love her dearly, I cannot condone the unfair advantage she has over oil fields in another man's nation."

"Perhaps then, you are in agreement with those who say that the split should be fifty-fifty?"

"Well, I know that many other foreign companies who are negotiating with oil rich countries are now of the view that an equal share is a fairer deal. And that it is time to end the outright exploitation. But I believe a country should be allowed to manage its own resources. It is true that many nations who discover oil do not have the capabilities of developing it themselves. And this is a problem. But the matter still remains: that a country should have sovereignty over its own oil. It may be that they have to invest in the expertise to get it out, and refine it and such things. But that is their prerogative."

Hajji-Hossein was silent for a while as they walked. It was not a view he was expecting. But this young man's demeanour was getting more surprising by the minute.

"And tell me, what about your colleagues. Do they feel the same way?"

There was a short silence.

"I cannot speak for them, but I suspect mine may not be the majority view. However, many have a great respect for this country, and enjoy living here. They may be concerned that nationalisation will mean the loss of their livelihoods."

"Hmm," Hajji-Hossein pondered. "Well I have heard that those in our government who are in favour of nationalisation are also in favour of keeping on the British staff, for they have know-how which we do not. But – there is also the matter of under-representation of Irani personnel in positions of authority."

Conroy nodded. "Yes, amongst other things."

"Well sir, I have reached my destination. I will bid you goodbye. It has been a pleasure to talk to you. Perhaps we will have the pleasure of meeting again soon when you visit with the details we spoke of earlier?"

"Certainly," said Conroy. "I will look forward to it."

Hajji-Hossein watched him walk away down the corridor towards the bazaar exit. He had a solid stride, but not an arrogant one. A very strange young man indeed. Was he being sincere? Still, he did not represent a majority view. So it was unlikely to make him look too differently at foreigners. Although he might, in future, give them the benefit of the doubt.

"Are you fraternising with the other side, Agha jahn!" shouted a voice across the way as he was returning to the carpet shop. It was Jamshid Dashti the carpenter calling from his woodwork chamber.

Hajji-Hossein walked to the open workshop where Dashti was in the process of sawing a piece of wood for a prayer book holder. Splinters were scattered here and there. A sea of sawdust covered the stone floor. At the back of the shop a young apprentice boy was sanding and shaping a variety of effects.

"Not fraternising. Enquiring."

"What of?" asked Dashti wiping his sleeve across his top lip and adding a layer of sawdust to his moustache.

"This and that. For an Englishman I find him surprisingly amicable. He works at the oil company offices and he was kind enough to deliver Parissa's letter from Karim."

"Ah, I recall his face now. I have seen it occasionally on my visits to pick up Karim's letters to his mother."

"Yes, he is nearly fluent in Farsi," said Hajji-Hossein.

"Indeed! That is very surprising. Very surprising," said Dashti. "Incidentally, I see your injury is taking a while to heal," he said pointing to the scar on Hajji-Hossein's nose.

"It's of no consequence and will heal soon. Parissa has been making me a poultice every night. I understand there were a number of arrests made on the night of the gathering."

"I have heard the same. And I heard today the date of the demonstration is set for three weeks from now. Our man Mossadegh is planning to have a bast in the grounds of the Imperial Palace to protest at the blatant election rigging and

I've heard Ayatollah Kashani is planning his return from exile in Lebanon to support the cause."

"You must keep your voice down my man. These bazaar walls have ears like donkeys," whispered Hajji-Hossein looking about himself furtively.

Since Mohebi's news from the grill he had decided to trust no one. And this demonstration had the potential to be a very important one. There were sure to be thousands of people attending. Mossadegh had complete support of the people. And yet he was being denied a seat in the Parliament because of his support for nationalisation. The very thought of it made Hajji-Hossein's blood boil. He thought back to his conversation with the Englishman. It seemed outlandish for Alec Conroy to originate from a place where liberty and expression were upheld – and yet the self-same nation was unashamedly encouraging repression and tyranny in another man's land.

"Help me gather our compatriots together Dashti, and we will have a meeting at my house tonight!" said Hajji-Hossein. "You know as well as I that Mossadegh *is* the voice of the people, and your son's future depends upon his success.

8

London, 2003

"Move in with you? Is this a joke?" said Alice. "I don't understand. And pass the salt please."

This was not going well. He'd spent the past week deep in conversation with various alter egos. He'd weighed up the risks and benefits of taking the odd gamble. And he had come to the conclusion that shacking-up might be the very thing to galvanise their relationship and inject the missing rainbow of colour into his life. But why was she not dropping down her cutlery and throwing up her hands in glee. No such reaction was anywhere in sight. Manu had introduced the topic in the wrong way. He should have rehearsed it more. He looked into her milky blue eyes. She looked away. He noticed her hair was different. Fresh blond highlights. Shorter. Her lipstick was light pink. She never wore light pink.

"What I mean to say is, I would like to be more committed to you. And I think it would be great if you would move into my flat with me," said Manu. "Unless. Unless of course, you'd-like-me-to-move-in-to-your-flat-with-*you*?" Was he seriously saying such a ridiculous thing? That certainly wasn't in the rehearsal. He hadn't even *considered* moving in with her. Still, it was too late now. His mouth had taken over. It was out.

"I *still* don't understand what's brought all this on?" asked Alice with a mouthful of food.

"Well. Right. I've been considering it. And thinking it would be doooood. Actually, I *have* been toying with the idea for a quite a while. You were right. I've been very aloof. Just – obsessed with my own needs, you know. But I think it's about time we took the plunge. Surely the answer can't be *that* difficult?"

"I'm not quite sure *what* to say" said Alice. She had stopped eating and was moving her guinea-fowl pie around the plate. Why did she have lacquered nails? And why was she looking so uncomfortable?

"You could say Y-E-S: yes?" suggested Manu – opening his eyes wide.

"I'm just no-ot sure if it would be a good idea."

"What? Why not? Hey – hang on. What is *actually* going on here? "

"There's nothing *'going-on'* here" said Alice "I'm just not sure I'm ready – that's all."

"Whoa," Manu held up a hand "You – not ready? I find that sooo hard to believe after months of dropping it into every single conversation going!"

"Keep your voice down Manu – please. People are staring."

"I really don't think I care right now actually. You know what?"

"What?"

"I can't believe I even bothered asking you. I had thought: I'll demonstrate my commitment – like she's always talking about. I'll put myself out. I'll offer to…."

"Excuse me. Let's get this into perspective shall we? *Yes* I've wanted that for a while. And yes, for me it was part of the grand plan. But – let's not forget –it *has* taken you a *while* to get round to it. And now – well, I, I just can't think about it."

Both of them said nothing for a few minutes. Each was considering their next rebuttal. The conversation seemed to have recorded itself into the atmosphere, and the words were, without doubt, ringing in the collective ears of the surrounding tables.

"Are you seeing someone else?" Manu asked in a ferocious whisper.

Alice swallowed hard. Then she took a large sip of her wine and whispered back.

"What kind of question *is* that?"

"Well why won't you move in with me then?"

A long silence ensued. Manu could see her going through different conjugations of phrases as she rubbed her lacquered index finger backwards and forwards along the tablecloth.

"More wine, Madame?" the vulture in penguin uniform swooped in to take advantage of the shipwreck of a scene in front of him. He topped up Alice's glass of wine and left covered in an irritating smile.

Manu lent forward and took Alice's hand. She pulled it away.

"Oh, I see where we're going with this now…" said Manu.

"I am, yes," Alice.

"This is, like, some kind of game and… You are *what*? What did you say?"

She looked down and began playing with the pie crust on her plate.

"Seeing someone," she said, in a resigned whisper. "I'm sorry, there's no easy way of talking about this."

"Christ. Is this some kind of joke? You've been with another man?"

"But let's face it Manu things were not going well were they?"

"Is that an excuse or an explanation?" he asked flatly.

She did not respond.

"I see," he said.

Another silence ensued. A wallpaper of murmuring from surrounding tables filled the void. Both of their very expensive meals sat waiting on the plate for a reconciliation.

"So who is it?"

"Why? Why does that matter?"

"Of course it bloody matters!" Manu raised his voice sharply and she gave him a frown.

"Keep your voice down will you. Do you want the whole restaurant to know our business?"

"I couldn't give a fuck at this moment in time. Who is it? Do I know him?" Manu felt like his heart was competing in an African drumming tournament.

"It's no one you know. I'm not that horrible," she mumbled.

Manu felt simultaneously sick, angry and jealous. He wanted to pour his Breton Lobster bisque over her red dress. No, he wanted to tap the side of his glass, ask for silence and publish her indiscretion to the whole restaurant.

"So, what? I suppose he's offered you security and children and all sorts of homely things."

"Not at all," said Alice. "Look I know you're hurting. And I don't know what the answer is. I'm just as confused as you are. I thought I knew what I wanted. But now I don't. "

"So you *did*, and now you *don't*. What *is* the answer?"

"I wish I knew."

They picked at their meals for a short while until Manu gave a long sigh and said he could no longer continue with a broth he couldn't taste and a girlfriend who had just thrown him over. That was one thing he couldn't' believe. She had dumped *him*!

Outside the restaurant he graciously hailed a taxi for her. She got in. "I didn't mean for it to end like this," she said.

"Yeah, yeah, yeah. So you were going to keep on lying behind my back?"

"No. No. of course not I was going to tell you soon. I still care about you, you know."

Manu sneered loudly "Yeah, I'll bear that in mind when I'm contemplating your infidelity." He slammed the taxi door and walked away without looking back.

It was quite a warm evening for March. He took the tube to Hampstead and ambled along the streets for a while, having a conversation with himself in various settings. Clutching a pint of bitter, on a bench outside The Flask, he pondered whether to sell-up his goods and chattels and move to a beach in Vietnam. Perched on a step outside the Everyman Cinema under a poster of a film aptly titled 'Down with Love' he rehearsed a confrontation with the phantom adulterer. He was probably someone she'd met at work: a pasty Caucasian with glasses. "Yes, I bet he is!" he said to himself loudly.

It was getting late and the bit of rain mist that had started to fall was making him cold. He wondered whether Laure would still be up at eleven o'clock and rang her on his mobile. She was about to go to bed but said she was happy for him to come round.

When he arrived at the door of her top floor flat she greeted him in some Winnie the Pooh pyjamas, her hair gripped back in a ponytail.

"I'm sorry to disturb you so late," said Manu throwing himself into her sofa.

"It's no problem," she said. "You look harassed."

"You're not going to believe this," he said and told her about the disastrous dinner with Alice, his attempt at reconciliation and her bombshell. Laure poured him a large whisky.

"How are you feeling about it?" she asked.

"I'm really not sure. At first I felt outraged and angry. Now I feel a little empty but strangely relieved."

"Well you've had your doubts for a while haven't you?" she said re-filling his whiskey glass in response to him thrusting it in her direction.

"Yes, you know what – I reckon he's some blonde, blue-eyed bookish type. Deep down inside she just couldn't handle an outsider. And her parents never liked me either. I wasn't catholic enough for them. Get this; her father's religious leanings are so extreme he was actually told by his priest to 'chill-out, because the Lord didn't like to have his glory eclipsed by over-zealous followers'!"

Laure laughed. "Well, there you go then. You have reassured yourself that it is all for the best!" she said tapping her wine glass with his. She had always found Alice pleasant but rather supercilious and secretly wondered if Manu had used her as a trophy to illustrate his British credentials.

"Yes, but let's just squeeze out some real perspective on this…." said Manu as he slid his tumbler on the coffee table, kicked off his shoes and stretched onto the sofa. "Let's see… aside from feeling like a complete outsider, and apart from my girlfriend plunging a sharp sword into our relationship;

there's the grey cloud over my career and, oh yes – I can't taste or smell my food. Some pretty good reasons to feel like shit – I'd say. Then there's all kinds of sludge at the bottom of the Zand swamp – which we don't really want to dredge up, but since we're on the subject let's just consider what kind of toxicity that could possibly contain. Twenty years of trying to convince people you don't belong to some backward, fundamentalist tribe. Too much of a coward to defend your roots. Continual suppression of a yearning for a past you know you'll never have again. Disconnected from everything that made you what you are. Tastes and smells that befriended you as a child – gone. Bonds of kinship that made you fit in – a hazy memento. You of all people – surely must know what it's like?"

"Being a frog you mean?" said Laure.

He laughed.

"Yes, I suppose," said Laure. "There's no easy way to settle into another culture. It is sad that even after so many years you feel like an outsider, Manu. My own experience of settling in Britain has been trouble free really; except my father-in-law's constant references to me being a Nuptial Tourist. Which, of course, you know about."

Manu grunted. The three glasses of whisky had joined forces with the bottle of wine he'd had earlier. And the room was starting to spin of its own accord.

"You know what? I think you need a holiday," said Laure

Manu opened one eye and tried to focus on her. Fuzzy golden candyfloss hair sat atop a bundle of arms and legs in the armchair. "What's the point. There will be no escape from the bitterness and resentment."

"It may not help the situation. But look – you've got a month off work. What better time to get away and do some thinking."

Manu closed his eyes again. He just couldn't think about it anymore. Whoever was up-there, out-there, or in-control definitely had it in for him. Was probably watching him right now: waiting to see exactly what he would do next.

“Do you want to stay the night?” asked Laure. He nodded with his eyes closed.

“I’ll get some bedding,” she said and disappeared off to the other room.

When he dropped off to sleep on Laure’s sofa he dreamed Alice’s pink, fluffy, rabbit (the one that consistently had its big blue eye on him when they were having sex) was impaled on the pink pole in the garden of his parents’ next door neighbours’ house – and he was standing aside it singing the Iranian national anthem.

9

Iran, 1950

The bus driver pounded his fist on the outside of the hot metal bus for attention. "You have fifteen minutes!"

First male and then female, passengers plunged themselves gratefully into the outdoor furnace hoping to catch a gift of passing air. Facing them was the carcass of a scene, bleached and desiccated. It was though God had, long ago, washed his hands of the landscape that lay before them. An acrimonious white sun had already scorched the scarce vegetation into submission with its pernicious blaze.

A few hundred yards below the dusty road, meandering through a few rocks short of a valley, an emaciated stream was attempting to trickle itself around a defiant set of boulders. Close-by, a huddle of parched walnut trees, wearily fought the heat to preserve the last of their ailing leaves. An orchestra of crickets, the only sign of life, filled the hot silence with its shrill siren.

Parissa and her friend Yasmin followed the other passengers as they scrambled down the formless path. Just below, an isolated tea hut took advantage of a morsel of shade bestowed by the overhanging crags. A glorious but intermittent pocket of cool loitered around numerous, small, scattered tables. Parissa pulled both sides of her headscarf outwards to refresh her damp hair. Most of the men, of which there were about nine or ten, had congregated by the stream to wash their faces. Some women waited their turn patiently.

Parissa sat with Yasmin and some other females to take advantage of a jug of water the hut owner had generously put on the table for those that could not stomach a glass of hot tea.

From a square of muslin in her bag she unravelled a flattened square of paneer and offered a piece, with a handful of walnuts, to her friend. Although they had done nothing but sit, Parissa was already tired of the fifteen hour journey. A defiant Alpine Swift flew down onto the table and cocked his head to one side, his large black eye focused on the cheese in hand.

Two young women and an old one, all of whose faces betrayed a restless night, sat in silence next to them. The old woman was falling asleep. From beneath the covered chest of the youngest one came the sound of a baby, aggressively sucking out every drop of lingering milk from its mother's parched breast.

"Are you visiting relatives in Abadan?" Yasmin asked the other.

"I am going to see my husband who works on the oil refinery," she responded. "And you?"

Yasmin pointed to Parissa who spoke. "We are going to see a friend of the family," she said.

She certainly did not consider Karim as her betrothed and would not allow herself to think of him as anything other than a family friend. The only reason for this trip had been to placate her father. And she was thankful he had been unable to accompany her, due to a last minute political rally.

"This is our first visit. What is it like?" she asked the girl.

"The refinery?"

"Yes."

The girl looked at the woman next to her and they laughed. "Have you ever seen the inside of a radio?"

"Yes, I think so."

"That's what it looks like!" said the woman. The girl with the baby started to laugh under her breath. Her quaking bosom choked the suckling infant who fired out a series of tiny coughs and then began to cry.

Parissa didn't quite understand the humour but said no more. A few minutes later they were joined by Ali who had been sitting with the men.

"I have so much to do. I cannot believe father has forced me to bring you to this stupid place," he groaned.

"It's not my fault, Ali," said Parissa. "I didn't want to come!"

"We should simply make the most of it," said Yasmin looking into a small mirror to poke and pry her thick red hair. Its bright, hennaed, glow disagreed with the azure green headscarf attempting to cover it, Parissa thought. She knew Yasmin had accompanied them with the intention of catching sight of some farangi men. And she often felt a pinch of envy towards the friend who had been granted immunity from her own custom by her free-thinking parents.

They had once been small parallel souls: she and her. And they had welded together in a week. Parissa's only week at school in the capital, before being extracted to care for the family, after her mother died. Nevertheless the intensity of their bond grew stronger, at the same time as the aspirations of their two families grew more polarised. Yasmin's home was a golden cloud. The only place where Parissa was permitted to take an untamed breath. The single spot where existence seemed silky and smooth. Where her glamorous mother floated in colourful clothes and coiffed hair. Where a silk scarf was an ornament, not a shroud. Where the status of beauty was treasured not blackened. In her mind Parissa would often reach out and touch the life that Yasmin had sprung from, with her painted face and big, sculpted red hair. And she often marvelled at how they were still united despite the different shapes their lives had taken. She, tied to a life of weaving, and Yasmin crossing boundaries by working as an assistant at the British legation.

Before long they were back on the scalding bus. Parissa fell asleep and was awoken much later by a sour stench which pierced the back of her nose. She peeled her cheek off the bus window and opened her eyes to assess where the smell was originating from. But the opaque afternoon sun forced down her eyelids, restricting her vision to slits of colour between her own thick black lashes. When at last the vehicle began to slow, passing through the shadow of some trees, she saw a gaggle of goats being directed by a goat herd alongside the road. The bus jolted and jumped to negotiate an incline in order to give the animals some room.

"What's that putrid smell!" said Yasmin, contorting her features.

"It's the oil. Crude oil," said one of the women leaning over. "And this place we are passing through is Ahmadabad, a district on the outskirts of the refinery. We are nearly there."

A group of skeletal boys with deep sunk eyes and oily faces were running for their lives alongside the front of the bus. Each time it slowed they would hurl themselves onto the front of the engine.

"What type of madness is that!" cried Yasmin.

One of the women laughed. "You will get used to it," she said. "They are trying to pull off the dead locusts and small animals that have stuck to the grill on the front of the bus. They will eat them later."

"This is the poorest part of the town. Some of the oil workers live here because they have no proper housing," said the woman with the baby.

As if to illustrate the point, shelters shaped from disused oil drums began to spring up along the side of the road. Outside, women squatted, washing and cooking. "I imagine it is because those contraptions are like a furnace inside," said Yasmin.

Parissa was aghast. "I hope Karim does not live in one of these!" she whispered.

In his letters to her he had alluded to the poor conditions of some of the workers. But she had not imagined it to be this bad.

When they eventually arrived at the bus station Karim was waiting for them with an umbrella by the side of the hot pavement. His face was blacker than she remembered, most likely on account of working outside. And when he smiled the whiteness of his teeth sprang out at them.

"You must be exhausted!" he said taking their bags. "I have arranged for you to stay with a family who live on the Iranian estate. I will take you there to refresh yourselves.

And Ali will stay in my communal quarters, where we have a spare bed."

As they made their way through the streets to their destination Karim pointed out occasional landmarks, many of which failed to impress Parissa. Did her father really imagine she would thrive in this colourless wasteland? The only sculptures on the horizon were monstrous, round, tanks and towering chimneys, retching out thick black smoke. It resembled, as the woman in the bus had said, the inside of a giant radio.

They passed by a concrete shed which Parissa took for a mosque, when she noticed an old megaphone hanging off the corner of small makeshift balcony. In front of the construction was a dry fountain. Evidently it had not played a part in any ablutions for some time.

"A letter from my mother tells me that the Suleymanis have sent their poor wretched child for an operation to be put right," said Karim. "It is wonderful how those American hospitals in the capital are able to cure the most peculiar deformities these days."

"Yes," said Parissa. "I hope his parents have made the right decision. I fear the child looks more like a flower ready to bloom, than a stallion ready to kick!"

He laughed at her analogy. "These are difficult times for all of us, that is for sure," he said pointing ahead. "Look, Ali – you can see the large port with cranes and tankers, with the British flags. These carry the oil for export to the West. And do you see those long warehouses there on the left?"

Ali nodded.

"That's where technicians like myself work and train."

"There is a lot of smoke. Does this smell ever go away?" said Ali.

"No, unfortunately not. It does get to the chest after while. And we need to wash it off frequently too!"

"It appears to add to the heat. I imagine it is stifling in your workshop," said Parissa.

"I am afraid so. At times I long for air conditioning – like the systems installed in the buildings where the British work.

But I think they assume we should be capable of tolerating our own climate!"

"Where do *you* live?" asked Yasmin.

"Living quarters for bachelors are behind these houses to the right. I live in a long bunker with six other workers. I am lucky to have accommodation in the town. Many lower ranking workers live in shanty towns on the outskirts."

"Yes. We noticed those on the way in," said Parissa.

When they arrived at the accommodation where the Parissa and Yasmin would be staying they were welcomed by an older looking woman– presumably the wife of one of the oil workers. Karim handed Parissa a map on which he had circled the social club where they were to meet at six, before departing with her brother.

The woman showed the girls to the room they would be sharing. It was compact and contained one large bed and a sink, underneath a small window.

"Perhaps tomorrow we can explore," said Yasmin as she unpacked her bag. "I have heard there are many western men here, looking for wives!"

"Yasmin!" said Parissa. "We cannot do that. It is forbidden!"

"I only mean us to take a glance," said Yasmin. "Who would know? We have *no* chaperone."

The flush of excitement in her friend's face was rivalled in iridescence only by her hair. For Parissa too, in that singular moment, it seemed to provoke an instant of madness more than her flesh and blood could bear. To be without guardianship was to swim an ocean with no circumference. Hafez's poetic voice sang in her ears: *I shall cease not from desire til my desire Is satisfied.*

"I don't think it would be wise," said Parissa stripping to her pantaloons and walking to the miniature sink to wash herself with the cloth the lady had left for them.

Yasmin pulled out of her bag a vivid green dress with blue flowers. It was creased and she sighed loudly.

Parissa turned around and saw the object of her sigh.

"I thought there may be somewhere for us to stroll and catch the eye of potential suitors?" said Yasmin by way of explanation.

This lay bare Yasmin's root. Her father was a legal officer and her mother a nurse in one of the hospitals. And they had instilled in her the universe. At times there were no frontiers to her conduct. Parissa vacillated between admiration and disbelief when confronted with her outlandish propositions. Hajji-Hossein had tried to discourage their friendship but the assignment required more effort than he was prepared to exert. Surveillance was the better option he had concluded.

"Yasmin! Have you failed to notice your surroundings? There is not a beautiful thing in sight! Merely ugly box buildings. No shade, no shelter… and – it seems …." She stopped as the tap in front of her coughed out a few drops of brown water. "…no water either!"

Yasmin came over to try the tap. "Perhaps it has been turned off?"

Parissa flung herself on the small metal bed at the side of the room. "I wish we had never come!" she said burying her head in the unyielding pillow.

Yasmin sat on the end of the bed. "We are just tired. Things will improve when we have had something to eat. Come. I have some leftover water in this bottle from the journey. We can refresh with that. We need to be at the social club in half an hour."

Parissa lay on her back and looked at the ceiling. A large green lizard was scuttling across. It froze mid-run, feeling the gaze of her human eye.

She sat up and took the bottle her friend offered. "You are right, of course. And I have decided this meeting with Karim is his chance to show he is worthy of my betrothal to him. By the end of tomorrow I shall have settled on a decision."

Yasmin laughed. "If indeed the decision is yours to make? I can picture your father's face at your rejection of the offer!"

Parissa laughed too. “It is unfair that your family is so tolerant and mine is so traditional,” she grunted as she tied a fresh headscarf around her head.

“It is merely the harvest of my father’s obsession with the Buick Super Convertible, which naturally he will never be able to possess,” said Yasmin. “And, of course, his love for President Truman.”

“Please don’t let slip those views in the presence of my father. You know how he feels about that president – with his Zionist footprint. And father already suspects I have become too wanton under your influence.”

“Well, I am sure he will be delighted to know that even *my* father has his limits. Last week he caught me applying some lipstick I purchased from Forooshgah Ferdowsi and was not pleased. However….fortunately for us…he did not confiscate it from his precious girl. Look!”

She pulled a silver bullet out of her pocket, unscrewed the cap and pushed up the bright red lipstick which throbbed with colour against the backdrop of the drab grey room. “Isn’t it delicious!?”

“That is beautiful,” said Parissa losing herself for a moment in the intensity of its shade. “But, if we wear it in this place we will be lanterns in the dead of night.”

“I shall keep it about me in case an opportunity arises,” said Yasmin with a fiendish smile.

“Very well. But please don’t brandish it in front of Karim. He will be sure to tell father,” said Parissa throwing the map in her direction. “Quick, find our destination while I put on my shoes. We are going to be late.”

****

The next day, at nine o’clock in the morning the girls stood by the solitary lamppost in their dusty street scrutinising a rudimentary map of the town they had been given. “I cannot see the municipal swimming pool on this map,” said Parissa impatiently.

“He said it was near the melon shop.”

Parissa turned the map around and looked carefully. “This looks like it might be it,” she said pointing to a small square in the middle of the map with a symbol of some waves over the top.

Karim and Ali were going swimming that morning and Parissa and Yasmin had agreed to get some food and meet them for a picnic at lunchtime.

"He seems very sweet," said Yasmin, as they progressed.

"I suppose so."

"You are not convinced by him?"

"He does not fit the picture I have in my mind for myself," said Parissa

"Did you not enjoy the evening?"

"Within reason. He is a nice man. In terms of practicalities I could not ask for more, I suppose."

"What is marriage if it is not practical?" said Yasmin uncharacteristically.

"I don't know. I simply think there must be something more. A spark."

"A firework perhaps? He was extremely attentive to you last night. Do you not think?"

She was right. On their arrival at the social club the previous evening Karim had been waiting for them eagerly, with Ali, on the steps of the porch. The newness of his suit was betrayed by the imprint of two small holes on the cuff where the label had been pulled off in a hurry. On his head was a western brimmed hat, a tight fit around his thick blue-black curly hair. She noticed his lips were dry and cracking.

He showed them into the main room of the social club which was furnished with metal tables and chairs. The club room was empty apart from an occupied table and there was no decoration. At the corner where there was a wooden counter, a man stood in a white uniform serving food, snacks and drinks. A few men who were playing backgammon acknowledged Karim when he entered. .

"Those are my working colleagues," he said.

They took some food and sat down at a table near the large glass window on the other side of which a small patch of grass was attempting to sprout unsuccessfully.

"It appears you do not get many female visitors here," said Yasmin looking around.

"Occasionally wives come to see their husbands. And a few wives live here too. But they do not often come to the club."

"And what about farangis. Do they come here too?" asked Yasmin

"The club is open to westerners but they do not come here in general. They prefer to attend their own club on the other side of the town."

"Can we go there and see what it is like?" asked Ali.

"I'm afraid not. Iranis are forbidden there."

"But if this is our country. Are they allowed to do that?" asked Ali.

"It's a complex state of affairs. But hopefully things are beginning to change. There is a British man who brings his Iranian wife to this club, I presume to allow her to mix with her own culture, and they are both very pleasant. But in general Westerners have no interest in coming here."

At that moment, to purposely contradict him, a group of well-attired, pale-skinned men strolled through the door of the social club laughing.

"Farangis!" whispered Ali tugging at Parissa's sleeve. Yasmin sat up in her chair and straightened her headscarf as she kicked Parissa under the table.

"That man showing them around is a high ranking Irani Official" said Karim under his breath.

The men approached the waiter and asked for some sharbat. Then, quite unexpectedly, they began to walk towards Parissa's table.

The Iranian official introduced himself and pointed to one of the sun-burned western men. "This is the editor of Naft, the Oil Company staff magazine, who is writing an article on the life of oil company workers in Abadan. Would you mind if he asked you a few questions and took a photograph of your group alongside these western oil colleagues as an illustration?" he asked Karim.

Karim was taken aback and asked Parissa and Yasmin if they were happy to appear in a photograph. Parissa nodded and Yasmin fidgeted with her scarf and hair. The editor sat down and asked some questions in English which were translated by the manager: did they frequent the venue often and what did they think of the social life in Abadan.

Karim was self assured and calm. He spoke in a measured way about refinery life. It impressed Parissa that he did not – as he had told her earlier – refer to the working conditions Iranian staff had to endure. He did not even mention his apprentice friend who had collapsed with dehydration after disconnection of the water supply to their quarters for most of the day. But he did draw attention to the issue of the staff magazine not being translated into Farsi, pointing out that the interview in which he was partaking now would not be available for indigenous workers to read.

The manager noted his concerns and pressed on with arranging the parties around the table for the photographic shoot. Parissa understood one of the gentlemen when he whispered to his colleague, in English, "This should convince them that all is well in Abadan!"

Within fifteen minutes they were gone. The only residue of their presence was the five empty glasses on the table. And the food and atmosphere had lost the little vitality it had, for which Karim apologised.

Parissa had spent much of the subsequent night awake and irresolute. Unwittingly her father had handed to her a profound truth. And it had enabled her to peer into the future and witness the loathsome existence of an oil worker's wife.

And even now, as she and Yasmin approached the dilapidated shop where a selection of lifeless tomatoes and cucumbers languished outside on a table, her sentiments were subconsciously ordering themselves into divisions and subdivisions of possibility and probability. And they questioned and cross examined each possible forecast. She knew not how she would escape it all. But escape it she must.

Outside the shop, a water melon seller sat with each foot buried in the flesh of half a large watermelon. He gave them a toothless grin as they entered the shop. On the shelves inside American and German imports sat uncomfortably next to native products. Parissa and Yasmin purchased some fresh fruit, cheese and bread before leaving to follow the route to the swimming pool that was shown on the map.

After passing through a repetitive lattice of drab bunkers the surrounding scenery seemed to recast itself. Dusty roads turned into well kept pavements. Pavements, at their sides, gave birth to lampposts, gates and fences. Fences began to skirt around leafy gardens, which themselves skirted around affluent cream houses. And from those houses little children were ejected to cool themselves amongst the water sprinklers which showered onto lush green lawns.

Parissa and Yasmin stopped.

"Where has all the water come from?" said Yasmin.

"I think we are lost. We appear to have entered an entirely different area?"

They both searched the map for guidance.

"Well, it seems the swimming pool is not far. Past that building. We had better run. We are late."

Behind a thick green bush to their right children were shouting and laughing. Parissa pulled Yasmin over to a large gate at the side of the hedge. They looked inside. A wealthy looking residence sat atop a heavily manicured green lawn. Outside, around a long wooden table with balloons at each end, sat chattering young children in pristinely colourful clothes, with immaculate hair.

"Listen," whispered Yasmin squeezing Parissa's hand. "It's the farangi quarter!"

As soon as she had uttered it, a woman dressed in a white uniform and wearing a cap came out of the house with a large candle-covered cake, followed by two more ladies. They all began to sing.

"Someone's birthday," said Yasmin.

"We must leave immediately or we will get into trouble."

"Wait," said Yasmin. "No one will know. Remove your scarf"

"What?"

"Remove your …"

"I heard what you said."

"Remove it. We're sure to be noticed with them on."

"People will recognise us nonetheless. We scarcely look Western."

At that moment a face appeared on the other side of the gate. It was the nursemaid with the white uniform. Her black hair was swept back under her cap and her pink lipstick was fighting to be seen over her dark lips.

"What business have you here?" she asked in Farsi.

"We are searching for the municipal swimming pool," said Parissa.

"You are on the wrong side of the city," said the woman. "You will need to take that road towards Braime Square, past the Gymkhana Club and turn right at Alfi's Book shop. It is approximately half a kilometre away."

And as they turned to depart she added, "if you do not wish to invite attention you would be wise to remove your scarves."

"There. I told you!" whispered Yasmin as they walked in the direction indicated by the woman, taking off their scarves as they walked. Yasmin produced the lipstick from her pocket. "I told you it would be useful!" she said excitedly as she put some on her friend's lips. Much later, when Parissa was back in the capital, the memory of this venture would be constant in her mind. It was the sun that never set, the moon that never waned. And with each whisper of the breeze upon her unsealed hair she craved more latitude still. Though she feared she would be unable to contain her thirst for it. Did Saadi not warn against destroying the fires of life by pursuing a heart's desire?

The two women walked for a while, following the directions they were given. Before long, they saw a large rectangular building with arched windows, open. Through them emanated the sound of clapping.

“Let us see what it is,” said Yasmin walking across the grass in a crouch. Parissa followed and they raised themselves to look over the window ledge. At the back of the large, ornately decorated room, an orchestra was preparing itself. In the centre, parallel rows of long tables were laced with men in suits, listening to a speech from an official who stood at a lectern in front of them.

Parissa studied the scene.

She was unsure how her eye managed to pluck out the detail which was later to beguile her appetite. But somehow her vision was drawn to a figure at the corner of one of the tables. And in the moments that followed she observed him slowly bat his golden lashes as he watched the speaker. She saw him place his elbow on the table and rest his dimpled chin onto his fist. She noticed the white dot of the sun flicker in his pupil, as his eyes absently began to scan the room. She witnessed him slowly rotate his head so that it came to a stop facing her. And she stood opposite the full moon of his face.

What followed seemed to persist over a giant second of time. As he squinted to discern her frozen countenance. As her eyes felt powerless to unlock themselves from his gaze. As his expression rotated from perplexed to astonished. As she raised her hand to cover her blood red mouth which was emitting a gasp. And as she bolted downwards towards the ground in shock.

“For heaven’s sake. What is it?” asked Yasmin squatting alongside her under the window.

“We need to get away. It’s him!”

“Who?”

“The gentlemen I told you about who came in the shop. I wish to leave immediately,” she whispered, shaking.

“Come,” said Yasmin and took her hand. They began to run replacing their scarves as they did, and did not stop until they reached the municipal swimming pool where Ali and Karim were sitting under an umbrella on the step outside.

“Where have you been?” cried Ali.

“We got very lost,” explained Yasmin as she handed them the picnic basket.

“I am simply happy you are safe,” said Karim smiling at Parissa. Her heartbeat was only now beginning to return to its original tempo and she returned the smile. For once, she admitted to herself, she might actually have been pleased to see him.

10

Iran, 2003

When Manu Zand marched off the plane onto the hot tarmac at Emam Khomeini International airport he was not consumed with nostalgia.

If this was the cannon's mouth, and if it were *here* his younger, less damaged, self would emerge, the process – he figured – had got off to a bad start.

No matter that it was only March, the heat was sandpaper against his skin and the sun had a brilliancy of a flashbulb. If nothing else, it was nice to feel the warmth, a permanent outsider to his recent life.

Once inside the terminal he was surprised at its modernity. Greeting him were escalators, tall glass walls and shiny marble columns – like you would find in most corners of the world these days. Clearly his perceptions of the country had not allowed for any kind of progressiveness, or wisdom, in action. The Iran in his mind remained an outmoded stencil, perforated with relics of the past. He began to feel nauseous. What if his memories turned out to be the antithesis of sober reality: and he was about to discover he had been living a lie for a quarter of his existence. Like the shock of discovering you were adopted or had accidentally married your sister.

After passing through customs (uneventfully, which was a nice change,) he made his way to the taxi rank outside. He would remember it later as his first thankful glimpse of familiarity. A long row of yellow taxi cabs, each with a smoking driver leaning against it, all beckoned in his direction. The rickety contraptions looked ancient enough to be the exact ones he had journeyed in as a boy, on his frequent trips to his father's office in the centre of town.

He decided to be contrary and approached the least interested driver, a Danny De Vito lookalike who alternated between a puff of his cigarette and the gnawing of a sandwich, whilst reading a newspaper off the bonnet of his car.

"Salam!" he said.

The taxi driver jumped and dropped his sandwich on the bonnet before looking up to see the cause of the distraction. On realising he had a fare, he hurriedly discarded his cigarette and wiped his hands on a handkerchief.

In private, Manu had been brushing up on his Farsi for moments like these. He followed up his initial overture with a confident – *can you take me to Laleh Avenue* – and was pleased with how it sounded and with the acknowledgement it received. He smiled to himself. He absolutely sounded like a local.

The driver looked at him and grinned: *a tourist without a doubt.* And he started to speak to him in broken English, whilst forcing Manu's case into the already cramped boot.

"Mister – hello. My name is Amir. I will take good care of you. You are Engeleesh?" he asked as they got into the cab. Manu flashed him a false smile through the rear view mirror whilst looking around for a non-existent seat belt.

"You are visiting our lovely country for how long?" he asked.

"A week maybe," said Manu, secretly grateful he was being forced to speak his mother tongue. This was no different to being in Spain.

"You will be seeing the Golestan Palace and the Museum of Jewels for sure!" said the driver. "I give you my card and I take you anywhere you want to go in your trip. Where you come from?"

"London."

"Ah, London. I never been. But I know Manchesterr yoonite."

Manu forged a smiled.

"Football?"

Manu nodded, not wanting to get into a conversation about his least favourite club. But he allowed the driver to continue practising his English which he did pretty much continuously without help. He would be an ideal match for Phyllis from Laure's café he thought, and momentarily felt a wistful twinge for his favourite homely eatery thousands of miles away.

As Amir 'de Vito' communicated through the rear view mirror, with the characteristic elbow out of the window, and a part-time hand on the wheel, Manu found himself assessing the percentage of time his eyes were on the road – twenty? No, that was generous – ten perhaps. He wanted to be amused but it really wasn't that funny. Hanging in front of the car windscreen were some colourful worry beads and next to it dangled a small square sign with writing on it which Manu could not translate.

"What does the sign say?" he asked.

"That is a Persian proverb my friend. It means: *Travel as far as you can see, and when you get there you'll see even further*!"

I presume that's if you ever get there in the first place, muttered Manu under his breath as they pulled into a lawless, five-lane freeway – on which a vehicle riot was taking place. His fears were confirmed when a man on a motorbike – with three young children clinging to his back – zoomed past on the wrong side of the carriageway.

This was the Grand Theft Auto of Tehran life – minus the crime and sex which (in this case) might have been a welcome distraction. As they progressed at great and random speed, huge highways attached and detached themselves from the road – weaving in and out of each other, with living and working spaces plonked down at various intervals in between. As far as the eye could see pubescent construction projects were in the process of adding to the swelling urbanity which ironically looked more like a Soviet replica of Los Angeles than a Middle Eastern conurbation. Manu could not believe this was really the outskirts of the small city he remembered as a child.

Snow tipped mountains in the distance looked like jagged teeth on the horizon and, as they drew closer, Manu noticed a growing patch of grey concrete cancer crawling up the bottom of the mountainous slopes. It began to transform more visibly into a cityscape by the minute.

"Alborz Mountains!" said the taxi driver with pride. He turned on his radio which frantically grappled around for a signal from the competing airwaves, before finally settling on a pair of arguing clerics.

By now Manu was feeling claustrophobic and tense. After nearly an hour in the car they were sitting in the biggest traffic jam he had ever witnessed on the outskirts of the city.

"Is it always like this?" he asked.

"Always."

Then without warning, like a scene from a car chase, the taxi driver revved his engine menacingly, reversed onto a small patch of grass at the side of the road and turned the cab around aggressively before heading down a steep dusty incline leading off the highway. Manu clung on for dear life.

"What are you doing?" he shouted above the noise of the engine and the rocks underneath the car.

"I have a short cut my friend. Do not worry!" the driver shouted back.

Manu's fingernails were his only safety harness, as his body was tossed up and down by the force of the bumpy ride.

When they finally reached Cyrus' house it was nearly dusk and he was exhausted. How they arrived at the destination alive was beyond him, terror having eradicated most of the journey details. The taxi stopped outside a large wall nestled into which was a small wooden door. De Vito insisted on providing Manu with a business card, emphasising the fact he knew the city like his grandmother's kitchen.

Manu paid him and got out of the car to ring the bell. After a few minutes the door opened and Cyrus stood in front of him.

"Man, you did it. I was convinced you would chicken out! Come in and meet my mother."

Mrs Jamshidi was a small plump woman who pulled Manu down to her level with great force to kiss him on both cheeks.

"Call me Nazrin," she said in Farsi. "I have heard so much about you!"

Manu handed her the large bag of chocolate he had brought, under instruction from Cyrus who had told him of her passion for English confectionary.

"Come let me show you to your room. We live modestly here. But you are most welcome," she said as she led him to a small cubicle with a camp bed, above which was a window overlooking the courtyard. She flung open the doors of the only other piece of furniture in the room, a skinny wooden wardrobe, before leaving him to unpack.

A short while later Manu stood by the window in Cyrus' equally modest bedroom looking onto a small courtyard. A rooster was walking up and down the side of the pond trying to make a decision about where best to dip its beak into the water for a drink.

"Man, I need a drink after that cab ride. And I'm not even allowed to have one. What am I even doing here? It's utterly ridiculous. I shouldn't have come."

Cyrus was slouching on his bed. "Oh come on. Don't create a drama! Anyway, I have a bottle of vodka… here," said Cyrus leaning over and extending his arm under the bed. He pulled out a box. "…for times like this."

He reached for two small spirit glasses off his shelf behind him and poured them each a large shot. Manu noticed the bottle had no label.

"Where do you get this? It's illegal surely?"

"Hey – they all do it. A friend's relative has his own secret brewery in the second toilet of his house."

"Fabulous," said Manu looking with dismay at his shot and wondering if toilet water had played any part in its distillation. There was no mistaking a faint yellow tinge.

"Look," said Cyrus, "think of it as a sort of toast? You have done a very important thing in your life, you know. You have simply boarded what was already a runaway train.

The destination was always going to be the same. That train was going nowhere but *here* – where you are now."

Manu knocked back the Vodka and thrust his glass towards Cyrus.

He poured him another.

"Let's hope you're right. I mean, let's face it. The place hasn't exactly kept its youth and charm has it? Anyway, I'm only staying a week. It may be a long time in politics, but not long enough to give my personality a makeover or unpick my world views, right? Talking of knots, what news on the carpet? Did you find anything out?"

Cyrus recounted a recent trip to the bazaar to ask locals if they knew of Mr Forooshi, the carpet seller who sold Mrs Garakian the carpet. A few aged stall holders recalled the noisy parakeet, and after further investigations Cyrus had found himself in the teashop of a Mr Shariati, whose grandfather had been a good friend of the carpet seller in question.

"Anyway, Mr Shariati has invited us to meet his father – in his eighties apparently – in the bazaar tomorrow," said Cyrus. "Unless you have something else planned?"

Manu was impressed. "I suppose it's what you get with an advanced and close-knit community structure. Everyone knows everyone else. If we were doing the equivalent in London, we would still be asking around this time next year! And no, I don't have anything planned. As you are aware, there wasn't exactly much 'planning' *involved*," he said.

"Well, I suppose I could show you some sights now you are here," said Cyrus.

"Sights? What sights?" said Manu. "There's nothing to see except traffic and concrete."

"Hey man. You gonna criticise my city without giving it a chance?"

"Sorry, yes. No, I mean. Of course not. Let's do the tourist thing tomorrow. I'm starving right now is there anywhere to eat?"

"Yes, but I can't go with you tonight. We've got this family gathering for a funeral of a relative. I can tell you where to go though."

"That's fine. I'm happy to explore."

Cyrus got out a map. "If you get a cab into the centre here, you can see some nightlife."

"Really? I thought that didn't exist?"

"What do you mean?"

"The guide books says 'dream on'."

"No kidding?"

"Yup."

"Ha ha. That's funny. Well depends what you're dreaming of in the first place I suppose…" said Cyrus.

That was a good point. What was he dreaming of? He simply wasn't sure. He wanted more than to just acquaint himself with an old story. He wanted to corroborate it: verify segments of his past which had been suspended abstractly in his head. Whether or not he was courageous enough, was the question.

It was getting dark when 'De Vito' dropped him in the centre of the city. Better the driver you know Manu had figured. Having delivered him to Cyrus' house alive, the man deserved a measure of loyalty.

Manu strolled down the main boulevard, lined with large trees, where he had been dropped. There was a fresh warmth in the air which took occasional companionship with bursts of exhaust fumes, provided by cars and motorcycles as they coughed their way past. At least there was one benefit to having no sense of smell. Although the sticky tar on the back of his tongue acted as a distress signal.

Outside a café, a pick and mix of males were sipping tea in small shot-glasses and smoking, or playing backgammon. He felt a swarm of eyes following him as he walked past. What? He looked like a foreigner here too? The phosphorescent neon sign above his head was something he had grown accustomed to. At this moment it was flashing: '*Farangi*'. Back home it read '*Arab terrorist*'.

How wearisome that he didn't fit-in here either. In the UK a type of normality had been established in feeling societally naked. The inherent belief had been that a return to the homeland would offer a sense of 'slotting-in'. How frustrating that twelve hours into the experience no slotting-in was on the cards. Did they not recognise the hawk nose and porcupine brows? How intensely native did he have to go to convince them?

Much to his own disgust he decided to locate as westernised an eatery as he could find. And he chose (probably) the city's only junk food restaurant, 'Sooper Bearger' – seemingly the focal point for the city's entire teenage population on a Thursday night. There was no denying. Back Home had a lot to learn from this scene. A gaggle of vivacious young men and women were being rowdy and joking with each other on an evening out – and not a drop of alcohol in sight.

Manu ordered a burger. The aproned man behind the counter bellowed it to a tong-wielding, beetroot-faced, man on a stool – who grilled whilst watching a video of Madonna singing 'Like A Prayer' on a bygone TV above his head.

He sat down at one of the tables. All around was chatter. He surveyed the scene. And in that thought-space he suddenly began to value something within himself which he'd previously regarded as cheap and worthless. Language. In this place it had currency. And although he had forgotten how to speak it, one thing was evident: understanding what was being said was surprisingly easy. He spent the next few minutes allowing his ears to decipher snapshots of conversations. A couple talking about divorce. A woman grumbling to her friend about her mother-in-law. The young people on the next table discussing a party they had been to the night before. It felt good. And he was pleased.

His burger arrived and he ate whilst flicking though the tourist guide. As he did a piece of paper lodged in between the pages jettisoned into the air and fell onto his lap. He picked it up. On it was his uncle's telephone number and underneath was written the address of his old house, in which he had spent much of his childhood. His mother had slipped it into his hand before he left. She had been devastated to leave the country she loved so much and was keen to know what had happened to the old place. She had also made him promise to contact his uncle. He had remained in the country when the rest of the family fled.

The teenage boys on the table next to him were laughing loudly as they discussed the party they had been to. Their hair was slicked back with copious amounts of gel. One of the younger ones explained how he had overdone it by drinking two glasses of pomegranate wine, supplied by a cousin of a cousin. The attentive girls had expertly managed to turn their headscarves into accessories of *such* temptation that even Manu's female friends would be impressed. He glanced underneath their table. Amongst the table legs, three pairs of colourful high heels were doing a coquettish dance with three pairs of loafers.

A stunning looking female recounted a party joke played by one of her friends. He had violently burst through the door of the room where the party was in full-swing – simulating a raid by the morality police, the omnipresent Basij. The partygoers had exploded towards the pre-planned exit routes before realising they had been duped. Manu wondered if it was really worth having a party if it was too dangerous to disco. But he supposed it was his age talking. He'd always been a boringly cautious individual himself. The only risk he ever took was, at the age of eleven, sticking a banana in the exhaust of his father's Triumph Stag, which Mehdi had taken great pains to transport over from Britain.

An older member of the group caught Manu's glance and noticed the guide book he was holding. He nudged his friend who also looked across.

"Excuse me sir, are you from the USA?" one of them asked in English.

Manu smiled. "Britain," he said. The whole table turned round to investigate. Manu's muscles tensed slightly and his throat tightened.

"London?" asked the guy whose beard looked so fertile it appeared to be growing even as they spoke. Manu nodded, hoping that would be the end of it. He wasn't proficient in chit-chat, whatever language it was in. Evidently they presumed he couldn't understand because one of the girls asked the boy to translate: "Ask him if he's heard of a band called Gorillaz."

The boy obliged and Manu nodded, which excited the girl no end. It seemed everyone had a question and all were waiting in turn for the English speaking boy to translate. In the end Manu decided to put them out of their misery.

"I understand a bit of Farsi," he said in their language.

There was silence.

Then – much to Manu's dismay – the conversation switched to Farsi.

"Are you Iranian?" asked the boy.

Manu's response was akin to a six year old boy struggling to make himself understood. It was his own fault. He had been given plenty of opportunities to practise over the years and had taken none of them: mainly because it had embarrassed him to be associated with a country that was continually portrayed as backward, uncivilised and oppressed. And here he was having a conversation with a group of young adults who, in the face of the most extreme peril, were merely daring to party. How brave was that?

But even as he toiled through the familiar but rusty dialect, in what seemed like slow-motion, he gained a kind of fulfilment from struggling through his own private alleyway of history. It seemed absurd that he had spoken this language every day as a child. And that a branch of the family, whom he had known for most of his childhood, was actually here, probably nearby, in this city conversing in the language he was battling, at this moment, to master.

For an instant the iconic scene of departure came starkly into his mind. It was 1979. They were leaving in the dead of night, by car, a few weeks after the referendum which installed the Islamic Republic. Rumours that a purge of westerners would be taking place were circulating and his

English mother was in the firing line at the very least. He was sitting on the rear seat of the car, in pitch black, whilst his mother put last minute items into the boot. Through the front window he could see his grandmother – her face caught in headlights. She was crying and pleading with his father not to go. Uncle Reza had stayed away. He had refused to say goodbye. It was the last time Manu saw any of them. And his grandmother would never see her son again before she died. So many families must have lived through similar traumas. He wondered whether, like himself, they had all cultivated that tough outer skin which acted as a barricade to future emotional injury.

He spent a little while longer fraternising with the affable teenagers before strolling back to Cyrus' house. It was dark and the air was cooler. He found himself actually enjoying the sound of distant horn-blowing from irate drivers, a familiar sound from his youth. Thousands of twinkling lights etched themselves around the branches of some trees under which an old man sat roasting cobs of sweet corn on his charcoal barbeque cart. They cracked and threw up little tiny red sparks into the black air. And he found his nose twitching and ascending in the direction of the smoke – for no reward. More than ever he yearned for the return of his sense of smell. He kicked a green walnut shell that had fallen off one of the trees. This trip was going to be more difficult than he had imagined.

11

Tehran, 1950

"When the oil company is in our hands," Parissa's father was forever saying, as though it belonged to them alone. "When it is in our hands, Karim will find himself wearing a cloak of authority and have an income to match. And your good fortune, my girl, will be awakened."

But, like two cockroaches in a cranny, their conversations about marriage kept colliding, knocking against each other's principles and concluding where they had begun: with Parissa agreeing to consider the matter further. At best she had convinced him they should await the outcome of the oil company negotiations before making any firm plans.

Letters from Karim had endeared him to her a little, it was true. He had shown himself to be a caring and stable man. He had written to her every week without fail, telling her of his oil company escapades. But his candidness often made matters worse and reignited her doubts. She did not want to hear how difficult it was for families of oil workers. After all, she herself may be in that very position in years to come.

And so those alarming threads of thought were left untied. Instead, she immersed herself in heartfelt stories of romantic love. She was the noble and clever Sheharezade, tongue overflowing with tantalising words in the Tale of the Thousand Nights. She was the moon-faced beauty in Saadi's Rose Garden, awaiting a sweetheart to take hold of her sleeve. In the Shahnameh chronicle, she was Princess Rudabeh, smitten with the white-haired Zal, who was raised by a bird.

"*Stronger and more long lasting is the love that faces impediment in its unwrapping,*" her mother used to say, and she believed this to be true.

Nevertheless, buried deep in her bone was a fleck of Eastern prudence separating the whimsical from the utilitarian. Her father was not getting any younger. It was important for his progeny to launch their life journeys when the time was right. He had allowed Parissa to remain when the majority of girls her age were already betrothed. This had been the undoing of them both. And she knew her plight to be the subject of gossip amongst many in her circle.

A few weeks before, on an excursion to the hamam with her sister she was accosted by Mrs Suleymani, her many daughters and the new baby boy who was now ten months old.

"Let Parissa hold the baby," Mrs Suleymani proudly ordered her eldest daughter who held him in her arms. Parissa's sister Soraya pulled at the swaddling clothes to catch glimpse of his face.

"What a very beautiful child," said Parissa moving the sheet to one side to have a look at him closely.

"Fine-looking, yes. Beautiful, no," said Mrs Suleymani with a sour look in her eye.

"Either way he will break many hearts," said Parissa. The baby, though small for his age, had large eyes laced with thick, black eyelashes that clashed together, like butterfly wings, with every blink. A dense mop of charcoal hair, cut close to the head, was assisted in its charm by a pair of pink pouting lips.

Of course, it was a pity about the red birthmark below his eye, the child's mother said making a point of drawing it to Parissa's attention. But the doctor had confessed it may disappear as he got older. Even though it was now the size (and shape) of Saudi Arabia. "We are praying it does not grow to match the enormity of the Soviet Union, or we are in trouble!" roared Shabnaz Suleymani with laughter, revealing a chasm in her gum where a large gold tooth no longer resided. Parissa wondered if it had played any part in the transaction for surgical treatment as she watched the woman's daughters falling about at their mother's repartee.

"Will he have to go to hospital again?" she asked.

"By heaven, no. The procedure went extremely well. They say it is unlikely he will need to have further surgery. I am glad it is all over. The doctors in the hospital were so kind and I thank Allah he was able to be cured. But tell me my dear girl. When are you to be married and have a child of your own!" she cried patting Parissa's belly. "I hear you are to be betrothed soon to Karim Dashti. A finer young man you could not find yourself my dear."

"It will be a little while yet before I have a child of my own. I am too busy looking after these little ones!" said Parissa putting her arm around her sister.

"Well you do not want to leave it too long. They tell me it was my *age* that was responsible for my poor boy's abnormality. You do not want to suffer the same fate."

Parissa handed the child back to her, politely ending the conversation. And they bade their goodbyes before proceeding past the arches towards the bathhouse.

Soraya pulled at Parissa's chador and whispered loudly when she was out of reach "Did you see it Pari? He looks just like a girl!"

"Don't be silly," she said, thinking the very same.

At the disrobing hall in the bathhouse they encountered Mrs Shariati, the teashop owner's wife, Arezoo, wife of the Silversmith and Mrs Bidandoon the wife of the tea-carrier, in deep amusement over the exploits of Mollah Arjumand, one of the local religious men who lived on the north side of the bazaar.

"Have you heard the story?" Mrs Shariati asked Parissa amidst fits of giggles. She admitted she had not.

"You know that he has been getting rather stout over the last few months due to his broken leg in splinters – which he has been resting at home? Well, he was due to give a sermon at the mosque and so Doctor Azizi went over to remove the splinter as his leg had healed. But when the Mollah tried to leave the house he could not get himself through the door, by all accounts."

Mrs Bidandoon continued the story with a shriek, "And there was no other option but for the congregation to pitch up in his garden to hear him give the sermon through the window of his house!"

"By all accounts, his wife has now tied him to the mother of all fasts. He is allowed nothing but water and three apples a day," said Arezoo, tears of laughter running down her cheek.

"I know a woman who lives in the same road and she says she can hear him moaning and groaning all day long," said Mrs Shariati.

"The poor man," said Parissa as she undressed with the others. "How did he break his leg in the first place?"

There was a guffaw from the female gathering.

"A stray dog had run off with the leg of lamb they had hanging in the porch. He was trying to chase it, tripped over a rock and..." said Arezoo her voice trailing into a squeal as she pealed off her clothes to put them in the locker behind her.

At that moment the arched blue door at the far end of the room opened and an ancient washer women, naked from the waist upwards, came striding through. She had one hand on her hip and the other threatened an uncompromising loofah which she waved in front of them. Her wrinkled breasts stretched down to the top of her thin grey pantaloons. They clung, soaking wet, to her thin legs. "Who needs their fantasies scrubbed out of them?" she asked with a toothless grin.

"Parissa!" shouted all the women in concert as they followed her into the bathing chamber.

Washing ceremony over, they raced from the sweltering hot room, through the small tiled octagonal chambers with their domed ceilings, throwing themselves into the vat of cold water in the cool room. There was an explosion of screams. It drowned the sound of their bodies hitting the ice cold water.

"I hear you are to be betrothed to Karim Dashti," said Donya Bidandoon to Parissa as they dried themselves in the locker room afterwards.

"Of sorts," said Parissa quietly, bending down to do up her shoe.

"You are not certain?" she questioned, her pink fleshy face leaning down to catch Parissa's eye.

"Truthfully, I'm not sure what is for the best," said Parissa. "He is a very nice man, full of promise and very considerate. However…."

"I hear his prospects are very good," interrupted Arezoo, who had been listening in to the conversation.

"A man with good prospects is always a golden opportunity. But a youthful age is an added bonus," said Mrs Bidandoon in earnest. "You should be grateful you are not duty bound to a shrivelled old prune, with loose teeth and stinking of urine."

"Oh yes," said Arezoo who was the same age as Parissa. "You know my sister has ended up marrying a man three times her age. She was waiting for a rose and has ended up with the thorn! By all accounts, he breaks wind each time he turns over in his sleep. And his flesh is so brittle that when she puts away the bedding she has to shake off the dead skin. You would not wish that upon yourself!"

"I'm grateful to have someone such as Karim interested in me," said Parissa. "I'm simply not sure I am ready for marriage."

Arezoo tutted, shaking her head. "Take note my girl. Should you wait until you are ready, you will end up with sorrow the size of the Heaven's Kingdom."

"Karim does not make my heart rush," said Parissa.

The women looked at each other and sniggered. "She wants her heart to rush. She has much to learn," said Mrs Bidandoon.

"Do you realise what befalls a rushing heart?" asked Arezoo.

"What do you mean?"

"Those whose bonds derive from a rushing heart are those who walk blind until the rush stops. And when the rush stops they begin to see. And frequently they do not like what they see," said Mrs Bidandoon.

"Do not allow your heart to get involved my girl," said Mrs Shariati. "It is like leaving a rickshaw driver in charge of a steam train. Like letting a child govern the country. Like expecting a spastic to win a race. There is only one purpose your heart has. That is to blind you and lead you astray. We women are cursed with an emotion which makes us weak."

Parissa felt herself to be more unripe than she previously believed. Since her trip to Abadan, she had harboured a small pocket of hope which was becoming evermore battered and bruised by the actuality of life. And, at its centre, Mr Conroy's sandy hair and ocean-coloured eyes were being gradually eroded by overheard conversations and overseen incidents. His lean body sitting upright and thoughtful at the table was melting out of focus with each passing day. And even the bubbling brook that had erupted in the pit of her stomach when he glanced in her direction through the window was now difficult to resurrect. She knew one thing for certain: Karim was not the instigator of such a feeling. Perhaps Mrs Shariati was right. No connection existed between marriage and an effervescent heart. She resolved to put Mr Conroy out of her mind and quarantine her vile and ailing imagination. Karim was a perfectly suitable match and she should be thankful he was interested.

Later that day she wrote him a letter asking him to send a picture of himself. She would place his photograph by her bed. Maybe she would grow accustomed to his inevitable face.

****

A few days later Parissa was weaving upstairs in the workshop. Her father had taken Soraya for an injection at the doctor's surgery and Ali, who was on holiday from school, was in charge of the shop below. She grew thirsty and went down the stairs to the shop to ask Ali if he would get some tea. As she approached the door leading to the shop floor she heard voices. Her brother was laughing, she supposed, with a friend or family member. Pushing the door ajar, she peered into the chamber. At once she recognised Mr Conroy.

Although his impeccable Farsi accent had fooled her into thinking it was a fellow countryman.

"It's only my sister," Ali said by way of explanation, for she had made them jump when she pushed the door open. Parissa turned to retreat up the stairs but Ali stopped her.

"Mr Conroy has come to see you about making him a carpet," he said.

"I must apologise," said Mr Conroy. "I had meant to come in sooner with the measurements that we spoke of, but I was called away to Abadan for a conference." His voice was thick with implication as he looked her directly in the eye.

A wave of heat launched itself in her chest and shot up to her face. She attempted to conceal it by looking down at her clutching hands. "I'm afraid you will need to come back when my father is here," she said. "He will be back this afternoon."

Although only brief, the intensity of his glance revealed volumes. Would he mention that he had seen her in Abadan?

"I'm afraid I shall be leaving for Abadan again shortly. But I have the measurements you required for the carpet here," he said.

A silence ensued as all parties weighed up the potential consequences of their future actions. Ali drew out from his pocket the pendant watch given to him by his father the week before, as a sign of responsibility for taking charge if he had to attend a meeting or a political rally. He looked out of the shop window pane.

"I will close the door and we can move into the workroom. This is business. Father won't mind I'm sure."

"I think father would wish us to wait," said Parissa with a glare.

Ali pushed the glass door to the chamber shut and locked it from the inside. "I am in charge in father's absence," he said in an uncharacteristically deep-toned voice. "Please come to the workshop."

He led the way up the stairs and Parissa followed. Mr Conroy's shoes tapped gently on the wooden staircase behind her. She wondered on which part of her back his gaze was fixed. Once in the workroom Parissa bid them to sit at the side table and Mr Conroy revealed to her the measurements he had written down.

"Is the size too small?" he asked. "Only I would like to have it for my porch just inside the courtyard, which is not terribly large."

Parissa took out her tape measure and estimated the size. And as she did she noticed him looking at her hands.

"You have very smooth hands for a carpet weaver," he pointed out.

She did not have the courage to look at his face. "Luckily I do not do it every day. Otherwise my hands would be cankered and rough," she said focusing on her tape measure.

"Do you remember Mrs Zardesh from the workshop in Tabriz Parissa?" said Ali. "The skin on her hands was as rough as a turtle's. I think she herself was about a hundred and twenty!"

"Perhaps my hands will be like that when I am old," said Parissa raising her head for an instant and finding herself entrapped by Mr Conroy's stare.

He gave an encouraging smile. "I cannot imagine that at all," he said.

And the more she lingered in the vicinity of his face with her eyes, the more she felt it to be the most sincere territory she had ever meandered. His features were exactly proportioned, as though he were the closing sum of a heavenly calculation. The pillow of flesh which formed his top lip would occasionally catch on his front tooth as he spoke. And when he blinked gold flecks of sun bounced off his eyelashes. "A small carpet will take less time, so you will be able to take possession of it sooner," said Parissa hurriedly when she became conscious she had been scrutinising aspects of his countenance. "Perhaps you would tell me the type of pattern you would like. I have some patterns which I use. Let me show them to you."

She stood up to fetch her pattern book from the back of the workshop and he raised his hand to stop her.

"Please. Whatever comes out of your imagination will please me," he said. "Besides, I would like it to be a surprise. I am no artist and would not know where to start."

"An artist? I don't consider myself to be an artist," she said, astonished.

"Well perhaps you should. After all, anyone who creates works of beauty is an artist."

There was a silence as Parissa considered this new perspective on her handiwork. A clatter at the side of the room drew their attention to Ali who was taking the opportunity to poke into a variety of his father's effects. And Parissa continued sitting and looking in her brother's direction.

"It was you in Abadan, was it not?" asked Alec Conroy in a low voice.

Parissa turned her head towards him with a terrified eye.

"Please do not tell my brother!" she whispered clutching the corner of the table.

"You mentioned you are an avid reader" he said suddenly changing the subject. "Do you know the story of Leyla and Majnun?"

Parissa attempted a swallow in spite of her dry throat. She knew it as she knew her own history. She had lived through every detail of their unfulfilled love. It was a story where she had been both the told; and the teller. And it was as fresh in her mind as the opening footprint in the first settle of snow, for she had recited it only yesterday as a lullaby to her sister. The closing scene of two dying lovers kept apart by Leyla's father forever left a residual ache in her soul.

"It is a heartbreaking story," she admitted.

"Made more so because she was betrothed to another against her will?" he proposed gently, to her awakening conscience. He then continued before she had time to react.

"I have recently finished reading it. It has taken me some time because my Farsi is poor. But I thought it the most poetic and beautiful tale."

As he spoke she was soaked up by his attentiveness and absorbed by the movement of his animated face. The strangest thing about the circumstance was how secure she felt. It possibly evoked her childhood of unrestrained indulgence. Nevertheless, that he was interested in her opinions on literature was inconceivable. And yet, here he was now enquiring about her taste in poetry.

"My favourite is Saadi," said Parissa. "I can lend you a book if you would like."

"That would be very kind. If your father wouldn't mind, of course. I have recently been very taken with the poet Omar Khayyam's work which has been translated into English by Fitzgerald, one of our own writers. He has made very good work of it.

The Moving Finger writes; and, having writ, Moves on:

nor all your Piety nor Wit Shall lure it back to cancel half a Line,

Nor all your Tears wash out a Word of it."

The poem itself he quoted in English, and Parissa whose knowledge of the language was rudimentary did not fully understand his translation.

Ali, overheard the English recital and stopped his occupation to join them.

"I'm afraid I'm not sure of the Farsi translation," said Alec Conroy and moved quickly to the issue of the train he needed to catch. He asked how long it would take for the carpet to be made.

"I estimate a month or a little longer. I'm afraid these things take a little time," said Parissa.

"I shall return when I get back from Abadan to discuss price with your father. Perhaps you could let him know," said Mr Conroy.

Parissa nodded and he stood up to go. "It has been a great pleasure meeting you again," he said shaking her hand. She watched the back of his tall figure moving towards the door and as he departed he glanced behind himself and proffered a smile in her direction.

12

Tehran, 1950

"Let me explain in simple terms," said Hajji-Hossein pulling the backgammon board on the brass table a little closer. "The red pieces *here*, are the members of the National Front. Of these, *eight* have been elected to the Majlis." He slid eight red chequers to the other side of the board and surveyed Bidandoon's face closely. "Are you taking note?"

Bidandoon's extra large head was cocked to one side, "Y-e-es."

"And their leader is Mossadegh. He was also elected and also joins them *here*." He slid a black chequer over to the red ones already at the corner of the board.

"Ah, this black piece, Mossadegh, is the Prime Minister now," said Bidandoon proudly.

"No, no, no, no! He is not the Prime Minister. He is a deputy. He is elected to help make the laws."

"But the laws are made by the Shah are they not?" asked Bidandoon scratching his large head.

"Hah! Some say everyone else *but* him!" laughed Mr Dashti who happened also to be sitting around the table listening to the conversation.

"Dashti, please. Do not complicate this matter with sarcasm. I am attempting to explain the latest elections, which as we know have been as opaque as a woman's chador! The man is quite right to be confused. "

"Nevertheless, he is inflicted with an innate chaos in his mind Hossein," said Dashti under his breath. "Forever inform him the hen is a cock; and he will *still* expect it to lay an egg!"

"And whom did I vote for?" interrupted Bidandoon, purposely illustrating the point.

"You voted for Mossadegh who leads the National Front and it is he and his group of twenty who are calling for honest elections, a free press and oil nationalisation."

"Good. It is him I desired. And now he is in command, we shall all be saved!" shouted Bidandoon clapping his hands.

Hajji-Hossein emitted a dog-like whimper and lent behind himself to pick up a ghalyan.

"I would stick to the carpet-selling Hossein," called the Mr Shariati from behind his tea counter. "Your teaching skills are several volumes short of a vocation!"

At that moment the door to the teashop opened and Ali Forooshi came into the shop, smartly dressed.

"Father I have outside, the cart with the carpet for delivery to Mr Conroy. You said we would deliver it to him this morning?" said Ali.

"I'm feeling exhausted my boy. Tell Hassan to drive you there but ensure you collect the money."

"Of course," said Ali. "Father, I wish you would let me oversee the shop more often when you are so busy."

Hajji-Hossein frowned suspiciously. "How do I know you are up to it?" he asked.

"I have been studying my calculation books every night father. Please let me demonstrate my proficiency! My class teacher always says that to gain a skill one needs to practise. How will I learn if I have no responsibility?"

"He is right. Let him shoulder a little weight, Hossein," urged Dashti. "Besides, you know well that our involvement in this campaign will only become more intense over the coming months."

"Very well," said Hajji-Hossein. "Perhaps I shall let you be in charge one day a week after school. We will discuss the practicalities at home this evening. But at the first symptom of trouble I shall be upon you like an eagle. I have already lost one business too many."

Ali nodded and departed, passing Dr Azizi who was entering through the teahouse doorway.

"It's mighty cold out there. This snow has kept us waiting for weeks."

"By the colour of your nose I would say it is immediately around the corner," said Hajji-Hossein, beckoning to the tea-carrier. "Bidandoon, fetch this man a glass of tea if you would."

Azizi sat at the table and removed his gloves. "I have come straight from the Suleymanis' house where there was a celebration for baby Arvin's first birthday."

"Ah! One year already! I admit, I am not at all convinced the medical procedure undertaken was well founded," said Hajji-Hossein gravely.

"What are you saying?" asked Dashti.

"If there was a quandary as to his genus at birth, what parent, when handed such a gift of choice, would not opt for a male when he already has his full quota of women in the house? But it's my guess the baby may be on the verge of starting the masquerade of a lifetime."

"Are you suggesting he will find himself walking in the shoes of a man, when in fact he has a woman's backbone?" asked Dashti, wide eyed.

"From what I've seen of the child's sum-total, my instinct tells me a larger fraction was born female than male. And as the child blossoms and bursts into character, it may begin to find its disposition out of kilter with its competency. Indeed, if it is to make a mockery of itself and its family – is it not fair they should be informed?" said Hajji-Hossein.

"I confess, I have been wrestling with this quandary for a while," Dr Azizi confided. "But, you see, there is great expense involved to rectify these kinds of problems – sums which, I imagine, Suleymani could barely afford."

Hajji-Hossein scratched his head. "It is a dilemma. But I would have done the same in his shoes. Surely someone must know the solution to all of this?"

"I intend to visit the medical school at the university after prayers. It would be useful to find out more information about what the man's options are before broaching the issue with him."

"I shall accompany you," said Hajji-Hossein. "I need to clear my mind. I tell you, it is a good thing Ali has settled well into running the shop. What with all these meetings we attend, I think I may soon pull him out of school altogether to help takeover."

"Well I suppose you know what you are doing," said Azizi. "There's every indication that, with things as they are, it's best to leave them in school and encourage them to attend university."

"University is for empty heads who need their minds filling with all kinds of ridiculous ideas. And ideas will not put bread in our mouths, Azizi. You know that!"

"I am merely suggesting things are changing fast. Simply look at the number of young people on the streets with nothing to do. There is no work for them in the bazaar, now everything is being made by machine. When you and I are buried, Ali may no longer have a trade."

"Nonsense. There is an untapped market in trade with the farangis."

"Perhaps. Though that too will be under threat if relations with outsiders are soured by this oil crisis. I have already heard talk that the West is on the verge of imposing sanctions, to force us to our senses."

"Let us not speak of the issue. It makes my blood boil!" said Hajji-Hossein banging down his tea glass on the table. "I'm going home to have a nap and rid myself of this headache. I will see you at the mosque," he said and strode towards the door muttering to himself.

"I fear you have hit a raw nerve there," said Dashti biting his lip.

"I believe you are right," said Azizi with a perfunctory nod.

****

The sun was low in the sky and it had started to snow when Dr Azizi and Hajji-Hossein made their way to the university medical school later that afternoon.

"I am surprised you are accompanying me to such a den of proselytising," said Dr Azizi with a mouthful of bread and paneer as they walked.

"What? Oh yes well, I'm curious to see the place where these young people get their modern ideas from. I heard the other day that the percentage of students joining our campaign is very high. I cannot understand it, since they seem to be driven by western ideals."

"I suspect it is an unease with the lack of accountability and representation in our current system. They do not feel their voice is heard. And they see Mossadegh as a vehicle for their desires. Students are, by nature, revolutionaries are they not?"

Hajji-Hossein was relieved his son had no pretentions of choosing such a pointless route. He would be all the richer for assuming the family trade and remaining self sufficient. Parissa, of course, would have given her very soul to be a literary scholar. But what good was musing over poetics in a world where hunger and thirst were everywhere?

By this time they had arrived at the university gates. Dr Azizi asked directions to the medical science centre from a young male student walking past.

He pointed them towards a tall whitewashed building in the near distance. On arrival they located the professor of Medical Ethics, with whom Dr Azizi discussed the psychological effects of gender change. "The question remains whether the Suleymanis are able to do anything about it *now*," said Dr Azizi as they left the medical science building. "And – more importantly- whether I should even tell them."

Just as they were pondering the issue, a woman came around the corner of the building in front of them. Dr Azizi stopped walking and cleared his throat.

It caught the woman's attention and she looked up and smiled. "Why, it's Dr Azizi isn't it, how are you?" she said holding out her hand, her tight-fitting orange suit reverberating in the foreground of the white snow.

“Ah, yes hello…” he stuttered looking at Hajji-Hossein. “We have been visiting the medical centre, just here.”

“I hope you are quite well…?” she said, her beetroot-red lips frozen into a concerned pout.

Hajji-Hossein surveyed the scene. Clearly his friend had met this embroidered woman before. Her fluffy hair cascaded like a black waterfall onto her shoulders, and these were enhanced with padding to render her full-of-point. Her carrot suit traced every hill and valley of her anatomy and rhymed perfectly with the tomato-coloured shoes now pointing like a compass in Azizi’s direction.

Despite the frost, diamonds of sweat were twinkling on his friend’s forehead.

Typical, thought Hajji-Hossein. This was exactly what today’s excessive liberalism produced: crude and unambiguous wantonness. How could it be *more* civilised? He watched her play a coded game with Azizi with her bright blue eyelids. And he, poor man, was being forced to respond to the signals.

“Miss Shabi, this is my friend and colleague, Hajji-Hossein. He runs the main carpet stall in the bazaar. Yes, indeed. And has a daughter, with extreme talent for carpet weaving. Do you not ?”

Nargess abruptly directed her attention to Hajji-Hossein.

“A talented daughter, sir?”

“Yes – indeed. What about her?” said Hajji-Hossein.

“Dr Azizi indicates that she weaves carpets by all accounts.”

“Yes. She already has a skill.”

“I’m sorry?”

“She has a skill. She is proficient. In no need of bettering.”

“I quite understand, yes. There is no better skill than that of an artisan.”

“That you give it recognition is to your credit,” said Hajji-Hossein loftily.

There was an awkward silence and Hajji-Hossein looked away while Dr Azizi conducted a brief conversation before bidding their departure.

"It was nice to meet you again," he said with a smile.

"Equally," said Nargess Shabi and – after shaking their hands – strode purposefully away.

"I'm not a man to give unrequited counsel as you know Azizi," said Hajji-Hossein as they made their way towards the establishment gates. "But I would advise caution where a woman like that is concerned. She looks like a pro-western royalist. It goes against everything we are fighting for. How long have you known her?"

"I've met her only twice, in the bazaar. But you are wrong to judge Hossein. Did you not hear her just now? She was speaking of attending the next nationalisation rally, in the palace grounds."

Hajji-Hossein paused on the path and put his hand on Dr Azizi's shoulder to look him in the eye. "Was she indeed? I did not notice. I must confess I found it hard not to be led astray by her lavish attire."

Azizi shrugged it off. "She is glamorous, that I admit. But more important still is what exists underneath. And you must admit, she has a benevolent manner."

"You know as well as I do my friend. A fair face does not require embellishment. On the contrary, it is at its most beautiful by moonlight - when one sees half with the eye and half with the fancy. Women like her, I fear, take up the *whole* eye, not half of it."

"Well, no matter- I am too old to argue. Neither of us need worry. She is a rose it is true – but not in any garden of mine!" said Azizi.

"That will be my last word on the matter, for you are a good friend and I would not like to see you taken for a fool. But do remember, *he who wants the rose, must respect the thorn.*"

Dusk was upon them and it had started to snow as they walked toward the university gates.

From an office window behind them, the subject of their conversation watched as the two men retreated from the campus, leaving behind a set of larger and smaller footprints in the snow. What a peculiar pair they made, thought Nargess Shabi. Her second encounter with Ahmad Azizi, outside an eyebrow threading booth in the bazaar, had yielded a short conversation about the role of women in Iranian society, which proved him to be thoughtful and broad minded. Yet here he was fraternising with a relic of the past who looked as though he kept his daughter under lock and key.

As the curious union disappeared into the distance something suddenly occurred to her. That was the remarkable feature of this creeping revolution: the offer of collective satisfaction to opposing angles of society. Freedom, independence and progression were rare issues on which the peaks and troughs of Irani humanity could agree. She, Ahmad, and his friend Hajji-Hossein exemplified the assorted mixture of people in their culture who were joined together, at that particular moment, to make a specific point. What would happen, she wondered, when that point had finally been made?

13

Tehran, 2003

A meteorological accident had brought about a British summer in Tehran. Manu and Cyrus were in the taxi, on a stop-go trajectory, heading towards the Grand Bazaar in the morning rush hour. Their journey was a confirmation of the guide book's terse review of Iran's transport system: *top of the global league table in road fatalities*. The uniform obstinacy of both driver and pedestrian were played out in a posturing dance for all to see. Large crowds of office workers tumbled off the pavements, blocking entire roads, seemingly willing to lose life and limb to attract the attention of a cab. Taxis bombed down the street their passengers bursting out of windows. It was Keystone Cops – Middle Eastern style.

At the same time, on the pavement sidelines, Manu witnessed the road-crossing crowd's collective will. A courageous pedestrian, about to cross the road, would attract a large cluster of like-minded jaywalkers, and the whole posse would heave across the road like a Chinese dragon, indifferent to the speed of the road or the colour of the lights (of which there were few). Death aside, it was really quite cool; there was not a single circumstance in which the Tehrani pedestrian felt intimidated by traffic.

Whilst Manu almost physically felt his first grey hairs germinating, his unfazed friend chatted with the taxi driver throughout the journey.

A short while later both stood at the Four Souk crossroads of the Tehran Bazaar. Surrounding them were richly decorative grottos, at the mouths of which sat men of a variety of ages, their hawk eyes – now here, now there – ready to spot the tiniest opportunity to do business.

Manu sensed the customary beacon above his head attempting to flicker into action as he walked past rows of turning heads and staring eyes.

"What is wrong with these people? Do I look like an alien or something!" he said, irritated.

"Chill out, man!" said Cyrus. "You don't exactly blend in with your straightened hair and confident swagger."

He probably deserved it all. Had he made any attempt to connect with his roots? Had he showed any pride in his ancestry? Did he keep in touch with any Irani relatives? No, no and no. His only loyalty had been in keeping his nose away from the plastic surgeons. The flashing sign was here to stay.

Nevertheless, there was something deeply innate about this place. The mountainous kaleidoscope of spices and patterned ornaments pulsated with intensity. And the bedlam of colours and competing patterns which argued with each other, and competed for attention, offered a richness of depth his eye had not beheld for some time. And the sound of itinerant bartering emanating from a number of corridors sent a tickle skipping over his ear.

Ahead of him a carpenter was shaping doors. Behind a silversmith was hammering his woes into silver pots. In a chamber to his right, an ancient baker had already spent three-quarters of his life kneading dough and throwing it over the coals with a large wooden pallet.

What did these people think of westerners? Manu had experienced only approval and solicitous pleasantries so far. He wondered in which nook and cranny could be found those vehement anti-western incantations, so regularly spoon-fed by the media to a blank British public.

The trouble with international reporting was its tendency to cherry-pick and magnify. As a peripatetic window on the world it could never really put things into perspective or context. It was hard enough for people to relinquish conspiracy theories they had grown to believe of their *own* governments. They were hardly likely to question reporting of events across the divide.

He noticed, to his right, a young American couple entwined in a tangle of words and gestures with a stallholder. It was making them all laugh. The absence of self-aggrandising was reassuring to note. Shopkeepers were neither obsequious nor obnoxious, and their genuine interest in foreigners was charming. He wondered if there was such a thing as an Irani character.

He considered *himself* to be a citizen of nowhere in particular. Sociologists would doubtless have some theory about the cause of that; provoked by the wrench from one's birth country, no less. A kind of inverted separation anxiety perhaps? Whatever the reason, he never could understand the notion of feeling love for one's country. You could love your family, and members of your family. You could certainly love your children. You should at least *try* to love your husband or wife. You might – at a push – love your friends. Loving a god he could vaguely comprehend in certain contexts. But loving a country seemed absurd. What was it, in the inadequacies of a mortal, that cultivated the love of a country? What indeed was there to love?

By now they were passing a juncture which, interestingly, resembled a souk in mall's clothing.

"Is this what bazaars sell nowadays?" he asked Cyrus pointing to a Spice Girls Dolls box-set, which shared a table with a few replica Rolex watches. "It's starting to look rather like the Camden of Tehran."

"Hey man. This isn't a bygone age you know! You wouldn't visit Covent Garden and hope to see Victorian butchers and barrow boys would you?" said Cyrus beckoning him down a narrow alleyway towards a small teashop.

He had a point.

Manu followed him sheepishly up to the entrance of the teashop where a shower of multicoloured beads performed the function of a half-hearted door, leading to an enchanting little cavern. A horizontal film of smoke slithered around the room, considerately avoiding the abundance of framed pictures on the wall. At a table in the corner a few middle-aged men sat smoking and drinking tea. Cyrus led the way to the small counter on which was perched the largest silver samovar Manu had ever seen. He began to chat to the man behind the counter who was holding a tall silver teapot. As he listened the man trailed a torrent of tea along a row of glasses, filling them in one swoop.

"Your grandfather has owned this teahouse for a long time Mr Shariati?" asked Cyrus.

"Indeed yes," said the man as he placed the filled tea glasses on the waiting tea-carrier's tray. "The only change has been the actual position of the stall. It used to – in the old days – be in the South Suq of the bazaar. Then the authorities tried to bulldoze their way through the place, attempting to build a freeway. So we were forced to relocate."

He passed Cyrus two glasses of tea.

"Please sit," he said pointing to the small table in the corner. "My grandfather will arrive shortly."

Cyrus and Manu sat down at a corner table. A rather bizarre looking middle-aged man with long grey hair, wearing a brightly coloured robe, approached their table with a rag. He offered them a protracted smile as he began to wipe the table in a slow circular motion. His long and bright orange finger nails looked a little too immaculate against the dirty rag they were clenching. Manu gave Cyrus an uncomfortable glance.

"Arvin! Can you come here and take over the counter please?"

The robed man responded to the call from the teashop owner and departed, flashing them another smile as he did.

"Is it my imagination, or was he wearing mascara?" whispered Manu.

Before Cyrus could reply there was movement amongst the door beads and an old man with white hair and a walking stick was helped into the shop by a middle-aged lady. People from all sides of the room sprang into action as he slowly made his way to their table. Glasses of tea and sugar appeared from the sidelines. Someone placed a tumbler of water in front of him. Another young person brought over some cushions.

"This is my grandfather, Mr Shariati, and my mother," said the teashop owner who had emerged from behind the counter, with a young boy wrapped around his calf. "And this," he said picking up the toddler. "This is my son!"

The little boy buried his head into his father's shirt as the collective gaze of the seated group shifted its attention to him like a searchlight.

Manu cast his eye over the family. A chain of squints ran through the grandfather, his daughter and her son, the teashop owner. Fortunately it appeared to have stopped short of the grandson.

After an assortment of pleasantries Cyrus steered the conversation to the point by briefly explaining their interest in the carpet and enquiring about the carpet-seller Mr Forooshi.

"Ah, yes. Hajji-Hossein," said the old man. "He has long passed away now. He moved back to his hometown of Tabriz after...." he stopped to put a sugar lump in his mouth and take a sip of tea.

"Hajji-Hossein's carpet shop in the bazaar was very popular," he continued. Some of his carpets came from Tabriz, from the workshop he had before moving to the capital. But many were woven by his talented daughter. She could command a very high price for her weaving work."

"This sounds very like the carpet my friend has, which is also very beautiful," said Cyrus.

"She was indeed a talented young girl," said Mr Shariati looking in the distance. "In those days aptitude of that calibre was gold dust. Now of course it is all made by machine."

"Her skills must have been in great demand," said Cyrus. "Perhaps she also did commissions for foreigners?"

The old man shook his head in disgust. "No. The foreigners were not interested in our skills and our crafts. Only our oil," he said gruffly.

"Perhaps she was schooled in English then?" said Cyrus.

The old man looked confused. "Why do you ask that question?"

"The carpet belonging to my friend contains a line of poetry from Omar Khayyam. However it's an English translation, which is peculiar. This is why I ask."

"I do not understand your meaning," he said, agitated.

"Do you mean the poetry is in English script?" asked Mr Shariati's grandson.

"What kind of question is this anyway?" interrupted his grandfather. "You said you were interested in the carpet. I do not know about any English translation."

A crimson rage began to march across the old man's pale face and he raised a shaking finger, pointing it in Cyrus's direction. His daughter was studying her hands and fiddling with the ends of her manteau.

"I'm sorry sir. It is the carpet we are interested in. It is not my intention to cause offense," said Cyrus.

"What do you do? Who are you anyway?" asked Mr Shariati, the creases around his already wrinkled eyes multiplying tenfold with suspicion.

"What do I do for a living? Well, actually I'm a television researcher. But that's not why we're here, Mr Shariati. It's the history of the carpet that interests us," said Cyrus.

Manu was horrified and kicked his friend under the table. What kind of idiot would admit to being part of the Western media, in a country whose pet hate was – the Western media. It was a no-brainer. Surely even Cyrus would understand this. Especially as eyes and ears were everywhere, he had been told. He tried repeatedly to catch Cyrus' evading eye.

"And," continued his oblivious friend, disregarding each frenzied kick to his ankle, "we're interested in what the English connection might have been. Could it have been something to do with the Anglo Iranian Oil Company which operated at the time perhaps?"

"Grandfather, you do not have to answer these questions. Would you like him to stop?" said Mr Shariati's grandson.

"Well, there are plenty of people to talk to about that – and I'm not really – I can't really tell you much myself," said Grandfather Shariati, shifting uncomfortably on his seat. "My compatriot Mr Forooshi, the carpet-seller, was far more involved than I in oil company matters. It's true we did take part in a number of protests, in support of nationalisation. But I'm not sure what you are suggesting? If you think there was some sort of conspiracy on the part of the bazaar community you are very mistaken."

There was a silent pause. Cyrus began rooting around his jacket pocket. Eventually he produced a photograph which he held up for the old man to see. It was a picture of the carpet which they had taken before the trip. He slid it across the table towards the old man, with a John Wayne-type gesture.

The old man picked up the photo and studied it carefully before handing it to his daughter whose eyes betrayed moderate surprise.

"We are not suggesting this," said Cyrus, "but you must agree...."

He was cut short by the old man who had clearly found himself on the cusp of a second wind.

"You young people have no idea what our generations have endured in our lifetimes. You go about parading this trophy called 'Freedom' above your heads, as though it will provide immunity from all woes. And you go as you please. And you say as you please, as though free will is the cheapest thing in the world. Let me tell you this from experience. It has taken many lives and livelihoods to provide you with a mere drop of this privilege. Do not allow this fact to slip from your memory."

He stopped to catch his breath. His grandson stepped behind him and put his hands on his grandfather's shoulders protectively.

"I think you are getting tired grandfather. I suggest you allow mother to take you home."

The old man nodded obligingly and began to reach for his gloves.

"Sir, thank you for your time. We did not wish to cause offense. We simply wished to find out more about the weaver of this beautiful carpet. What was her name?" asked Manu tentatively in Farsi, and felt an immediate glow when the man responded un-perplexed.

"Parissa."

"Parissa. And I presume she could speak English?"

"Yes, some," said Mr Shariati rubbing his back as though in pain. "She had been schooled in English at a young age. But she – of course – had nothing whatsoever to do with the protests, or the oil company. "

"Yes, yes. I quite understand," said Manu, not wishing to cause any further commotion.

The old man softened his stance. "If you require more information on Mr Forooshi I suppose you could talk to Karim Dashti," he said, standing with his daughter's help and picking up his cane. "He spent a good deal of time working for the oil company refinery in Abadan and is, of course, married to Mr Forooshi's daughter. He can tell you many stories of how it was in those days. And there is Mr Forooshi's son Ali – who lives in Tabriz. Hassan joon, give the gentleman his telephone number."

The old man rose from his seat and pointed his cane towards Cyrus' face. "I would be careful if I were you, young man. All these questions will only open old wounds. And you may well get into trouble with the authorities. They do not appreciate people digging around for information."

Cyrus led him to the door of the teahouse. And as his daughter left the table she touched Manu on the shoulder.

"It's not my business. And it is not my family," she hissed. "But if you want more information you should ask Karim Dashti about the English man who ruined a generation of lives – including his own. There are rumours that have hovered over this family for too long," she muttered, shaking her head.

For the first time Manu felt quite uncomfortable. Was it really that sinister? Perhaps the daughter, Parissa, had become involved with an English man in some way. Did he abuse her, or just use her? He felt sick at the thought. Uncovering a story of abuse of an Iranian girl at the hands of an Englishman was something he simply couldn't face, even if he *was* lacking a few patriotic bones in his body. What if the man had done something horrifying to this girl and her family?

None of these issues seemed to be affecting Cyrus in any way. As they walked back to the main boulevard to find somewhere to eat, Manu expressed his reservations about the whole affair.

"I've been thinking and reckon we should abandon this," he said.

"Abandon what?" asked Cyrus.

"It's just. What *am* I trying to say? I just don't think this issue, this topic, this story – whatever you want to call it, is worth pursing - is what I'm trying to say. Look, we're running around like idiots chasing a stupid story about a *rug* for God's sake. A *rug!* Who cares? Do we really want to go digging into these people's lives like this?

"Of course not – but we wanted some background and, you forget, people here can be reserved about their personal lives to outsiders. Man, sometimes you need to shock them into confession."

Manu burst out laughing. "This isn't the Spanish Inquisition you know. And it's not like we're private detectives either – is it? I'd really just rather enjoy my holiday."

"Yeah. But man, maybe this girl, whoever she was, was in cahoots with the British; an agent maybe. It's well known that CIA and the SIS did manipulate Iranian citizens. In order to spread propaganda - you know, against the people's prime minister, Mossadegh. We just need a little more information – it could be interesting! Let's see this guy Karim and if he doesn't come up with the goods, we'll drop it."

"Yes but – even if this girl *was* involved – so what. It's all water under the bridge now."

"Water – under what bridge?"

"You know – history. Finished. Oh never mind."

"History man is what makes life interesting. History is where the story is. And history is where the money is too. And supposing we discover some secret history. Especially now – with all this tension over Iraq. It's gonna be like *be careful what you wish for*."

"Hey, this isn't downtown Shepherd's Bush, you know. This is Tehran. You, of all people, should know what kind of trouble you could get into. That journalist, what's his name I can't remember – anyway that guy who recently poked his nose into some conspiracy or other – look where he ended up – in Evin Prison. He's there now isn't he? If we're not careful we might be joining him."

"Nah, we will be fine. They *want* you to feel like that. They like to put the frighteners on you. But they can't police *every* little thing."

"OK. But the moment it starts getting uncomfortable I'm cutting loose."

"Fine by me if that's what you want."

They walked along silently for a while. Passing shops proffered plates of sprouted green lentils on tables outside, to celebrate No-Ruz. A young boy chased after them with a barrow full of water-filled plastic bags, each containing two goldfish bouncing against each other. A blind, old amputee and his young grandson sat on the pavement selling multicoloured hand-painted eggs.

Egg painting. That was Sami's favourite No-Ruz past time.

A torrent of images came into his head. Sami egg painting under the willow tree. His grandmother piercing eggs with a pin to empty their contents. Sami on the balcony throwing a raw egg into Mrs Garakian's garden next door. *Mr* Garakian's angry face at their front door holding a statue of Saint Nino covered in egg yolk.

Further retrospection of this kind was likely if he was to spend No-Ruz day with his uncle.

Ahead of them outside a little café, a crowd of agitated people were heckling a television in the window. As they approached, Cyrus clutched Manu's arm.

"What's up?"

"Look."

Manu pushed past a tall man in the crowd to see the mother of all antitheses on the TV screen: George Bush conversing in Farsi. (over-dubbed of course – but it still looked crazy strange).

"It's happened. Iraq has been invaded!" said Cyrus.

"Nice one. In the face of near-global public opposition, a minority of world leaders have seen fit to dictate," said Manu. "There you have it, a mere taster of one of the incompetencies of the democratic process: the myth of political self determination. And what a surprise. Its perpetrators *still* hawk it around the globe as an example of good governance. What's he saying?"

"Usual stuff. *We won't be at the mercy of an outlaw regime that threatens the peace with weapons of mass murder.*"

The small gathering watching TV was becoming rather agitated.

"It's a joke!" shouted a man in the crowd. "It is they who give Saddam the power he needs and now they want to disarm him. The victims caught in the middle of this mess are the Iraqi people!"

"Do you think we'll be able to get out of the country?" Manu asked.

"What do you mean?"

"You know. Fly. Be allowed to return to the UK!"

"Ha ha. You're not used to war are you?"

"You take it in your stride, obviously?"

"It's part of life around here," said Cyrus. "Wasn't that long ago that we were fighting Saddam ourselves remember? My uncle is still driven mad with skin rashes from the poison gas during the Iraq war."

Manu felt abashed. At the start of the first Persian Gulf war he had just arrived in the UK and been thrust into a sea of British middle-class schoolboys who were on the hunt for nonconformity. Finding a niche was never going to be easy – especially with the nickname 'My New Chair' and its associated verbal paraphernalia. Then came the bitter Middle Eastern squabble in which the bouncers of the western world supported Iraq's use of nerve and mustard gas on Iranian civilians. 'New Chair' was lying low, watching from the sidelines and developing a chip on his shoulder as a result of being associated with the underdog. No one likes being a loser. And Chair was by now feeling like a loser. So when Ethan Bell-Parker and his gang came gunning, the only option was to run with the Anglo-Saxon pack. This resulted in a kind of ethno-infidelity, whereby vestiges of Persian ancestry and history were consigned to the bin. And Manu would employ elaborate tools to untie himself from any remaining Middle Eastern tethers. One happy outcome: he was no longer referred to as a piece of furniture. But there was a kind of internal damnation for crossing to the other side.

Manu surveyed the petulant crowd of (mainly) men watching President Bush and grumbling over what they saw as history repeating itself. Cyrus had a point. There was war and fight in every one of those faces. And the evidence was all around: it had trickled down even to the animated three year old who hung about his father's trouser leg.

Cyrus pointed to a nearby restaurant with a crackling coal stove outside on which slabs of sizzling kebab were being rotated by a man with a shaved head. Smoke from the meat juices burst vertically into the air and unfurled themselves in front of them. Manu was conscious his nose was rummaging around the air for a smell. These days it had assumed an exaggerated twitching motion, very much in keeping with a marginally deranged dog. And it was becoming a subconscious habit at the sight of cooking food. What's more, he had often caught his own reflection during 'the act'. It resembled the pose of a man about to shape-shift into a werewolf. At best it might be mistaken for a microscopic epileptic seizure. And now the barbeque chef was staring in his direction, a half-loaded skewer frozen in mid air. Manu smiled and nodded as a reassurance of his sanity.

They sat outside at one of the tables and ordered their food whilst Cyrus used his mobile to telephone the number they had been given for Karim Dashti to arrange a meeting for the next day. Manu lifted his face towards the sun and closed his eyes. It was the one thing he had consistently appreciated since his arrival, and would be sad to be parted from.

The silky megaphoned voice of the muezzin echoed out across the rooftops in the midday call to prayer. In symphonic waves came the distant cry of the almond seller. And an old man on the next table advised another on how to tend to the blight of his apricot tree. It was all starting to feel so very correct.

Tomorrow was the day before new year. The day after that he would be returning home: if indeed that's where home was.

14

Tehran, 2003

"So my friend – this is where you used to live," said De Vito as he pulled in to a small road and pointed to a large pair of black metal gates which were invitingly open.

Manu stepped out of the car and walked towards the entrance gates of the square detached house, one of three similar designs on that side of the street. The outward appearance of the surrounding buildings themselves remained unchanged after all these years, but their purpose had evolved from residential to commercial. Additional shops and offices had been squeezed in between and around them. Where once family life had passed its time, now enterprise had muscled in. And as he approached the entrance Manu noticed a discreet brass sign on the right-hand side gate which read: Zagros Nursery. His own family's history, it seemed, had been devoured by market forces too.

He surveyed the scene inside the small garden which was open for all to see. About ten small children were playing chase around the weeping willow tree where his brother and he used to play. The house itself had retained its facade: wall-to-wall sliding glass doors opening onto the garden, from the ground floor; and above, large glass-fronted rooms overlooking a balcony, with two planters built into the metal balustrade. The lady who was supervising the toddlers saw him looking through the gate and called her superior, an older woman, who came over.

After explaining the reason for his visit, the supervisor looked hesitant.

"I'm afraid I cannot allow you to come in," she said without explanation.

Manu watched as she went into the house.

To the left of the willow tree, the fateful pool was now a sandpit in which two small children, toasted by the sun, built sandcastles. It appeared much smaller than he remembered. How was it possible for a child to drown in a pond that small? The sight of Sami's small body floating in the water face-down had, for years, been outlawed in his consciousness.

It had been shortly after Manu's eighth birthday, the gift of a Batman utility-belt (with radio receiver buckle) having rocked his world the week before. A pair of bat-cuffs completed the set, and had been used to apprehend a range of toys and small domesticated animals. It was whilst he was frantically looking for the key to the Bat-cuffs, which he had dropped in the grass, that his mother's screams pierced his very soul into the future. Mrs Garakian's cat had witnessed the whole sorry saga whilst neck-cuffed to the garden gate.

The small blue body was pulled from the pool and various fruitless resuscitation procedures had ensued before he was pronounced dead at the scene. A gigantic wall of shock tumbled down upon them, and had continued tumbling ever since. A persistent image which took Manu years to lock away was the thread of water leaking from his brother's small, ash-grey, mouth as he was being cradled by his crying mother at the side of the pond. Now, in that sacred spot, two little laughing children were throwing sand at each other. It was as though the incident had been erased.

Manu was turning to leave when a young man appeared at the side of the entrance where he stood. "My colleague has asked me to show you around," he said standing to one side and putting out his hand in the general direction of the house.

"That's very kind," said Manu nodding to the manager who stood in the doorway smiling as he went past. What a surreal feeling: being ushered through the front door of one's own house by a total stranger. In front of him were the marble open-slatted stairs, under which he and his brother used to play hide and seek. These memories had been a mere speck in his imagination. Now they seemed to be gathering legitimacy. Hardly any photos of his past life existed. All superfluous memorabilia had been shed like a dead skin before flight. The only snapshots which had survived the purge were those of his brother, caught, frozen, mid-life. All else had been left to memory and its whim. And now, like a dormant seed given the right conditions, his narrative was beginning to unfurl. It was true. The place really did exist. The space under the stairs, where the oil stove used to be; now usurped by a reception desk. Leading off the hall, the plush living room: transformed into a toddler-sized play kitchen. And in it, two little girls were making a meal out of Lego bricks. How bizarrely pertinent.

The man led him upstairs to the bedrooms where Manu walked round the edge of the landing area and into his old room, which now hosted four miniature beds. It had shrunk to a quarter of the size he remembered.

A fog of melancholia hovered. The place of his youth: he never thought he would see it again. This was, to a small degree, what people felt like when identifying a dead body, he imagined. The final chance to commemorate something beloved they could never again experience. He walked across the room and stepped through the open glass door onto the balcony, into the bright sunlight. Below, Mrs Garakian's old garden next door into which Sami had thrown the egg, was now a builder's yard. He stood there for a few minutes with the man watching behind him.

Immediately beneath him, on the grass next to the old pool, the children were being coaxed to sleep on blankets under the shade of the willow tree. A mosaic of swirls and patterns were engraved in the sand where they had been playing earlier. And from the composition Manu could make out the shape of a child's giant arm and hand, waving – to him, it seemed.

He stared at it for a while. "Goodbye Sami," he murmured.

He turned and nodded to his chaperone waiting in the hallway and they made their way downstairs and back to the front gate. As he left the house he took some surreptitious pictures from the outside to please his mother. What had become of Mohammad, in the house opposite theirs, with whom he used to play football in the street? And the girl he had a crush on at the end of the road. Where were they all now? Perhaps they ended up scattered across the globe too.

"You are looking a little sad my friend!" said De Vito as he came out of the gates.

"It may have been better to leave the past alone, I think," said Manu as he climbed into the hot back seat of the taxi cab.

"This is advice that is hard to swallow my friend. Whatever is in the heart will eventually come up to the tongue!" said Amir, pointing to his own by way of illustration.

There was a grain of truth in that maybe. But at the moment this homecoming felt like an error of judgement. He had always hoped an experience of this ilk would offer some cathartic outcome: improve his ability to make sense of life – to progress. But Sartre's speculation about life beginning on the other side of despair was nonsense. Here was a clear sign being held up to his face stating: don't be deluded; life is *exactly* how it appears. History was best left unexamined.

"Do you have a family?" he asked Amir, who was nudging the bumper of the cab against the rump of a donkey in the road to convince him to move out of the way. Behind them a cavalcade of horn-blowing vehicles, with their worldly belongings atop, were becoming irate.

"Hey! If you don't want his ass to swallow my car then move the donkey!" shouted De Vito out of the window to the man who was trying to encourage his furry friend out of the way with an apple. He turned to Manu. "It is the New Year tomorrow and everyone is leaving the city today. Excuse me Mr Manu. You ask a question?"

"I was asking if you have family in Tehran."

"My sister only, sir. Only my sister. I lost all of my family in the Rudbar earthquake thirteen years past. My children, my babies: two boys and a girl. My wife dies also. My brother and my mother too. It was very sad day for me."

He caught his driver's eye in the mirror – they were wet with tears.

"I am so sorry to hear that. It's terrible!"

"Yes. Me and my sister we lose everything. Our house, our families. We came to Tehran. There was nothing left. Fifty thousand people dead."

"How do you recover from such a tragedy?"

"They say rain is of no consequence to a drowning man," said Amir in Farsi. "Do you know that proverb?"

"I think it means…"

"When you suffer the worst things in life, everything else – is, is… .. Ahsan."

"Easy."

They sat in silence for the rest of the journey, until reaching Karim Dashti's house where Manu had arranged to meet Cyrus. They were a little late, the sea of traffic having regimented their every move. Cyrus was sitting smoking on a wall outside a block of whitewashed flats when they pulled up.

When Cyrus told him he had fabricated some story about being research students studying the history of the Anglo Iranian Oil Company, Manu was horrified. Too late now. They would have to go along with it. Hopefully this would be the last step in unravelling the whole riddle. His friend was clearly itching to break the story of British infiltration within the bazaar community.

But Manu was otherwise engaged. He was wandering around his own private emotional territory, interrogating his own personal memoirs. And at this moment he was mentally dramatising a particular scenario. The one in which he stood facing an uncle he'd wiped out of existence. How did one actually articulate a phrase like: *I'm sorry I haven't been in touch for twenty years*? A self-help manual would be useful: Conquering estrangement for beginners? How to bury the hatchet in one fell swoop, maybe. Or, simply, a dictionary of fawning phrases. That would be better than nothing.

A few rings on an infirm looking doorbell eventually produced a small, thin woman with grey hair tucked neatly under a brightly coloured headscarf. Striking remnants of beauty, from a younger time, had left a shimmering bloom around her aged face. And she smiled to show she was expecting them.

This was surely the very woman who had woven his carpet. It was at this very spot where the past and the present were now colliding. And he, Manucher Zand, was the crossroads between them. An unexpected tingle of anticipation flickered through his body.

They followed her into the alleyway and up some stairs.

When they reached the top floor she showed them into a small and very basic flat with a nougat colour scheme of fluffy-white, tinged with flecks of green. She led them into a room where an old man sat in an equally ancient sofa, from the arms of which the marks of twenty years of elbow activity glared out stubbornly.

The man did not appear to be in the best of health and attempted to rise, but was stopped by Cyrus. He had lost most of his hair apart from a few thin shreds which were sleeked down with gel. From the lenses of his thick glasses bounced out a mirage of gigantic eyes. He held up his blue-veined and warped hand for a shake.

The wife scuttled off towards the kitchen. "She will make us some tea," said the man.

They sat down on the carcass of a grey sofa, through which Manu felt a large angry coil pushing up into his thigh. Cyrus offered introductions which he proceeded to decorate with Middle Eastern pleasantries before explaining their presence in a few deceitful phrases. Each one pierced Manu with shame and guilt.

"I'm not so sure how m-much….." the old man was halted by a juddering jaw, further impeded by a set of false teeth. "…help I can be," he finished finally.

It could be a long afternoon.

Cyrus leaned forward on his chair. "We are very interested in the history of the Anglo Iranian Oil Company and in particular the English contingent who were working there at the time. And we would like to know a bit more about the oil nationalisation campaign. I believe your wife's father was involved quite heavily in that?"

"It's true Hajji-Hossein was part of a group of people supporting the campaign to nationalise the oil industry. However, he was not doing anything subversive – if that's what you were thinking."

"And I suppose you were involved too?" asked Cyrus.

"I wasn't involved directly but was based at the oil company headquarters in Abadan."

"That's interesting," said Cyrus. "You obviously experienced first hand what life was like during that time."

"Yes I did, and they were hard times. If the n-nationalisation had been successful I would have been in a better position. And my wife and I would not be living in these c-conditions now. But that's the way of the world."

"What was your experience of the British who worked alongside the natives?"

"They did not work alongside us in a- a-any way," said Karim Dashti sternly. "They were kept separate from us. Had they been integrated with the indigenous workforce from the start, or if there had been equal treatment of all nationalities, perhaps nationalisation would n-n-never have become an issue."

Cyrus nodded his head. "And did you yourself ever have cause to build any relationships with English staff?" he asked.

The old man shifted himself in slow motion on his chair, at which time his wife came through the door with some tea and sweet meats. She put her hand on his shoulder and said she was going out to do some shopping. He waited until she had left the flat before answering.

"I did not know any Englishmen personally. However, my wife's father had dealings with an Englishman whose behaviour did both his own country, and our culture, a disservice."

Manu looked at Cyrus who did not reciprocate the glance but instead continued his line of questioning.

"Was this someone from the oil company?"

"Yes it was. And in a reasonably senior position," said Karim, his cheeks glowing and his breathing laboured.

"Are you able to tell us any more about it?" asked Cyrus, gently, having seen the agitation brewing inside the old man.

"C-Conroy."

"I'm sorry I didn't hear. Could you repeat that please?"

"Mr A-A-Alec Conroy." His voice was trembling.

Cyrus looked over to Manu who shrugged his shoulders.

"This is the Englishman you were referring to?" asked Cyrus.

The man nodded, trying to catch his breath.

"Let me fetch you a glass of water," said Manu getting up from the sofa, glad to be relieved of the spiteful metal spring which was getting more aggressive by the minute.

He headed down the corridor towards the small kitchen. The thin, plaintive whine of a fiddle emanated from a radio in another room. In a tiny glass bowl, on a sideboard outside the kitchen, a goldfish chased its tail a circuit of infinity.

"I know how you feel pal," Manu muttered.

The kitchen was the size of a large bed. A degenerate stove had been kept sparkling clean. A box of antacid was the only sign of nourishment on the single shelf. Manu found a glass by the window and filled it with water.

When he returned to the room Karim was showing Cyrus some pictures.

"These are pictures of my workplace in Abadan. Things changed after nationalisation. British staff sabotaged the machinery before they left the complex. They did not leave any information on how to operate it. The company offered jobs to Western staff but their government would not allow it. Once the British had left, sanctions were imposed to stop countries from buying Iranian oil. Eventually many of us were put out of work, including me."

"I'm sorry to hear that," Cyrus said "I hope you managed to find another occupation?"

"Yes, finally I returned to Tehran and opened a small shop, which my wife and I ran very successfully."

Manu passed him the glass of water which he took gratefully and began to drink.

"We will not keep you much longer, sir. But we do have a question about a carpet, which we believe was woven by your wife."

The man's face brightened up. "Ah yes. She is an exceptionally talented weaver," he said, pointing to the carpet in front of them, the only glorious thing in the room.

"Back in England, we have a carpet which we believe may have been woven by your wife some time ago. It has an inscription by Omar Khayyam. We would like to find out a little more about it."

"It may be wise to wait until she returns and ask her directly yourself. She will be back shortly I am sure. What line of poetry is it?"

"It's from the Rubaiyat and woven in English," said Cyrus. "That is partly why we would like to find out more."

"What do you mean?" asked Karim.

Cyrus explained and added in the detail about the municipal swimming pool on the back of the rug.

As he spoke Karim's furrowed mouth remained open and began to quiver. Manu noticed him clutching the arm of the sofa so vigorously with his bony hand that his fingers blanched.

"Are you alright?" asked Cyrus.

There was a silence as Karim swallowed to alleviate his dry mouth.

"I, I , you, I cannot…." he spluttered.

The sound of the door opening in the hallway interrupted them.

"My wife must not – on any account – hear this conversation," said Karim in a frightened whisper. "I am not in a position to talk about this with you."

"But surely she can tell us more about the carpet. You said earlier she would have more information," said Cyrus, confused.

"N-No. On n-no account must she be questioned about this. You must leave immediately. Immediately!" he raised his voice.

His wife entered the room smiling with a bowl of fruit.

"These gentlemen are in a hurry, my dear. They are just leaving. Please show them to the door," said Karim Dashti to his wife.

She looked surprised but followed his orders and led them to the door.

"We should ask her," whispered Cyrus.

Manu frowned at him and shook his head.

She showed them out. "Well that was mighty frustrating!" said Cyrus as they stood outside on the street. "And just as we were beginning to get somewhere. Why do you think he changed his mind?"

"I'm pretty sure the English guy must have done something to his wife. But it still doesn't explain the inscription," said Manu.

"We could wait until she goes out again and ask her," said Cyrus.

Manu shook his head. "I really just don't have the stomach for it, Cy. I've got enough on my mind with this family reunion tomorrow. I'm in favour of dropping the whole thing. Really."

"Man. So much for the detective work. If we were pros we'd be sacked for incompetence!" said Cyrus.

"Yeah. Incompetent and broke, that'd be us," said Manu as they got back into the cab.

15

Tehran, 1951

Hajji-Hossein Forooshi was exhausted and ecstatic. He had arrived home late most nights. He and his colleagues had been protesting all winter: outside the palace grounds, outside the Majlis Parliament and wherever his coterie could gather without fear of arrest. The rallies and demonstrations were beginning to take effect. It was a triumph for the country. And most of all it demonstrated the might and will of the people. In all of his sixty years of existence he could not remember a more exciting time to be a mortal.

It was past midnight when he returned home that evening, after having been to a late meeting at the Mosque. His mind was running wild with spirited thoughts. Grasping his opium pipe from the shelf he sank with a sigh onto his usual red cushion at the corner of the room.

"My daughter, fetch me some tea if you would," he groaned for Parissa was in the habit of waiting up until his return. "My feet are as fat as a pregnant ewe's belly. I need to rest them."

Parissa undid the nationalisation ribbon around his arm. "I'm worried about you father," she said. "You are working too hard."

"Nonsense. There's no need to be concerned my girl. We have won a significant victory tonight. Prime Minister Razmara has been assassinated outside the mosque. He was the last enemy of the process. And he is out of the way."

"How can you be so sanguine about someone's death father?"

"*You* may not understand. But your children will. If you ever *have* any that is! From time to time sacrifice is needed for a better future. This is that time. How do you think the constitutional revolution, giving rise to the birth of our parliament, took place all those years ago!"

"But what about the fifty-fifty deal that you spoke about the other day?"

"Too late for that now. All possibility of compromise has been thrown out of the window. If the British had been willing to negotiate earlier perhaps an equitable distribution would have been possible. But they have been as stubborn as a goat on a hilltop."

Parissa loved her father but felt him to be rather antiquated in his thinking. It was true, the need for more freedom was as clear as the way to mosque. But she was doubtful that traditionalists like her father would serve as capable masters of that freedom.

Only a few days ago she had experienced what life might be like should the knot of tradition be untied. Her father would have been enraged had he known of her assistance at a British Legation function in the centre of the city. Even though she was there simply to circulate trays of food, she had allowed herself to be swept into the revelry and had found it enchanting. Yasmin had looked so proficient in her white uniform, with her long hair bundled into a chignon and floating gracefully in between the immaculately dressed guests with a silver tray. Parissa's own uniform was slightly less fitted, having belonged to the maid she had replaced. And she found it both alarming and thrilling to be without her headscarf once again. The guests laughed as though their shoulders were universally unburdened. And the women matched the men, in a commanding fashion she had never seen. Was this not the type of society their people should be striving for?

She looked at her father's tired face as he puffed on his ghalyan. The musty smoke was making her light-headed. Before long the bubbling sound of the pipe mutated into the distant pulse of a troupe of Tonbak drummers at a Persian wedding. And she imagined it to be hers.

"Anyway," continued her father. "I've said you will bring some refreshments along to the gathering. It will be a long day and we will be hungry and thirsty."

"The gathering?"

"The gathering. Are you not listening? Where is your head today? I know we have not seen each other much since I have been busy with the protests. But you need to keep your wits about you. Things are changing by the minute."

"Sorry father. You were saying there's a celebration next week and Deputy Mossadegh will be speaking to the crowd."

"Indeed he will. People from all over the city will be there to hear him speak. We are moments away from victory against the British."

It sounded so hostile. Perhaps it would culminate in a war. And she could not imagine the British conceding defeat so easily. And what about Karim? Where would that leave him? She had been receiving regular letters from him every week for over a year. And each time he returned to visit his parents – which was not very often – they would invite her over for tea.

His apprenticeship was due to end this summer and she had overheard exchanges between his parents and her father about imminent nuptials. It made her nauseous to consider it.

"But perhaps I am being overly strict. I suspect you are pondering your future," the voice of her father seemingly read her mind in a stroke. "There is talk of Karim being promoted which is good news. We would do well to hasten your connections with him, now he is in such a good position," he muttered through half-closed eyes.

Parissa did not reply. She could see him drifting off, waking only occasionally to take another automatic puff of his pipe in his sleep.

Quietly she slipped into the sleeping quarters she shared with her sister Soraya, who was asleep in the small mattress next to hers. She sat on her own bedding and reached across to fetch a small wooden box from its perch behind her pillow. The light from the room next door fell onto its contents as she opened the lid. She pulled out the pamphlet of poems by Omar Khayyam, translated into English. It was given to her by Mr Conroy during a visit to the shop a few months ago. She ran her fingers gently over the stanza next to which Mr Conroy had written its Persian translation in pen. It must have taken so long for his hands to master it. She mouthed the lines to herself:

Ah, Love! could thou and I with Fate conspire
To grasp this sorry Scheme of Things entire,
Would not we shatter it to bits – and then
Re-mould it nearer to our Heart's Desire!

For the thousandth time she replayed the scene where his hand reached into his pocket and pulled out this same small book which he handed to her whilst her brother's back was turned. She heard afresh his whisper, "take this gift with my interpretation beside it." And once more she evoked his attentive face. His pallid skin, having been challenged by the sun, had retaliated with collections of freckles so plentiful they were beginning to join together in defence around his cheekbones.

This was one of the mementos of their infrequent encounters. Another was the thimbleful of air that caressed her face when he brushed by to examine the rug she had started to weave for him. It seemed like yesterday and yet it was three months ago.

Where was he now she wondered as she lay down onto the bed and closed her eyes.

She imagined him and Karim passing each other in some quarter of the oil community and wondered if they would bond. Although Karim had told her the British and Iranian contingents never really met.

A crashing loud snore from her father in the adjacent room severed her train of thought. He would be outraged if he knew she was entertaining these ideas, and enraged if he knew of her exchanges with Mr Conroy. If he had not been so preoccupied with his protests not a thing would have taken place. Although she recognised this did not absolve her of any blame.

Since the previous summer her brother, without realising it, had acted as accomplice. He had been simply attempting to demonstrate his merit and maturity as supervisor during his father's absences from the carpet shop. And one day when Hajji-Hossein returned to the bazaar to pick up his goods at dusk, Ali had a proposition for him.

"Father I have been thinking. I know you have allowed me to occasionally mind the shop. But as you're so busy with your meetings now, perhaps you should leave the management of the shop in my hands for a short while. You have been pleased with my capabilities before. You said that yourself. So perhaps I can be in command for the summer when there is no school. I am perfectly capable of bartering with customers."

"Really?"

"Yes, of course. Indeed I sold a carpet and two saddlebags to some tourists today!" said Ali smiling.

"That's excellent!" said their father and slapped him on the back. "Have you been continuing the book-keeping exercises I've given you?"

"Of course father!"

"Show me the accountancy book," he said.

Ali pulled out the large leather book from the mouth of wooden desk and waved it under his father's nose.

"Here you see. I've entered the sale and transaction details of both items."

"You're growing up, my son," said their father with a sigh. "I think you are right to have more responsibility. Let us see how you do over the summer."

The summer arrived and trade was tighter than a tambourine skin.

"What we need is more orders," Ali told Parissa one day as he was flicking through the books. "Mr Conroy likes you Parissa, I have noticed that. So I think we should certainly encourage him to put in more orders. He must have family and friends abroad. I am sure they too would be interested."

"Father would not approve Ali," Parissa had said to him.

But he was in no mood to listen. "Leave it to me Parissa. Father is extremely preoccupied at present," he said.

So Mr Conroy was encouraged, more than once, to attend the bazaar and view other rugs she was weaving. "You must visit and see the latest rugs we have brought in from

Mashad," Ali would say in frequent, deliberately contrived, visits to the oil company headquarters where Mr Conroy was based.

And there had been the start of it. And the start of them. And the beginning of a miniature maze of interactions which had at the outset made her acutely self-conscious. Nevertheless as time progressed she became more comfortable with each exchange. At its crest had been a private encounter in the shop when Mr Conroy had come to settle his account, at a time when Ali was taking an examination at his school. A broken discourse, a fumbling of hands, anxious breaths and a stampede of heartbeats had followed before Mr Conroy's exodus, which left Parissa jubilant though bloodless against her father's desk.

Then it reached a juncture whereby Parissa was unable to stop herself forever gazing out of the shop window, waiting for him to walk by. And she felt him to have taken root in her. In the same way that opium had taken root in her father.

And the root was growing more quickly than she could control it.

And her brother continued to lubricate the relationship, all the while leaving out of his calculations the emotional cost of his transactions.

It was upon such a random day, when Parissa was in the workshop weaving, that a feast of such rapture was laid squarely at her table. A loud scamper of footsteps up the stairs was followed by her brother bursting into the workshop, breathless.

"Parissa, Mr Conroy is downstairs and has brought two of his British colleagues to discuss an export order to the West. I have told him father is away and I am in charge of the shop. So I will be discussing the matter with them. Please don't interrupt us."

He retreated back down the stairs and she closed the door behind him, leaning against it with her chest. Was that the beating of her intense heart knocking against the door, even through her ribs? Each breath she took was like drawing water from the deepest well, using a bucket with a hundred holes.

After a few minutes she opened the door again, tiptoed onto the landing and crept down the stairs. The door at the bottom was closed. It was dark, except for a line of light escaping from bottom of it. She could hear her brother's half-broken voice attempting to plunge into manhood with every phrase. In between his utterances were voices she did not recognise. But occasionally breaking through the noisy exchange was the silver toned melody of the voice that was now engraved on her memory. He was translating the words of his colleagues for her brother. She adored the struggle of his tongue around the R in her language. And his melodic laugh was like the tickle of a Persian flute, which made the hairs on her arm stand erect. She stood quietly listening for a while. Suddenly she heard him utter the words "perhaps Parissa would know," as though the door was transparent and he could see her figure standing there. She froze to the spot momentarily. The sound of footsteps coming towards the door unlocked her from the floor. She sprinted up the stairs, her heart three steps ahead.

Moments later there was a knock. She had, by then, seated herself on the weaving scaffold. In her shaking hand was the comb she used for packing down the wefts. She had no breath to answer but simply sat in silence panting in anticipation.

The door creaked behind her back. She turned around. An eye she recognised as being Mr Conroy's was looking through a gap in the door. He asked whether he may enter and she nodded, putting her hand up to her head to straighten her scarf. It wasn't there. She had taken it off to cool herself earlier. She immediately felt unfortified. He apologised and said he would leave. But she reassured him and he came into the room, shutting the door behind himself.

"I have come to ask about the length of time it would take for you to weave three carpets to order," he said in a quiet voice.

She stood up and went to the desk in the corner to retrieve a pen and paper.

"I am afraid you will need to tell me of the quality and size of rug you require, as well as the type of design, before I am able to be exact," she said looking at his face expectantly. His straw-coloured hair had grown a little since she last saw him and had developed a kink in front which dangled over his forehead.

"Oh," he looked disappointed and remained standing.

"There is a reference book I have which has some details but it's in Farsi," said Parissa and made her way to the shelf at the other side of the room which was packed with a combination of books and weaving materials. Ali had taken the stool so she stood on her toes to try and reach the book she referred to.

Alec Conroy followed her to help. As he stood behind her and reached for the book above her head she could feel his breath on her hair and his chest brushed against her back. She did not turn around for fear of being caught in his embrace but continued standing with her back to him. He brought his arm in front of her offering the book, which she took

"There is a table here which has details of timings – you need to refer to the size of the rug, and the number of knots per day – to make your calculations. My rate of knots is approximately ten thousand per day," she explained turning to show him the table in the book. As she did it fell from her hand. They both bent to pick it up in unison. His hand overlapped hers on the spine of the book. There was a moment of apology. A shared gaze embraced a multitude of things unsaid. To Parissa it felt like her heart was in his chest and his in hers.

"I had better go. They will be wondering where I am," he said smiling. His face was close enough to hers that she could see his front teeth were wet and the inside of his bottom lip was pink. He let go of her hand.

"Please take the book," she said offering it to him. He obliged and began to walk towards the door then stopped.

"I too have something for you," he said reaching into his pocket. He handed her a small pamphlet. "I have attempted to translate it, but very badly. Perhaps you might let me know where there are flaws. I am often in the Park e Shahr eating my lunch when I am not in Abadan, if you are ever passing."

She blushed and looked down, all the while noticing the small dent at the bottom of the wall where Ali had tried to kill a fly with a hammer when he was younger.

When she looked up moments later he was gone and the door was shut.

She sat down on the scaffold and put her head in her hands.

Each encounter was like a delicacy laid at her feet, with a lure into the unknown. Where would it all end? She could not, even for the smallest speck of time, allow her imagination to speculate.

16

Tehran, 2003

"So how are you feeling on your last day in our city?" De Vito's bushy black eyebrows danced to and fro in the rear view mirror as he spoke. Manu grinned. He had become very fond of this little man who had taken an active personal interest in his welfare since he arrived.

"It will be strange to be back in England," he said, this time in Farsi.

"Bravo, you are getting back your language!" cried Amir in English "I am so happy for you!"

"It feels good – like pulling back the curtains to see the sun. I am going to practise when I get home."

"Yes. You take proper teacher of Farsi I think. You are saying you will fix your brother's hand when you get home."

"Really?"

"Yes, but s'ok you will do good," said Amir as he pulled in to the side of a pretty, tree-lined road and parked. "We are here. Your uncle's house."

Manu left the car and headed to a modern house sitting behind large gates over the top of which tumbled dramatically a Bougainvillea plant, spitting out radioactive-looking purple flowers. He rang the bell. And a short while later the door, embedded in the gate, opened slowly. A small unexpected child no higher than his waist stood in front of him.

"Are you Manu?" he said with the confidence of a teenager.

"I am, yes. How did you know?"

"You are my English cousin."

An air of precocity wafted around the miniature gentleman in a purple waist coat, from whose wrist was dangling dramatically to-and-fro an expensive compact camera. It brought to mind a scene at his father's fortieth birthday party in which his father was swinging Fatemeh, the neighbourhood's annoying little girl, around in her pink frock. Her small spidery legs were flying through the air. She could only have been around six but articulated herself with the vigour of a middle aged woman: "Oh Mr. Zand, if you were my father we would have so much fun together!" Meantime, her younger brother was in conversation with a banker about the compression ratio of a Bentley. Maybe Manu had never really appreciated how growing up fast was a life skill, a survival mechanism, in these parts.

"Did you bring a present?"

"Yes, I have brought some Sohan," said Manu, half expecting him to take the gift and rubber-stamp his hand on the way in. He was not good with kids. Was this really his cousin? He thought not. Surely his uncle wasn't still having children at this age?

He followed the boy through the small garden and into the hallway of the house. A face appeared around the doorway of one of the rooms. It was his uncle, twenty years smaller, older and thinner. Surprisingly, though grey, his hair remained thick and vibrant. His father would be envious without a doubt. But the two dimples, which had forever been his uncle Reza's defining features, were now camouflaged by a mesh of random lines of various intensities all fighting for seniority. Thankfully his features were still prominent enough to surface through the folds and furrows. How he wished he could reach in and pull out his uncle's younger self.

The old man threw up his hands and clutched his heart "ghorboonet beram!" he cried with tear-welled eyes. He clutched Manu to his breast, buried his head into his neck and sobbed unashamedly. A spear of remorse struck Manu. His moist eyes were posed to erupt like a dam. He swallowed hard through the dry throat and prickly tongue. It seemed to last forever. His tin of Sohan was sandwiched between them both, pressing into his belly. Then a quip released the tension like a spring.

"I thought you would be grey by now!" said his uncle tugging at Manu's hair.

"Would you have recognised me if I was?" asked Manu

"How could I not recognise the family nose!" joked his uncle. "I said to Simin, I bet he's cut it off by now. That's what they do here of course."

Manu laughed. "They don't mind it so much in Britain."

"No?"

"Not really," he lied, remembering his own cycle of paranoia, discomfort and eventual resignation when it came to all things nasal.

"Let's find your auntie. She's strapped into a conversation with her sister and needs rescuing," said his uncle as he led Manu into the main living room where decorations hung on the walls and a large table covered in a white cloth was laid with a variety of colourful items symbolising the traditional New Year.

"You remember your auntie Simin?" asked his uncle interrupting the conversation of two grey-haired ladies whose waistbands had seen better days.

Auntie Simin had fared rather well in the ongoing battle of years, the fleshy properties of her face having defended her against the assault of creases and crows' feet.

Simin punched her husband on the arm light heartedly.

"Of course he remembers me!" she squawked grabbing Manu by the neck and pulling his face down to her level and pecking it with kisses.

Manu had been close to Auntie Simin. It was she who had bundled him into the cupboard away from the revolutionaries when the hospital was invaded. They were on a visit to the ward where his mother was recovering from an operation. A terrified nurse came running in to warn that Khomeini supporting revolutionaries had occupied the building and were demanding the eviction of all westerners from their beds. Aunt Simin had grabbed his arm forcefully and pulled him into a nearby cleaning cupboard. Through the door Manu could hear the muffled argument between the doctor and revolutionary guards about the numbers of westerners they were treating. His younger self had swallowed back the silent tears with the help of Auntie Simin's hand over his mouth – for he could hear his mother's soft weeps as they squabbled above her head. Fortunately, in the battle of wills between science and political ideology, science had been the victor. The revolutionaries departed empty-handed.

Without any warning, Manu felt an agonising pain on the right side of his face. It was Auntie Simin. She had pinched his cheek like she was breaking off a square of chocolate from the corner of a chocolate bar. "My darling baby," she uttered, breaking off another piece from the opposite cheek. She looked from right to left across his face, as if attempting to read the last twenty years in every pore. That was the thing: he was as dear to her as her own children.

And this had been one of life's great vacuums. The revolution had swallowed up his extended family and scattered them across the globe like marbles. Defenceless and isolated he had been rolling round the battlefield of life ever since, hoping to bump into other marbles like himself.

He asked his uncle how things had been for them all this time.

"You know Manu, you get used to what each day tosses in your way. Our family has never been overly religious or political. And I suppose that puts us forever on the sidelines. But I feel sorry for the children," he nodded towards his grandson. "Their future is not stable. And I would like to die knowing they were in safe hands – whoever those hands may belong to. And how is your mother?"

"She is fine, of course. And sends her best wishes."

His uncle looked sceptical.

"And your father?" asked his uncle.

"He is fine. But lonely, I think," said Manu recalling very well the argument his father and uncle had had during a family meal in a restaurant after returning from skiing in the mountains.

"You're an opportunist!" his uncle had shouted.

"If I'm an opportunist, you're a fence-sitter!" had been the response from Manu's father. And so it went on.

The argument had been over Mehdi Zand's decision to leave the country when the revolution took hold. As a hard-nosed business-man he a) wasn't about to see his business flushed away and b) had no time for religious jiggery pokery and political interference. So he went about recasting his vocation – from an importer of Western artefacts to the *East*, to an importer of Eastern artefacts to the *West*. He had not spoken to his brother since.

"Yes I've often wondered how lonely he must be nowadays, so far from his friends and family," said his uncle. "I'm sorry to say that loneliness is the curse of the dispossessed my son. But those that have their freedom snatched away are powerless. So at the same time as he is lonely; we are powerless. *Which* is worse I'm not sure. Although I do admit things have improved somewhat since the tenure of President Khatemi. We are slightly less stifled these days. But we cannot cool our heels for long, lest our shoes be stolen when we are not looking. What is a manageable risk today – may tomorrow be the spark that ignites a barrel of gunpowder."

Manu thought of his own charmed existence in leafy Hampstead where the only manageable risk was evading a parking fine for outstaying your welcome. How easy it was to take it all for granted. The revolution itself was nothing but a collection of cotton-wool memories. He supposed because his thirteen year old self had been perpetually bedazzled by Isabel Gonzales: five years older; and a sexy adaptation of Violet Elizabeth Bott – something to do with her Spanish lisp perhaps. Her father was a handsome Castilian racing driver who frequently returned home smeared in oil and reeking of Champagne. And her mother was forever entertaining ambassadors and starlets in their smart modern pad across the road from his house. This was a much more important focus in his mind at the time. He remembered only that the atmosphere was one of happy chaos. Schools were closed frequently, there were power cuts and shortages. But a feeling of excitement and opportunity lingered in the air. Even his apathetic parents frequently spoke of the timely birth of a republic. Little were they to know what was waiting around the corner.

His uncle clutched his arm and took him proudly round the room introducing him to a variety of vaguely familiar relatives. And a short while later they sat down to lunch and a range of favourite foods he had not experienced since he was a boy. The yogurt and egg-yolk rice-terrine, layered with chicken, took pride of place in the centre of the table, painted bold yellow with saffron. And piled high to the right was the traditional new-year dish of herbed rice with layers of salted fish and broadbeans. His favourite dish of all sat steaming in front of his eyes in a copper pot: lamb stew infused with poached, sour greengages.

Manu set to work serving himself a variety of food whilst answering questions being fired at him by his eight year old removed cousin. Yes it was very cold in Britain, no he'd never met Robbie Williams, and yes, he would post him a copy of Finding Nemo on DVD. But what was that? Manu felt a feint electrical impulse tingling across his taste buds. He had recently concluded, worryingly, that over-dependence on imagination in the discernment of flavour might stop him differentiating reality from fantasy on a plate. But there it was again. An undeniable sour tang. The tart flesh of the greengage. It was trying to fight through to his palate. As though someone had pierced his tongue with a pin.

"Is everything ok?" asked his aunt across the table as she saw him put his knife and fork down in shock. "Have you bitten on a stone?"

Manu had refrained from disclosing the story of the missing senses and wasn't about to explain now.

"Everything's fine," he smiled. "I just remembered I had asked the taxi driver to pick me up at four. What time is it?"

"Oh plenty of time it's only three," said his uncle

Manu continued with his meal. Part of him did not want to resume the process in case he *had* imagined the experience. He sipped slowly from his glass of water. After a short while he put a second greengage into his mouth. A definite but minute sharp tang ensued. He took a deep breath in an attempt to conceal the bout of internal melodrama taking place at the peak of his emotions.

"What a fantastic dish this is," he said to his oblivious relatives. He found himself plugging his ears with imaginary cotton-wool as he tried to block out the noise and zoom in on the atom of taste that was dancing around his tongue, in case it evaporated before he had time to savour its impact. There is was again. Like the tiniest acerbic punch from the tiniest heavyweight boxer. He had never felt so grateful to feel something so familiar.

After the meal, there was time only for quick pleasantries as Manu's taxi had arrived. He felt angry with himself for not keeping in touch with his family. And it was ridiculous that his father and uncle had not spoken since his father left the country.

"Please will you contact my father?" said Manu as he hugged his uncle goodbye. "You need to talk to each other."

"I promise," said his uncle. "You're right it has been too long."

And then came the ultimate dilemma: what to say when parting from loved ones not seen for decades and may not see again for equally long? Conventional farewells seemed absurd. 'See you soon' had a preposterous ring of insincerity to it. Why had someone not cooked up a new-fangled vernacular for tribes who interact over wider zones of space and time in the sub-cultural world of today? A special set of laws too. In fact a whole new governing code would be useful for all those global nomads, displaced people, separated families and would-be lovers across the world. And, in the activity space where these communities wander, special rights could exist – unconstrained by national boundaries. A type of cyber-citizenship and the start of a new political order.

For the moment the only etiquette at his disposal was the clunky vocabulary formulated by those who would never need to experience relations across forbidden boundaries.

And as Manu said goodbye he wondered if he would ever see these people again.

17

Tehran, 1951

It was a seasonal crossroads where the anaemic rays of early summer competed with the boisterous wind of spring for pre-eminence. A white-tipped snow finch swooped past Parissa's head on its way to the cooler mountains in the distance. Clumps of blushing blossoms hung, like paperweights, along the branches of the cherry trees. And their sweet fragrance interlaced itself with the smell of melting tarmac rising from the paths, as Parissa passed through the park on her way to the palace grounds.

The large hessian sack on her shoulder was filled with food and refreshing drinks. It was well past lunchtime. Her father and his friends would be hungry. How ironic she should be providing succour for a faction whose deeds had the potential to put to an end the wishful thoughts she harboured daily.

As she neared the palace gates the sound of chanting thumped around the tips of her ears: 'Mossadegh, Mossadegh'. On turning into the grounds, she was confronted, in the near distance, by a sea of people, thousands it seemed, sitting on the grass, reciting in unison. She scoured the heads of black hair and religious turbans. Nothing resembling her father stood out. She decided to push her way through the crowds despite the unbearable temperature. Unexpectedly, a soft shower of fine water scattered itself upon the crowd. They uttered a collective scream of pleasure, opening their mouths to catch the precious miniscule drops bestowed upon them by a generous palace gardener and his hose.

Parissa spotted Dr Azizi sitting under a cherry tree in deep conversation with a glamorous woman. Her hair was scraped into a bun and she was smoking a cigarette. The usually reserved and gentle man she knew as her father's friend seemed to be summoning, in his female companion, a certain vibrancy of character. She tossed back her head and laughed without restraint, in between the occasional touch of his arm, or turn of her head to blow cigarette smoke away from his face. Parissa stood for a moment watching them until Dr Azizi spotted her and waved. She walked over and asked whether he had seen her father.

"Last I saw he was at the front," said Azizi pointing to the large pond ahead of them. "You look hot. Sit with us in the shade a while," he suggested, patting the grass before him.

Parissa sat down. "I can't stay long. They are waiting for refreshments," she said smiling at the lady who was studying her with equal intensity. It suddenly occurred to her this was the lady her father had spoken about. His description fitted her perfectly. "She wears her hair as if it is a work of art!" he had said more than once.

"Nargess," said the woman holding out her hand as though attempting to complete the picture.

The intensity of her red lipstick singled her out from most of the crowd. And where she had recently started to drink from a bottle, little drops of water glistened like baby rubies on her lips. She did not seem like the woman of easy virtue her father consistently referred to. She had overheard her father say: "Azizi thinks because she's educated he has found himself a gem!"

The woman leant over to Parissa, her brown linen suit wafting a smell of lilies and cigarettes in her direction. "Dr Azizi has told me about your carpet skills my dear," she said, her white teeth catching the sun as she spoke.

Parissa handed her a pack of salted greengages from the bag. "It's really not that exciting," she said. "I would so much rather be studying at university."

"What stops you doing that?" asked Nargess biting into a greengage.

"Apart from not having a proper education you mean?"

"Ahmad tells me you have great love of poetry. You must have *some* skills to be able to understand and appreciate that, surely?"

"I suppose so. But, I left school when I was twelve, so my skills were only ever rudimentary. I am afraid much of what I learned has perished along the way."

"To dismiss the rudimentary is to dismiss the best," said Nargess pulling out a piece of paper from her bag. "Here take my details. If ever you would like some tutelage I would be happy to assist. I'm a teacher of literature."

"That is so very kind of you! It would be an aspiration I would love to fulfil. But my father…."

"Your father is an important person in your life, of course. But never forget whose life you are living," said Nargess. Then she lowered her voice so Azizi could not hear. "From time to time change needs to occur *behind* the scenes, if you understand my meaning."

"I understand. That's very kind of you," said Parissa. "I promise to consider your offer."

She picked up her bags. "I must find my father now. He will be parched and wondering where I am."

How wonderful it would be to have one's own tutor of literature! What would her father say? She could not imagine he would be supportive. After all he didn't even like the woman. Would she dare go behind his back?

In the distance, to her left, she heard someone shouting her name. It was her father looking agitated and beckoning to her.

"Where in God's name have you been?" he said as she approached. "We're famished and our throats are as dry as Lake Orumiyeh!"

As she was unpacking the food the crowd roared and people started to stand. "It's Mossadegh," said her father, he has come to the podium. Someone had erected a temporary platform made of planks on top of grocery boxes onto which the statesman was clambering. Although she had often heard her father talk about the man, Parissa had never seen him before – except in the newspapers. He was so small and frail, she had to stand on her toes to catch a glimpse of him above the crowd. How could someone so slight have motivated so many thousands of people?

"My fellow countrymen," he started with a high-pitched tone which sliced through the murmur of voices. "By now you will have heard of the assassination of Prime Minister Razmara. And although he and I fundamentally disagreed over various items of political policy, my heart goes out to his devastated family. But I am here today to thank you for your support, without which we would not have got as far as we have. You believe – as I do – that it is the right of every nation to nationalise what belongs to them. To usurp it for their people; their forebears. The oil committee – of which I am a member has today passed a resolution adopting the principle of Oil Nationalisation. I do not have to tell you how significant this moment is. Our long years of negotiations with foreign countries... have yielded no results this far. With our *own* oil revenues we could meet our entire budget and combat poverty, disease, and backwardness among our people. And if we eliminate the power of the British over us, we would also eliminate corruption and intrigue by means of which the internal affairs of our country have been influenced. Once this tutelage has ceased, Iran will have achieved its economic and political independence."

The crowd roared with delight. Parissa covered her ears. She was not interested in these demonstrations, due to the violence it attracted. Thankfully there was no encouragement from her father. According to him there was little place for women in politics. It was, perhaps, the only thing on which both they both agreed.

Parissa decided to slip away just as another roar took hold. She squeezed through the bodies to the palace gate and walked down the main boulevard to Ferdowsi department store where she had arranged to meet Yasmin after her work day at the British legation.

"Come with me!" said Yasmin leading Parissa up the stairs of the store and pushing her way through the crowds of women who eyed the latest imports from Paris.

"Look. Don't you think it's beautiful?" said Yasmin running her hand over a velvet dress with bright yellow flowers that was on a manikin.

"Would you like to try it on?" asked the shop assistant who herself was dressed in a smartly fitted, white, figure-hugging manteau. Yasmin nodded and was led away to the changing room by the assistant.

Parissa ran her hand over the dress and imagined herself in it. Her father would have a seizure if she was to wear such a thing. She noticed herself in the reflection of the mirror stand to her right. A plain girl, with hair flattened by a headscarf, returned the stare. In the top corner of the mirror she noticed two American women dressed in brightly coloured full skirts laughing. One was pointing at her like she was an animal in the Mellat Park zoo. She looked down at her feet. A toe was pointing out of a hole in one of her moccasins.

A torrent of shame engulfed her and she pushed her way though the crowds towards the revolving doors at the exit. The warm dry wind which hit her face was welcome after the cold pretend air indoors. For a few minutes the sun wiped out her vision as she stood outside the department store, blinking blind.

"Parissa?"

A black figure in front of her bloomed into colour as she grew accustomed to the light. It was Alec Conroy dressed in a short-sleeved shirt and wearing a hat.

"Are you alright?" he said bending his head downwards to try and catch her gaze which had shot to the floor.

"Yes, thank you."

"Perhaps you are not well. Would you like me to accompany you somewhere?"

"No! No. That will not be necessary thank you. I have recovered and need to get home."

"Of course. But before you go I simply wanted to offer my thanks for the carpet which Ali delivered last week. It is truly beautiful. And for the book on Saadi which you sent me."

"Did you read it?"

"I am struggling, of course. But what I have managed to understand I am enjoying. In fact I have asked the company to provide me with some more Farsi lessons. It has made me realise I do not know as much as I should."

"Well you know more than at least three-quarters of the foreign population here currently!" said Parissa without thinking and wished she hadn't. She gasped and put her hand in front of her mouth.

"Do not be sorry. You have every right to say such a thing. And I have every reason to deserve to hear it."

She could not help but notice his feet opposite hers. And hers opposite his. Her big toe, which she was trying to pull into her moccasin, kept sliding back out. And his black shiny leather shoes in front of her made her feel ashamed. Separating them was a small puddle of dirty water. In its centre a fly was struggling to swim.

They both gazed at it for a while. "Do you think we should save it?" asked Mr Conroy.

Parissa smiled. "We should let nature take its course," she said, glancing for a moment into his eyes. She continued to watch the fly struggle aimlessly.

He touched her arm. "You seem preoccupied."

These encounters were beginning to etch his modest charm onto her heart. And with each brush-by, she felt it to be deeper and more indelible than before. And for the most part she could not determine whether to consider it a wound, or a bond. Whatever it was, it seemed to be rearranging her being. What a curious thing alteration was. For the most part, she had been so unaware of its impact, it was hard to remember at exactly *what point* she felt one thing, before she felt another. And now, the thing she was before, she was no longer.

She apologised and said she needed to get back to the workshop. And as they parted she noticed the fly in the puddle had stopped writhing against its fate.

18

London, 2003

When Manu opened the door to his London flat the sober décor hit him like a brick. Walls and floors seemed strangely bleak. Each piece of furnishing spoke of functionality. All were out of keeping with the ornate Middle Eastern style with which his eye had recently bonded. In culinary terms, the underlying theme facing him now was a bowl of consommé – a kind of bland minimalism. No embellishment, garnish, chintz or truss was anywhere to be seen. He closed the door behind him with his foot, placed his suitcase on the pristine birch floorboards and laughed.

"Don't tell me you've become attached to the gold trimmings and ornamental nonsense?" he asked himself out loud.

The red Persian carpet, the start of it all, lay smugly in front of the fireplace, disassociating itself from recent events.

Manu threw himself into the grey velvet armchair. Work seemed more abstract than ever now – and so beside the point. The little red light on his answer phone flashed angrily from across the room: payment for leaving his mobile behind. In that machine a queue of worried, needy and earnest voices were waiting to unfurl themselves upon him. He couldn't face it.

He turned on the TV. BBC news: President Bush inarticulated his way through an inflammatory soundbite prescribing a 'decapitation attack' on members of the Iraqi leadership. It was the type of absurd threat that a small boy would use as part of his toy soldier's prattle when delivering an ultimatum to a miniature regiment in the back yard. Manu switched off the TV. He could not stomach his beady, sharkish eyes and perpetual astonished look. There was something rather inverted about a man who only smiled whilst using hostile words.

Manu needed to get out of the house. So he took a walk and savoured the cold prickles of rain which relied on the wind for their direction. He had forgotten his scarf and pulled up his collar to protect his neck from the wet. The fresh warm climate of Tehran with its fumy bouquet had become a mere memento of another life. He made his way to Laure's café and was surprised to see a note on the door announcing closure until further notice. She had probably gone to see her father. But it was quite curious. Normally if she closed the café she would specify a re-opening date. Surely she hadn't just left the country? He looked through the glass door. Dust was beginning to form on the tables.

He went home again and decided to confront the answer machine. Two from his editor (had he decided on a date for his return?). Four from Alice, the last one quite frantic – she was worried about him. One from his mother welcoming him home. And the last one from Laure. Her father had taken a turn for the worse and she had gone to Cogolin to be with him. Her voice sounded despondent. She must have had a great deal on her mind but had kept it to herself. Suppose her father was dying? It had been selfish of him not to ask about her father's health. He groaned as he flicked back through the scenes where they were in each other's company. How could he have been so consumed with his own frothy predicaments at the expense of her more significant ones? She probably thought *exactly* that before deciding there was nothing left for her here and jumping on a flight to France. He tried to ring her on her mobile but there was no answer. A shiver of anxiety rippled through his spine.

What to do now? Everything seemed so quiet. The momentum on the streets of London seemed to have shrunk from a stampede to a stroll, compared to the tempest that was Tehran. Coming home had been like turning off a monotonous freeway into a quiet country lane; like stepping from a funfair into a library. How one extricated oneself safely from the intensity of that kind of emotional experience was yet to be seen.

Over the following week he assumed the impetus of pinball: bouncing randomly from one activity to another. What was propelling him it was difficult to say. Occasionally he would be motivated to hunt out a nugget of history on Iran. Other times he would attempt to conjure up a replica of a dish he had not tasted for years. But mostly he would ignore the phone ringing.

He frequently wondered if he had made himself more – not less – depressed by dabbling in the past. He was definitely bored, being back in London. And simultaneously he divided his time between the supermarket, where he trawled for morsels of food, which now promised the lure of tastes and tangs, and the computer, where he foraged amongst online records looking for any crumb of information on the man they called Alec Conroy. He seemed to have vanished into thin air. At one point after several hours pilfering the depths of the cyber underworld, he latched on to a promising lead. But it climaxed in a bizarre dead end: a photo-montage of an old man in various uncompromising positions at a fetish club called Whip in Sweden.

A couple of days later, after being given some contacts by an old journalist acquaintance, he spoke to the secretary at the BP Society who identified an Alec Conroy on their list of active members until a few years ago. Following a merry dance she provided Manu with a last known address. It provided the surge of adrenalin he needed to release him from the apathy that had grown over him like a mould since his return.

He ventured out of the house for a second time to visit his parents, something he had, thus far, been postponing. In the event, he was glad to discharge some of the emotional drama which had been circulating within. Something he had been unable to do in the presence of Cyrus. And, all the while, as he offloaded, he was aware of his parents' frozen faces and paused cutlery as he recounted his disbelief at how much the country had changed; the atonement in confronting the swimming pool; the cheer of discovering the community of children who kept company with Sami's spirit in the old house; and the joy of seeing his uncle and aunt.

At the end of the performance his mother threw down her fork and burst into tears.

The look on his father's face vacillated between bewilderment and distress, as he leant across the table to comfort his wife.

"All those missing years!" his mother kept repeating in between sobs.

His father remained silent with his arm around her, looking at his half-eaten meal.

"Well say something!" she sniffed as she got up from the table to fetch a tissue.

"What do you want me to say?" said Mehdi in an unusually quiet voice. "I cannot undo the past. Like thousands of others we had no choice but to be blown about by the winds of change. Don't you think I have my own regrets?"

There was a silence, punctuated only by an occasional sniff from Rebecca at the corner of the room.

"Perhaps it's time to act on those regrets," said Manu. "Uncle Reza and Auntie Simin miss us terribly."

His mother began to cry once more. And Mehdi rose from the table to go to her.

"You are right my son. The time has come to put our differences aside. I shall contact him and we will invite them over. Or maybe even go and visit."

"Really Mehdi?" asked his wife.

He nodded.

They continued with their lunch during which Manu excitedly described his recent encounter with a greengage. Since the incident he had experienced two other such saporific events: one with a slice of marmite toast and the other with an anchovy.

"Do you think you're recovering?" asked his mother after his father went to have his usual postprandial nap.

"I can't be sure but it looks promising, although I still can't smell a thing," said Manu, picking up a lime from the bowl on the table and sniffing its skin. "More importantly, do you think dad will keep his word about going to visit Uncle Reza?"

"Who knows. I don't presume to understand the man's mind anymore," said his mother as she loaded the dishwasher.

"I'm sure he will. I mean, look at him. He's got nothing to do in his life. He surely must be wondering if there's more in this world than spying on the neighbours by *now*?"

His mother laughed.

"Oh Manu. You'll be glad you weren't here. I've been going through sheer hell," she said putting a plate of sweetmeats on the table and pulling a chair out to sit down. "I didn't tell you because I was too embarrassed, but before you went away the neighbours had found him in their garden attacking their new conservatory with a hammer!"

"What?!" said Manu as he sat down and took a chick pea cake from the plate in front of him.

"Don't worry – it's all ok now. But it was touch and go for a while. He said he had spotted boxes of alcohol, a mirrored disco ball inside – whatever and...."

"Disco ball? Come on, dad wouldn't know one of those, even if it rolled in front of him, surely?"

"Well anyway, he was obsessed with this notion that they were opening a night club next door."

"Oh for goodness sake."

"I know. Anyhow, cut a long story short. The police were called and the council threatened to charge him with anti-social behaviour. Damage to property. Trespassing. That kind of thing. Anyhow...."

"On no. Why didn't you tell me?"

"I was too mortified and I thought it would pass. But at one point I was embarrassed even to show my face in the village. Honestly. I had to apologise to the woman for your father's behaviour Manu. I really did. And thankfully she was very understanding. In her late fifties I'd say. Apparently they've just returned from living in Morocco for the last five years. The husband still goes back and forth for business purposes and doesn't seem to be around much. And, you can imagine, for a woman who's in the house on her own much of the time, it must be quite frightening finding a stranger attacking your property. Even if it is an old man! So really it was charitable of them not to press charges. He could have ended up in prison!"

His mother went on to describe the session of neighbour mediation his father had been forced to attend by the council whilst Manu was in Iran. It was here the issue of pink poles and alcohol had been resurrected and the embarrassing truth arrived at. *A wedding*. The neighbours had been planning for their daughter's wedding. And it was the foundations of the marquee which had consisted of a pink pole. The sound system and alcohol were, of course, for the reception. A humiliated Rebecca Zand had spent a good few days with her head in her hands.

At that moment his bleary eyed father appeared at the kitchen doorway, dressed in pyjama bottoms and an old vest.

"If you are going to talk about me, at least do the decent thing and wait until I have fallen asleep," he observed. "I see your mother is exaggerating as usual. I only wanted to have a look at the pink pole and examine the conservatory they are building. I tell you, it didn't look safe and I was worried that it might fall on top of your mother when she is cutting the hedge!"

His father's bony shoulder clicked as he waved his finger around to make his point. Over the last few years everything about him had shrunk – apart from his nose which had insisted on staying its rightful size. This new-found delinquency was clearly a final exertion of authority, before the loss of all his pride. The poor man still found it difficult living in England, even though he had been in the country for twenty-five years. But he missed the culture, and the weather, and had found it difficult to make friends. In all their time in St Margaret's, Mehdi had not made a single close acquaintance. Whether it was because he felt like an outsider, or whether he was simply too proud Manu could never be sure.

"Anyway," continued his mother. "After all that, he's now decided that he's going to help them with the wedding. Can you believe it? Apparently they're planning a Moroccan extravaganza. So of course your father – he couldn't just leave them be could he? Has been telling them what to do…"

"Do not talk *around* me like you are at my wake, woman! I have not been *telling* them. I have been *suggesting* that he should also try some Persian delicacies, so the guests can experience tastes from a variety of regions."

"Wow, that's fantastic, Dad. Did he agree to that? After all it is a *Moroccan* wedding?"

"Of course he did my boy. I took him some of your mother's Kookoo Sabzi which he tried and he absolutely loved it. He thinks it is a marvellous idea!"

"Hang on, hang on…" said Rebecca "This food you've offered – *who* exactly is going to cook it?"

"Well you, of course," said Mehdi opening the drawer in the sideboard next to where his mother was sitting.

Manu's mother turned to Manu and screwed up her face "Oh Mehdi, you do realise they have about 150 guests coming. That is a lot of food. "

"Nonsense my dear – it's nothing. Anyway I've said we will provide aperitifs. So it won't be the whole meal. Anyway – you can ask Farzaneh and Samira to help you. They love cooking."

"So I take it you are now best buddies with this chap next door, what's his name?"

"Abdul. And I'm not best buddies – just neighbours. He's been involved in buying and selling pottery so he understands that kind of business. We have something in common."

"Incidentally Mehdi," said his wife rising from the table to smell her husband's head. "What is that *awful* smell about you. I've noticed it recently. A sort of musty smell you have every time you come back from their house."

"I don't know what you mean," said Mehdi with a frown.

“Well I can’t explain it. Sort of...” she leaned over to him and smelled his thin blue jacket. “There it is. Sort of sweet. Smokey as well.”

“It must just be their house. The woman’s always cooking these things over coal.”

Rebecca gave an unconvinced look as she walked to the fridge.

“Have you been on the hookah dad?” Manu asked with a smirk.

“I may have had a small puff – earlier today. It was offered to me and I had to accept.”

“Hmm, well I wouldn’t make it a regular thing. You know your lungs are not good and the doctor said no more smoking,” said Rebecca as she fetched a box of eggs from the fridge and began to crack them on the side of the bowl.

“Anyway,” said Mehdi, ignoring her and moving a chick pea cake around the plate with his bony finger. “I have also agreed to organise the music.”

Rebecca Zand stopped her egg cracking halfway, allowing the white of the egg she was holding to run down the side of her arm.

“That’s ridiculous Mehdi. You know nothing about Moroccan music!”

“Not Moroccan music, no. Traditional Iranian folk music,” said Mehdi with a smile.

Manu laughed. “This seems to be turning into an Iranian wedding not a Moroccan one!” he jeered.

Astonishment bled across his mother’s face. “Are you seriously telling me that a Moroccan family, whose daughter is getting married to a man from Scunthorpe is happy to have traditional Iranian folk at their wedding?!” she said, wiping egg white from her arm with a tissue.

“Well, I said I would take this music over for them to listen to – they’ll make a final decision when they’ve heard it,” said Mehdi shrugging his shoulders, whilst placing a very old cassette tape on the table.

Manu shook his head and laughed. He couldn’t bring himself to remind his father that the cassette tape had been consigned to the dustbin of musical history. And he felt sorry for his mother who would have to go through yet another saga. He watched her close her eyelids whilst putting the back of a now flour-coated palm up to her forehead in resignation. There were few inevitable things in life. But one thing *was* quite certain: life with Mehdi Zand was anything but dull.

19

Tehran, 1951

Hajji-Hossein Forooshi was undertaking his customary weekly duty. This involved strolling past the police station in the centre of town, stopping at the end of its long dusty road, confirming nobody was in the vicinity, before walking over to the grill in the pavement.

Mr Mohebi's wife had come to rely on the weekly news from the grill underneath which her husband had been imprisoned for the past two years since the assassination attempt on the Shah. Often the prisoner had not much to say – aside from describing the insipid fodder he had been given for lunch, or the latest torture methods. Hajji-Hossein would dilute these accounts substantially before relaying them to the man's wife, lest she foisted upon him a hysterical fit. On the whole, it provided a morsel of comfort for her, knowing he was still alive at least. Both Hajji-Hossein and Mohebi knew that surviving the system involved accepting one's punishment and occupying one's mind until whosoever was in command had a change of heart. It was frequently as arbitrary as that.

Hajji-Hossein squatted over the grill and performed his habitual blow – a sign that he had arrived. And for the first time Mohebi's customary finger never appeared. Hajji-Hossein blew again. But a response was no where to be seen.

"Mohebi," he whispered gruffly "Are you there?"

There was a rustle of sorts and Hajji-Hossein jumped at the sight of a large and official-looking white eyeball blinking ferociously at him from in between the bars. A loud banging ensued as the eyeball's owner began to batter the grill with a blunt instrument.

"Who is that?" came a shout so mighty Hajji-Hossein could both smell and feel the stale breath of fermented whey against his face. "And what are you doing conversing with prisoners of the crown!"

He scrambled to his feet wrenching up his jacket which was caught under his shoe and ran as fast as he was able down the road, without looking back.

The exertion did not suit him and he arrived, quite breathless, at a coffee house outside the bazaar where many of his friends were seated at a table in the sun, playing backgammon.

"What on earth is the matter? You look as if you've seen a flying carpet!" said Mr Hakim the silversmith.

"I had rather a scare during my visit to Mohebi. Instead of him I had an encounter with an unpleasant guard," said Hajji-Hossein gasping for breath.

"He has probably been disposed of," said Bidandoon unsuccessfully chewing on a piece of nougat. "I've heard they are having a cull because the chambers are getting too full."

"In God's name I hope not! What will I say to his wife?" said Hajji-Hossein, pouring himself a chai from the samovar on the table.

"I would let it lie for a while. He may have simply been taken away for a spell of torture. He will likely be back before sundown," said Mr Hakim.

"Well, I fear neither torture nor death will make his wife happy. I will refrain from mentioning either to her until we know more."

Dr Azizi came out of the coffee shop with a newspaper in his hand. "Have you heard they've settled on a name for the oil company, now it's been nationalised. The National Iranian Oil Company – it has a certain authority to it, don't you think?" he said.

"It certainly does!" said Hakim.

"Mossadegh has called for a day of celebrations – and I think they will be hoisting the national flag over the offices in the centre of town this afternoon. We should attend," suggested Dr Azizi.

Hajji-Hossein peered at him oddly. "You look rather smart today Ahmad. Are you going to a wedding?"

"No. I am wearing a new suit. The old one was rather decrepit."

"Hmm. Blue. Rather progressive for a doctor," said Hajji-Hossein picking up the corner of Azizi's shimmering blue jacket. "And in answer to your question, Yes we should support the hoisting of the flag – after all, it may never have happened without us. I wonder if Karim has he been affected by all of this nonsense," he said, rifling though the newspaper Dr Azizi had handed to him.

"Odd you should mention it," said Mr Hakim. "Dashti told me he received a letter from him only yesterday. Things have been a little tense in the Abadan refinery. Apparently the Iranian workers have been protesting outside British residences and there have been some skirmishes. Karim wasn't involved, but he has some friends who are not as apathetic as he. There is talk now of evacuating the British workers."

"I suppose that will be true also of our friend Mr Conroy," said Hajji-Hossein.

"*Your* friend Mr. Conroy you mean. You seem to have become very friendly with him these days," said Dr Azizi jovially.

"Not friendly, no. He is putting plenty of trade in my path. In the past few weeks he has given my son Ali a list of farangis interested in importing carpets to the European territories. It's an expanding market."

"I think he may be expanding into forbidden territory himself," muttered Bidandoon under his breath.

"What exactly do you mean by that?" asked Hajji-Hossein filling his pipe with tobacco.

"Are you *sure* he's not *only* interested in the carpets, Hossein?" asked Mr Hakim.

"It's not the only beautiful object in your workshop after all," said Bidandoon with his hand in a silver bowl of syrupy sweets.

"I do not know what you mean?" said Hajji-Hossein. "What more could he be interested in. I do not have any other lines of business."

"I don't like to speak out of turn as you are a close friend. But there is talk he has his English eye on your daughter," said Mr Hakim.

Hajji-Hossein's confident expression unravelled into incredulity.

"What in God's name do you mean? Do I hear wagging tongues again?" he shouted.

There was silence amongst the clan.

"Well, reveal all. Who *exactly* has been saying these things!" Hajji-Hossein asked.

"Not so much saying but seeing really," muttered Bidandoon under his breath.

"Seeing? Seeing what? And with whose eye?" said Hossein banging his pipe on the table so that the tobacco came flying out.

"Now don't get cross, Hossein," said the Mollah. "It's simply that we've noticed the man going to and fro from your shop quite frequently over the last two months."

"Well of course you have. I have already told you he's been purchasing carpets and talking to Ali about exporting."

"Oh, has Ali been involved then. I do not think we realised," said Mr Hakim. "In that case, I'm sure we have been mistaken."

"Well, yes. You have," grumbled Hossein, re-stuffing the tobacco in his pipe and puffing to re-light it. "I mean, how is a shopkeeper to make a living if he is not even allowed a foreigner in his shop!"

At that very moment they were interrupted by a woman. Mrs Mohebi the wool-carder's wife came flying into the overwrought scene, her arms and hands everywhere. "Oh Hajji-Hossein, I have such good news to tell. My husband has been freed this very morning!" she cried kneeling to the floor and putting her head at his feet.

"Get up woman what are you doing?" he said tapping her head gently with the stem of his pipe.

“Oh Hajji-Hossein, I cannot thank you enough. You kept his hopes alive for two years. If it wasn’t for you I am quite sure he would have perished in that godforsaken place. And now, well now he has been released. And…,” she cried excitedly, “for *no* reason that we can think of!”

“Well,” said Hajji-Hossein with a snort. “He has been released for the self-same reason he was arrested then.”

“Yes. Oh yes. And I have sent him to bed for twenty-four hours – saying to him he is not to leave the house. He is very pale and ill. And I think he should not join any of the gatherings. It is too risky.”

“I am pleased for you,” said Hajji-Hossein, relieved he would not have to deal with any more bad news today. “Azizi, you’d better go round and check on him later.”

“Yes I will. Please do give him our regards,” said Dr Azizi.

Just then a boisterous crowd, which had been getting nearer and noisier with every minute, lumbered slowly by. The large procession of people was being led by what looked like some university students holding banners.

“They must be heading into town,” said Bidandoon. “Where are you going?” he shouted at one of the students.

“We’re heading to the AIOC offices!” shouted back the young man. “Come and join us. Mossadegh will be speaking.”

As they passed, Dr Azizi spotted Nargess Shabi, in the crowd. She smiled and waved a ribbon at him. “Come and join us!” she shouted above the clamour.

Dr Azizi felt himself blushing and turned his head so his friends did not notice. “Shall we join them?” he asked when she had moved on.

“Yes,” said Hajji-Hossein pleased to be putting the subject of his daughter behind him. “Although I’m not sure you should be fraternising with that woman, Azizi. You know she’s a royalist don’t you?”

“I’ve already told you. She is a republican,” said Dr Azizi.

"A royalist in republican livery then, I would deduce," said Hajji-Hossein under his breath as they left the café to follow the crowd.

The throng wound its way through the streets, attracting people to itself like pins to a magnet as it progressed.

When they reached the oil company headquarters a large mass had already gathered. The offices were shut and metal blinds had been put up in anticipation of disruption. Young men being goaded by the crowd were standing on each other's shoulders and pulling down the large signs above the offices. As they did roars of approbation followed. Police were attempting to halt them but they were outnumbered.

"Oh dear, what a shame," said Azizi. "I was sure it could all have been done so amicably."

A young man had climbed up to the roof of the building and was fixing an Iranian flag on top. "This oil company is now the property of the Iranian government," he shouted and the crowd bellowed.

"Do you think anyone is inside?" asked Nargess who had worked her way to Dr Azizi's side. Hajji-Hossein looked at her from the corner of his eye. He didn't trust the woman. She could very well be a plant. The crowd was mainly male which made the sprinkle of women in colourful clothing all the more conspicuous. Before long the shutters of the oil company headquarters were being pulled down and youths were attempting to get inside.

"Do you suppose your friend Mr Conroy is inside?" Dr Azizi asked Hajji-Hossein.

"I imagine all the English have been told they must keep away," said Hajji-Hossein picking up a discarded banner from the ground.

"Yes, I would not like to be one of them facing this crowd."

The conversation prompted Hajji-Hossein to consider what his friends had been saying earlier. It was preposterous to think that a man of Mr Conroy's calibre would even consider setting upon his daughter. He could not imagine it of him. At all times he had portrayed a well-meaning and courteous front. Despite his suspicion of foreigners, he had almost grown fond of the young man who had an obvious admiration for their culture. He could not believe Mr Conroy would not respect his culture and family. And Parissa herself knew better. There was no point or prospect in a marriage to an Englishman. Even the thought of it made him shudder. And as he shuddered he abruptly recalled an incident which, at the time, appeared perfectly benign. In the light of matters present, he wondered if perhaps more weight should be given to its importance.

A month ago he had been returning from a political rally and as he hurried down the bazaar corridor he had seen Mr Conroy leaving the carpet shop. That alone was insignificant. However, being in a hurry, he had continued home and on arrival was confronted with Ali who had, at that moment, returned home after taking an examination at school. Why did he not question this at the time? And, more importantly, who let Mr Conroy into the shop? He would surely not have been alone with Parissa. Even Parissa would not be that foolish. She was quite independent it was true. And he had often struggled with her discordant nature. But ultimately she knew the difference between right and wrong. And even she would count the costs before bringing that type of shame on the family. These thoughts twisted and turned through his head as he observed young men shaking and pulling down signs and railings in front of him. There was a loud crash as the main company sign above the door of the building fell to the ground. Did it wake him from his unworldly ignorance? It was hard to say. He dropped the banner he was holding and began to run.

20

Tehran, 1951

Alec Conroy sat on a wooden bench beneath the ungenerous shade of a walnut tree in the city park. In his hands was a typed letter. He read it for the fourth time.

Dear Mr Conroy

We regret to inform you that since you have declined to accept employment with the National Iranian Oil Company your continued residence in the country has ceased to be effective and we therefore must ask you to refrain from reporting to your place of employment as from Thursday 27th September 1951.

Every effort will be made to extend to you all the necessary assistance as hitherto in order that the remaining days of your stay in Iran should be as pleasant as possible.

Yours faithfully

Temporary Board of Directors; National Iranian Oil Company.

He walked towards the commotion emanating from a small bird cage at the end of the path, in the hope it might drown the pandemonium at large in his own head. A crowd of fat little lovebirds were in a heated debate over space, which was tight. Soft and bright little green feathers wafted about above their heads. Huddled in the corner were a bonded pair, their bright red beaks locked in amorous concentration.

If only life could be that sincere.

Assorted flares of his future prospects exploded before him. The starched look of his puritanical parents who never understood his affection for the East. The cold, grey light back home, which seemed even to run through the sentiment of his own people. And the forthcoming empty space in his throat, where the ache of love would once have resided. He could not survive the unbearable vacuum of this.

He looked about himself. The park was almost empty. His eye was drawn to some leaflets on the ground directing people to a gathering at the oil company headquarters. He would have been there today if he had not been dismissed.

He looked at his watch. Whatever calculation that came next, into his head, was strong enough to propel him immediately towards the park exit and through the narrow streets, as fast as he was able. It was not long before he was walking swiftly through the bazaar with his heart crashing against the wall of his chest.

As he neared the carpet shop he noticed the door was shut. A sign hanging in the door read 'closed'. The beats of his heart came to a momentary halt.

Whilst he stood for a moment considering what to do, he noticed a patch of movement at the back of the dimly lit shop. He peered through the dirty glass. The scene overwhelmed him with comfort. Ali was sitting on a pile of carpets, about twenty high, with a parrot on his shoulder and an abacus on his lap. He was pushing the abacus beads to the side of the frame and recording his calculations on a piece of paper, his teenage fingers working their way into adulthood by the minute. Parissa was flicking through a large pile of rugs as if it were the biggest notebook in the world. Her scarf had fallen away from her head and her thick black hair was twisted, like a rope, around itself. It shimmered as if it had just been polished. He could hear the very faint sound of their voices.

"Six Kermanshah," she counted – "all silk".

Ali echoed her, "Six Kermanshah, all silk".

"Six Kermanshah, all silk," echoed the parrot.

The hour had come. He needed to act fast. He knocked franticly on the pane of the shop door. Both looked up. Ali jumped out from behind the desk, to open the door. The parrot flew onto Parissa's shoulder.

"Hello Mr Conroy," said Ali as he opened the shop door. "Your carpet is not ready yet."

"Hello Ali. I was just passing and thought I would... Do you mind if I come in?" He stopped to look behind himself.

Ali obliged by standing aside to let him into the shop.

"I thought I would drop in to see how far Miss Parissa has progressed with it. I have heard today about…" he stopped to swallow a ball of tension that had built up in his gullet. "The Nationalisation. It is not good news for me. I've come to say that I will be leaving the country."

"Leaving the country!" screeched Shikar the parrot at the top of his avian lungs. Parissa raised her arm and clutched his beak, which he did not approve of. He lifted his foot to his face to try and push her finger away with his claw.

The silence that followed was like a hammer against Alec Conroy's skull. Perhaps they did not care? Why *should* they worry? The parasite exploiting their country had, at long last, been removed.

"What I mean," he said with a long sigh. "Will the carpet you are weaving be ready before I go?" He looked pointedly at Parissa.

For once her eyes met his, squarely. A yellow flicker from the oil lamp danced around the centre of each of her large black pupils. He yearned to jump into those fires. Perhaps he was imagining the shimmer of moisture which seemed to be working its way across her eyes. She blinked it away.

"When do you mean to leave, sir?" she asked with a tinge of concern.

"It's not certain yet but in a few weeks' time."

"But that's – that's so soon!" said Parissa. It was the first hint of real earnestness he detected in her voice. The wash of colour that existed seemed now to be draining from her cheeks.

"I mean. How will I have time to complete the rug? Does this mean you will never return to our country?" Parissa continued in a shaky voice.

Alec Conroy did not look up. He could smell the scent of the wool rising from the pile of carpets next to his waist. "It is a penance," he said. "I will not be able to return for the foreseeable future. And I thought perhaps…"

For a marginal second of time it seemed they were alone. He and she. That he could surrender every little feeling that had washed over him throughout these long years. And it would awaken in her a sense of sovereignty in which she would play his counterpart, and match his confessions equally with hers. Like a young bird that had, this very minute, discovered how to use its wings.

A cough from Ali, who was standing behind his shoulder, disabused him of this notion. It would never be. The hand of naked truth reached into the bottom of his spirit, pulled out the last morsels of hope and flung them into the abyss.

Then, without warning, a loud thump drew his attention to the figure before his feet. Parissa had slid onto the stone floor in front of him, unconscious.

He leapt to her aid. "Ali – fetch some water and salts– quickly!"

Ali ran out of the shop and down the passageway.

Alec Conroy gently lifted her head from the stone floor and leaned to pull over a small rug which he placed under her head. Her scarf was around her neck and her long rope of hair had worked loose, spilling like a stream of black oil over the rug.

"Parissa," he whispered as he stroked her face – "wake up."

She stirred, licked her lips and slowly opened her eyes. He noted her shock at seeing his face so close to hers, and helped her sit up before moving away to give her space.

"I'm sorry," she stuttered. "I – it just went black."

"No – please, don't stand up."

"I must – someone will come into the shop."

She stood up and went to sit on the chair by the table. He followed her.

"I'm tormented at having to leave the country Parissa," he said looking solemnly into her face. "But I am more heart-broken to leave the people I have grown close to."

Each word was strangling her. She found it difficult to breathe. But he was compelled to continue before Ali's return.

"I know you and I are from different cultures and that it's not right for you to consider me as a potential suitor. But if there was any way you could be released from your obligations, to come to England with me as my wife – I would be the happiest man in the world," he said.

Parissa began to wrap her headscarf around her head. The blood which had earlier drained from her face was reappearing in an impactful way. Her cheeks were overwhelmed with crimson. She picked up a piece of accountancy paper from the table and fanned herself.

"Your kind offer is one I wish I could accept. I would do so in the blink of a bird's eye. However, I need to have the permission of my father. I , I –" she trailed off.

The sound of running footsteps echoed down the bazaar corridor.

"I understand perfectly and would accept any decision that was made by you. I will await any answer you have for me. And will respect your father's and your wishes," he whispered as quickly as he could.

At that moment Ali ran into the shop with a glass of water. Behind him followed Hajji-Hossein looking enraged.

"In front of my ancestors' spirits – what has taken place here?" he shouted.

"Oh father I'm sorry – I fainted in the shop and Ali went to get some water," said Parissa

"This is a mischievous scene. I do not like the look of it. Mr Conroy, what are you doing here with my daughter? Have you no shame in forcing yourself on her company at this vulnerable time?!" he shouted pointing his finger into Alec Conroy's chest

"Please father! He has behaved with dignity at all times!" cried Parissa.

Hajji-Hossein thrust himself within breathing distance of Alec Conroy's face. "I have heard rumours I do not wish to believe. I was of the impression we had a measure of mutual respect for each other," he growled softly with more composure than he felt within. "Nevertheless, it seems that those rumours may very well be true. For that reason I ask you to refrain from ever entering my quarters again."

"But father," interrupted Ali. "Parissa has not finished the rug she has been weaving for him."

"Well she will finish it as quickly as possible and you can deliver it," said Hajji-Hossein.

Alec Conroy walked towards the entrance of the shop and looked back at Parissa who offered a sad departing smile. He felt Hajji-Hossein strutting in his wake and heard the glass door slam behind him as he stepped into the bazaar corridor. He stood for a moment by the side of the shop, out of view.

"Is it that you wish to bring shame on what remains of this family?" he heard Parissa's father shout from the other side of the door. And Parissa's plaintive response in his defence followed. His many years in the country had familiarised him with the tradition of Iranian families and he knew the power of honour in these relationships. He prayed Parissa would not be in trouble on his account.

"What would Karim say if he could see you now fraternising with him in the shop alone?" came the booming voice of her father through the pane.

"Father, I am not betrothed to Karim. I do not love him. And I know he is not for me!" he heard her shout. It took him by surprise. She was evidently more passionate than her external demeanour had hitherto revealed.

"Ah, I see, So now you know what's best for you…? Your father, who has all this time had your interests at heart and has made all attempts to secure a good future for you – he is now ignorant of your needs. Is that it? So – now it is about romantic love is it?"

Alec heard a loud thud as he threw something heavy down onto the desk.

"Do you know how hard I have worked to keep the family in food and clothes since your mother died?" continued Hajji-Hossein, the echoes of his loud voice reverberating faintly down the bazaar corridor. Alec was glad that most of the bazaar community seemed to have shut up shop to take part in the procession. A very old man slumped on a chair outside the spice shop was attempting to wrestle with the tide of sleep that was washing over him.

Then Parissa begin to sob and he found this unbearable. Perhaps he had made a mistake in growing so close to her. The consequences could be devastating.

He began to walk away from the shop. It was the only way to distance himself from the sound of her weeping.

****

An hour later, Parissa sat atop a pile of carpets in the shop, her head in her hands. Her father had departed with Ali in a whirlwind of obstinacy and nursing a headache. It seemed to her that life was truly a sealed pot. From this, emergence was hopeless. Why did her father see the world with such a jaundiced eye? He had, it seemed, become a bitter man. He and his antiquated friends were determined to close the door of progress to her generation. And as each thought ground itself through her head, she became more vexed – with her father for his thoughts and deeds; with herself for enduring these unnecessary shackles.

In God's name what was she to do with the volcano that was boiling inside? Tears were an inadequate conduit for its caustic spit.

She walked to the small mosaic laced mirror which hung on the wall at the back of the shop and examined her face. The sockets of her eyes were swollen with tears yet to come. She remembered the counsel of Dr Azizi's friend, Nargess: n*ever forget whose life you are living.*

If she did not act now, she would remain forever regretful of the path she had allowed herself to choose. She removed her headscarf and threw it behind herself in a defiant gesture. Then she walked with embellished confidence to the door of the shop, let herself out and stood outside in the corridor for a few minutes, looking about. She turned, re-entered the shop, picked up the headscarf and put it in her tunic pocket. She walked back out of the shop and out of the bazaar into the melting late afternoon sun. The beat of her heart was lagging a few paces behind her new-found motivation.

The streets appeared to be somewhat deserted, to do with the oil company gathering she supposed. She lifted her head to the sky and sighed. How rarely she was allowed to feel the caress of the sun on her hair. And a gentle breeze wrapped itself like nature's silk scarf around her neck. A good many of her fortunate sisters were accorded this freedom by the authorities every day. And for them there was no dishonour in accepting a marriage proposal from a Westerner. What kind of misfortune was it that had thrust *her* into such a bygone tribe?

Sitting under a withered tree, a beggar woman held out her arm, the other arm clutching an open-mouthed, sleeping, baby. Parissa gave her a little money and wondered if there were beggars on the streets of Englistan. Unlikely, she decided. The English quarters in Abadan had attested to that. She had seen it for herself. Clean-shaven men emerged from white houses into green-lawned gardens. Their milky faced wives were elegantly poised at polished gates with their cherry cheeks. On the tennis courts, small children, with rackets as big as themselves, expressed ripples of unfettered joy. It was a wantonness even her own excitable sister would find difficult to comprehend: having life's full charge on her shoulders at the age of ten. If only she could free her brother and sister from these obligations. If only her father would comprehend the life that could be available to them, if he would simply allow her to follow her heart.

"Is that you Pari?" she heard her father call as she opened the door to their small lodgings. She remembered her headscarf and immediately replaced it before entering the room. Ali and Soraya were preparing food in the kitchen.

"Come here my girl," said Hajji-Hossein, beckoning to her to sit by his side.

Parissa sat next to him on the large floor cushion. A waft of opium emanated from his arm which he put around her. "I have been thinking that I have been a bad father to you," he said looking at her with his sad and pink intoxicated eyes.

"Oh father please...."

"No, let me finish," said Hajji-Hossein holding up his finger to her face. "When you were a young thing I mistakenly thought of you as a surrogate in the absence of a male successor and put much responsibility on your shoulders. I see it was wrong. And it is because of this, and because of me, your mind has been led astray and your character has become entangled with itself. For too long I have forced you to take on a multiplicity of roles, when all the while you should have been married, long ago– for your own sanity and safety."

"But father..."

"Please, Parissa – allow me to have my moment.

"Sorry Father."

"It has been made clear to me that I have damaged your credibility as a potential wife. An older woman like yourself becomes steadily set in her ways and less adaptable. There's no doubt we should have started formal Khastegari proceedings with Karim much sooner. So I want to apologise and say that I understand why you have been led astray. And I accept some of the blame must be laid at my door. I have taken my eye off the ball and it has bounced outside of my reach. I regret bestowing on you such an injury and I intend to do everything I can to help and support you in your future happiness."

"Father, you do not have to apologise. I understand your position and would not have had my life any other way," she said gently, holding his hand.

"I am an old man now my dear. I wish you to have security in your life. So I have this afternoon had a serious talk with Dashti senior and we have agreed a date for your wedding to Karim. That way you can settle into your new life and have no worries. There is a holiday planned for the workers at the end of the month when the farangis are expelled from the country. It's an ideal time for the wedding ceremony."

The cold blade of grief sliced through her. And as it did she heard no more. She simply saw her father's mouth moving amongst the stillness of her thoughts:

O father, cease to advise me about my love, cease!
For your daughter will not be tamed with this disease.
The dust that lies before my door
Love's long desired elixir pour
Upon this wasted heart of mine
Bring me a promise and a sign!

"Did you hear what I said?" he asked putting his fingers under her chin and lifting it up so her eyes were level with his.

"Yes. Of course father."

"Good. That is settled. It may seem daunting to you now. But in a year or so you will be happy with the outcome."

Parissa sighed and endeavoured to concoct a smile through the remnants of her misery.

"I will change my clothes and help the children prepare the food," she said standing up.

After she had changed there was a knock on the bedroom door and Ali entered, shutting the door quietly behind himself. From under his jacket he took out a small book and handed it to Parissa.

"I should not be doing this. But he asked me to return it to you in confidence."

It was her book of Saadi's poetry which she had given to Alec Conroy. She held her breath. It was surely a sign of his disconnection and change of heart. This accelerated the march of wretchedness that had already begun to circulate in her veins.

"Did he say anything?" she asked as she took the small book with her trembling hand.

Ali shook his head and left the room.

Parissa leant with her back against the nearby wall clutching the book to her chest, her dry throat aching with anticipation. A moment later she shook the book to see if any note would fall out. It did not. And she knew he would not have risked it. Ripe tears began to tumble down her cheeks.

How often had she been told not to heed a rushing heart? It was her own fault that she had been ensnared. She flicked through the book repeatedly to make certain there was no letter tucked in between the pages. Some black markings on a page caught her eye and she hastily re-located that page. On the chapter on Love and Youth, in the margin beside the verse, was some small writing in black ink.

Dear Parissa, thank you for lending me this book which I loved. I would like to have had the opportunity to say goodbye to you before my ship sails from Abadan. But it seems this will not be possible now. I wish you the very best and thank you for being my teacher of poetry for the short while we have known each other.

He had underlined faintly one of the verses:

I shall not let go my hold of thy skirt
Even if thou strike me with a sharp sword.
After thee I have no refuge nor asylum.
To thee alone I shall flee if I flee.

She shut the book and tucked it underneath her pillow. He had conceded defeat. Surrendered himself to life without her. Severed their connection. And in weeks he would be gone. A seething anger arose in her belly. Her father had put in her way a barricade of such enormity that it would require either a work of utter brilliance, or a singular stroke of good fortune, to conquer it. And she sensed she lacked both the intellect and the auspiciousness for the prospect of either.

She lay on the bed for a short while examining the options open to her. The hand of kismet offered her but two paths. Each as treacherous as the other. She must either accept the future her father had proposed. Or become an infidel, a heathen and a traitor. Perhaps, in her heart, she was already all of these. She sensed this to be the case. And the more she sensed it, the more she convinced herself the tide could not be turned. She was determined to have her future. Even though the intoxication both suffocated and liberated her in the same breath.

Her sister's loud chatter came and went in between the walls. How comforting that she was safe and happy in her world. If only she could be protected from all that was about to come. It was for Soraya's sake that she couldn't allow others to have the last word.

What mattered now was how the story was told. Gossip and rumour would cling to her repute without mercy. People she loved would bury her character with shame; in private they would deny her an existence. Much later, when the hurt had faded, her ancestors would use the fable to teach their children a lesson. Until then others would whisper and speculate. The name of Parissa would linger on the lips of mollas and beggars alike and there would be a thousand and one versions of her chronicle, like the tale of the Arabian Nights.

But there was not a single drop of doubt that remained in her mind. She would not allow herself to perish from grief, as the lovesick Leyla had done. Many of her sisters had followed their hearts. She must indeed follow hers.

21

London, 2003

A cacophony of noise emanated from the hallway of 53 Salford Gardens in Kensington, contesting its record as the quietest street in Britain. Fortunately, a two-ton, Edwardian, oak door proved an ample barrier between passers-by and the lungs of a woman with an overly generous ribcage.

"You'll be late again! Get yourself down to this door RIGHT NOW!"

Reluctant foot thumps retorted down the stairs. The door burst open. A skinny young boy of about seven, with a rucksack on his back, was ejected from the front of the house, like a baby bird from its nest.

"I'm confiscating that computer game before breakfast! Now get yourself to that bus stop and no messing on the way," screeched a portly woman with black curly hair, a feminine moustache and an apron. The boy slithered down the road dragging his feet.

"Love you!" she shouted with a smile and the wave of a handkerchief. She subsequently bent down to wipe the noses of three small children who were dangling like human tassels from her flouncy skirt. As she twirled to go back indoors, the infant frills rotated with her. Luckily she had enough surface area to accommodate a whole nursery.

"Well now children. We have a lot to do today," she said, nonchalantly picking up the smallest by the arm and swinging her around to land squarely on the hip.

"Let's see, we've got Mrs Blythe on the third floor – needs her ironing done and – Tony, get that out of your mouth!

She snatched away the muddy golf ball her two year old had found on the stair and put it in her pocket.

Talia Christou's daily grind began with an early rise to feed her husband before he set off to plumb his way around

London. She then dressed and fed the children and – as warden of number 53 – checked on the six tenants in the building to ensure all were still alive and breathing (her take on it).

She banged on one of the doors as she went up the stairs "You ok in there Miss Devon?" she cried

"Mama, I'm hungry," grizzled the third child. "When can I have biscuit?"

"When we get top of the stairs baby – Miss Devon you hear me?" She put her ear to the door.

"Yes dear just having my breakfast" called a thin (but living) voice from inside.

The doorbell rang.

"Oh Jees. I just got up here!"

One by one she placed the three children on the top stair. "Alexa. You stay here. You hear? Look after the babies."

She ran down the two flights, grunting as her heel hit each step, and opened the front door.

"Yes?"

"Hello, I'm looking for a Mr. Conroy please. Does he live here?"

She looked the man up and down. He looked Greek and returned a frosty stare.

"Are you a relative? You don't look like it," she said surveying his face stridently.

"No I'm not a relative. Are you?"

"Huh?"

"I mean – are you his *daughter*?"

"You're joking me – eh? No!" she stifled a disparaging laugh deep in her belly. Then she glanced upstairs and squinted her eyes, her ear leaning towards the stairway.

"So – does he live here then?"

"Well yes, But is he expecting you?"

"No I'm afraid not"

She humphed.

"Who's calling please?" she asked, her preoccupied eye wandering to the side.

"I am Mr Zand. I'm doing some research on The Anglo Iranian Oil Company. I'd be grateful to….."

"Wait here."

Manu was about to follow her into the hall but she kicked the door shut with her foot as she went, slamming it in his face.

"Charming," he muttered.

A short while later she reappeared at the door, this time with a small baby on her hip and another attached to her hand.

"He says you can come in and see him. But I'm the warden of this place and I don't like my tenants getting too tired – so please don't keep him long. He's a very old man and not at all well. And if he gets tired, I got twice as much to do."

She led him to a large door which was ajar, off the hallway, and pushed it open.

In front was a wide corridor, along the length of which a snapshot of history paraded itself. A range of assorted beaten copper and brass trays glistened on the wall interspaced with photographs of other times and places. And darting out from under the soles of his feet as he progressed along the passageway were a collection of blue and red deer, bringing an intricately woven carpet-runner to life.

The large imposing living room he entered next took Manu's breath away with its busy Eastern theme. In between giant canvases of royal hunting scenes, tiny Lilliputian people acted out their stories in miniature paintings.

Delicate boxes, bejewelled with mosaic scenes, were perched here and there on shelves and tables. A large wall next to the fireplace exhibited a gallery of carpets of all sizes. Ornate patterns and flamboyant colour monopolized every bit of space available. It was, indeed, Little Persia.

Manu felt strangely envious, having just arrived from minimalist bland of upper Hampstead. A month ago this hectic setting would have made him feel nauseous. How quaint that it now seemed homely. The only marginally plain item in the room was the large expensive-looking cream white sofa, and the matching curtains which hung in front of the bay windows over looking the street.

"I've told Mr Conroy I'll make you both a cup of tea. Please sit down. He will be with you shortly," said the caretaker and disappeared back into the hallway.

Manu strolled around examining some of the artefacts. A large Victorian desk at the corner of the room had been kept in immaculate condition. On it there were a number of small copper pots and a sculpture of an Asian hunter on horseback. Behind the desk, white shelves ran floor to ceiling with books: some of Persian poetry; others political and historic books on the Middle East.

Above the fireplace hung an arresting fiery red carpet at the bottom of which was an inscription in Farsi – which he couldn't understand. A feeling of excitement passed through him when he noted its uncanny resemblance to his own rug, only larger.

"I see you've found the prize possession. It's lovely isn't it?" A voice behind made him jump.

A frail old man, with white hair, languished in the doorway in a wheelchair.

"Yes. Beautiful," said Manu.

"The inscription is a line of a poem by Hafez, the Persian poet," he said pressing a knob on his wheelchair, which Manu was thankful to see was electric.

"Please do take a seat. Bear with me. I have rheumatoid arthritis and..." he tried to manoeuvre himself round the side of the coffee table, occasionally crashing into the corner, "as you can see – I'm not a terribly good driver!"

Manu smiled patiently, wondering if this was what lay in wait. A life of loneliness, incapacity, and accommodated in a museum of one's own creation?

"So Talia tells me you doing some research on the AIOC?" said Mr Conroy having settled himself.

Manu explained his interest in the life of British workers at the AIOC, flexing the truth where he thought it might benefit the outcome. It seemed to come naturally to him these days, having been in Cyrus' company. And he was horrified at himself for appreciating the tangible benefits a little white lie could bring.

"Are you of Iranian origin yourself?"

The question threw him. His usual response would involve denial of some kind. But these days it seemed rather extreme.

"Yes. My father is Iranian."

"Ah, I thought I could see a glimmer of the Middle East about you," said the old man shuffling about in his chair.

At that moment the housekeeper (and her children) came in with the tea and some biscuits.

After they had left, Manu took out the list of questions he had prepared,, concerning the history of the AIOC. Mr Conroy, understandably, was an authority on the subject. Manu listened intently as the old man recounted the company's history beginning with the wealthy Englishman who bribed the Shah for exploitation rights to the country's oil, and finishing with eventual takeover by the British government. He scribbled copious notes and, much to his surprise, he found Conroy's detailed account to be of genuine interest.

Alec Conroy had been head of finance and administration, travelling between the Abadan and Tehran offices to ensure payment processes were in order.

"It must have been difficult for you, when there were calls for nationalisation and when riots broke out," said Manu.

There was a short pause in the conversation and Alec looked into the distance.

"Yes, indeed. I've always been interested in the politics of the country of course. You have to be. It involves a highly complex collection of overlapping ideologies held by nationalists, modernists; and Islamists – all tugging against each other, both outside and inside the country. But of course, at the end of the day, I was merely a pawn in the process. As we all were. And many of us did not want to leave."

"If you loved the country so much why did you not take the contract?"

"I was told, in no uncertain terms, by my British employers, that if I stayed in Iran there would be no future for me in the UK oil industry."

"So basically, they had you over a barrel?" said Manu, oblivious of the pun.

Conroy laughed. "Yes I suppose they did!"

"Tell me a bit more about your life in Iran."

"It was a charmed life in a sense, "said Conroy. "I first arrived just after the Tehran conference where, quite ironically, Churchill , Roosevelt and Stalin had made a pact to ensure Iran's independence. And the longer I stayed the more I grew used to the place and particularly the people. I found the Iranian people to be amongst the most generous and selfless people I have met. Unfortunately there was much poverty. Centuries of no universal education systems had taken its toll. But I have very fond memories. I'll show you some photographs."

Conroy manoeuvred his wheelchair around the table and headed for the desk where he retrieved an album from the drawer. Flicking though some pages he pointed to a collection of photographs. "Here you are – this is me outside the AIOC offices. Not sure of the year – 1949 perhaps?"

A striking young man with blonde hair and a dimple smiled out of the picture. He had his arm around the shoulders of another young man – a native.

"That was a young gentleman called Jamshid. He was a lovely chap. Worked in the AIOC offices with me. Quite sad really, he was badly injured – lost his arm in the riots that followed during the oil nationalisation. There was a lot of bad feeling amongst the public and the company offices were smashed and burned after nationalisation."

Manu looked at some of the other photos in the album. Quite a few were in social settings with Conroy appearing in a variety of party shots. At the bottom of one of the pages, the photo of a pretty young Iranian girl in a headscarf caught his eye. The shot was relatively blurred, snapped without consent perhaps. Nevertheless the camera had caught the beauty of the moment.

"A friend?" Manu asked, pointing to it.

"Yes. And tell me," said Conroy changing the subject. "You say your father is Iranian. Have you lived there in the past?"

"Until I was thirteen or so."

"Left during the revolution I suppose?"

"Yes, that's right."

"And have you been back since?"

"I have just returned from a trip to Tehran, this week."

"How wonderful!" said Conroy, with an enthusiastic tone but a gloomy demeanour on his aged face.

"Yes it certainly brought back a few memories," said Manu wandering over to a small upright piano nearby where he picked up a small leather Khoran. "It made me realise what I had been missing. And looking at all the wonderful things you have in your room I realise I had purposely, and subconsciously perhaps, distanced myself from all things Middle Eastern."

"Whilst I, on the other hand, have surrounded myself with all things Persian, to prevent me forgetting the most definitive period of my life."

"This carpet must, indeed, bring back exactly such memories for you," said Manu wandering over to the shock of colour on the wall that demanded attention. "Can I touch it?" he asked.

"Of course, please do."

Manu ran his hand over the silky pile of the rectangular carpet that cascaded down, in splashes of eccentric tone, from a horizontal pole halfway up the stark white wall. The blood-red and gold border played fortress to a chaos of entangled flowers and leaves of differing sizes, all spilling over themselves in the fight to influence the eye.

Conroy smiled "Beautiful isn't it?" he said, wheeling his chair over to where Manu was standing.

"What is the inscription?" asked Manu.

"*I gave up my desires straight, when beloved took my heart's rein and made me her slave*."

"That's beautiful."

"Yes it is, isn't it? I find the poetry of your country most beguiling."

Beguiling? Really? He could not quite believe his ears. The sketch of his teenage life had, running through it, a strand of inflammation caused by persistent anti-Middle Eastern dogma: hidden in an ostensibly anodyne turn of phrase; conspicuous in overheard conversations; and vented in bad politics.

What a pleasant change it was to be on the receiving end of a compliment about the country of his birth. Quite unusually, a moment of profound cheer and pride overwhelmed his mainly sour temperament. It was as though – for an instant – a kind soul had offered to relieve him of the rucksack of xenophobic postulations he had been lugging around for the past twenty years.

"You are smiling," said Alec Conroy, as if surprised.

"Yes. I was just considering how rarely I hear these types of accolades about Iran."

Alec Conroy shrugged his shoulders. "It's terribly unfortunate; the relations between East and West. And I fear I shall not live to see any kind of rapprochement. It saddens me."

Just at that moment there was knock on the door and the caretaker squeezed her plump face through the crack. "It's time for your morning walk, Mr Conroy," she said. "Mr Jones is here to take you out."

"I'd love to keep chatting but I'm afraid I have this '*morning walk*' which they take me on to get me out of the house. If you'd like to come back another time I'd be happy to talk further."

Somewhat flustered by this unexpected interruption, Manu took the card that Alec proffered. How frustrating. He had been so absorbed in their conversation he had failed to use the opportunity to introduce the subject of his own carpet, or to press Conroy on where he had acquired his.

“That would be nice,” said Manu forlornly. He saw himself out of the door being held open for him. And, on stepping from the house into the (unusually) sunny afternoon, he was overcome with a strange sense of levelling off, as though his infuriated and angled edges had been filed down. Had his embittered soul been marginally disinfected?

22

Tehran, 1951

There was a Door to which I found no Key:
There was the Veil through which I could not see:
Some talk awhile of me and thee
And then no more of thee and me.

The chamber in which she sat was as familiar as her own breath. For ten years or more she had perched on the same seat, adopted the same posture and embarked on the same motions. The warp-threads rained down before her face and, above her head, brightly coloured balls of silk were suspended like planets in the air. Her arms were the strongest thing about her. For they had been used to years of extravagant animation. Of stretching upwards to cut the string and then downwards to knot each single strand. Of wafting across the loom, quick-as-a-rabbit, fingers zig zagging through the warp. Of beating down each thread with a comb.

For the past week she had done nothing but this, from the sprouting to the dying of the sun.

And dusk to dawn she had lain in bed examining assorted combinations of solutions, to rid herself of the calamity that now blocked her life. Of ending it. Of succumbing to it. Of challenging it. Of bearing it. Of escaping it. On all these she deliberated. And then she deliberated on them again in the days following, knotting every anxious rumination and every utopian fantasy into the carpet she was weaving for him.

She felt comfort in the notion that when he took possession of it he would acquire her most inmost wishes and fears. The beetroot-red border with its dying autumnal leaves screamed of the cruellest adversity that might await her. And the scenes of pale blue, summer flowers – abundant stamens and rich foliage, whispered the paradise in which she walked alongside him in her dreams.

She stopped for a moment and wafted her hands about her to catch a little air and allow the blood on her fingers to dry. The span of a hand and the carpet would be nearly finished.

She had read widely, in the papers her father had left in the house, that British personnel were to be forced out of Iran in three weeks. Mr Conroy was anticipating a line of verse. And today, of all days, her poetic mind was threadbare. Tears rolled down her cheeks and dripped onto her apron. She searched in her pocket for rag to wipe her dripping nose. And with it emerged a miniature red leather bound book: the English translation of the Rubaiyat given to her by Mr Conroy. Her trembling hands flicked through the pages. The words were as unfamiliar to her as raindrops to the Dasht-e-kavir. She became agitated and began to cry again. Then the voice of her mother intervened to calm her. *Locate the granule of serenity within yourself – and you will feel crystals falling from black clouds*. She thumbed through the book once again and the occasional meanings of words offered themselves to her.

And then at once she saw a simple line which revealed itself like gold. For it condensed all that was in her heart at that very moment and the words she was desperate to impart to her beloved. It revived each filament of flesh on her bones. And it ignited every nerve and neuron in her body. The whirlpool of thoughts that had been circulating around her mind, day after recent day, abruptly arranged themselves into order and purpose. Like a regiment of soldiers being called to attention. She needed to work fast. There was much to do.

For the rest of the afternoon she worked faster than ever she had done, with pure intent and direction. With the progression of each minute, in front of her eyes and up the warp of the loom, evolved the words which made her nauseous with excitement the more visible they became.

By eight o'clock when light was starting to evaporate she accomplished the final knot and, exhausted, she briefly rested her head against the woollen consequence. And when she lifted it again to look at the sentence complete, she felt dizzy, leapt up from her bench, ran to the corner of the room and began to wretch with uncontrolled trepidation. Night's greedy shadows were beginning to stretch themselves around the room. She lit the oil lamp. Fingertips of warm light skimmed the rims and edges of the room's protuberances. She held the lamp in front of the carpet. Each dense black word bellowed above the noise of colour surrounding it. She mouthed the words to herself: *All things end in yes.*

It was the response to his proposal and the decree of her own fate. Quickly she undid the carpet from its frame, rolled it up and hid it behind the shelf of yarns. She heard the shop door downstairs close with a bang. Outside, two wild street cats attacked each other. She gritted her teeth and descended the stairs. Her father was sitting on a wooden chair, reading the newspaper. He was keeping vigil. This was how it was now. And she detested him for it. He had closed the door to the modest freedom she had been able to snatch whilst his back was turned. And, with it, her esteem for him.

"Have you finished for the day?" he asked, looking up.

"Yes father."

"You look much better today my girl. There is uncharacteristic flush in your cheeks which I am happy to see. I have been very worried about you."

"I have not been sleeping well. But now I understand there is much to look forward to. Father, I've been thinking about it. I would like to marry Karim as soon as possible."

He looked at her quizzically from the corner of his eye as they walked to the door of the shop to depart.

"Well, he takes a holiday at the end of October."

"The end of October is too late," said Parissa, as she marched forcefully down the bazaar corridor towards the exit.

Her father cocked his head in surprise at her terse tone. "Too late? Too late for what?" he said scuttling to keep up with her pace.

"I would prefer the wedding to take place sooner. In Abadan," said Parissa turning to him as she began to walk down the path toward their lodgings.

"Why should we do that, when it is far easier to have it here?"

"It is far better for me to immerse myself in oil company life as soon as possible. After all, it is where I shall be spending most of my time. And if we wait any longer I fear his parents may think we are not suited."

"Why? Have they said something to you?" asked Hajji-Hossein opening the door to their home.

"Not directly. But there are rumours that a sister of an oil worker colleague of Karim's has been visiting him at the compound," she lied.

"I see," said Hajji-Hossein gravely as they entered their abode. He had contested many things in life, but was wise enough not to question a woman's intuition. "Very well. Let us discuss some dates after supper and I will speak to Dashti tomorrow."

Parissa went to her room to wash and pray. Of all the tightness inside her the most piercing came from her conscience. She knew God to be full of loving kindness, merciful and compassionate. And she was breaking a promise to him. Why was it Haram for a woman, but not a man, to marry outside of the faith? Once, a long time ago in class, she had infuriated her teacher by questioning the justice behind such a tenet – and suggesting it should be included in the Doubtful Matters. They sent her home from school.

And now, as she put the full force of her face to the ground, she was fearful that perhaps God was retracting from her the faith that had kept her whole all these years. And she repeatedly told herself this would not be so. That God, wide-awake and vigilant, had accepted her prayer to leave the comfort of her devotion for a brief while. And that he was confident of her return, in good time, to be called to account for her deeds on the day of Last Judgement.

The following week she quietly disregarded a good many of her father's demands to scheme for herself a plan of action. At times she could not believe the strength she had found to do such godless things. For many of the lies she was forced to tell were tangled and fat. She alternated reassuring chatter about her upcoming marriage with furtive acts of defiance. She tricked her father into signing her travel permit document whilst inebriated, his head tilted backwards and his mouth thrown open like a fish out of water. Into a letter she decanted her confessions and apologies, to be discovered on her departure. She consorted with Poupak Dashti to orchestrate the detail and occasion of her own delusory nuptial knot. She arranged with Hassan the delivery of the carpet to Mr Conroy.

What penalties lay in wait at the end of this long line of misbehaviours she wondered? Each day she ached with remorse when she saw the painful arrow she was on the verge of propelling towards Karim's heart. And she found herself keeping score of the number of transgressions, so when the time was right she could offer reparations to cancel them out. Collectively they hung like a giant, wrought iron, bell on her conscience. How wretched that the joy she felt for her destination was being overshadowed by the struggle of the journey itself. And she begged her mother for forgiveness every night.

When she had presented the carpet to Hassan for delivery, he questioned both its provenance and destination.

"There is no need to worry about that Hassan," she said firmly. Ali must have told you to expect this for delivery?"

He could not remember having had such a conversation with her brother.

"Well I am telling you now this has been arranged. And if Mr Conroy is not at home you must leave it on the porch. Now hurry. His belongings are being packed tomorrow for shipping," she said. "You must not delay."

She strode away, without looking back. Later when she checked the yard, the cart had gone and she felt another degree of thankful relief. She was confident that Hassan would not have the prudence to inspect the carpet, and even if he did, what would he see? He was from a long line of illiterates and had spent his life a mere go-between. It was doubtful he would even recognise the scripture of his own mother tongue. Thus, he would be sightless to the message scrawled in black ink on the back of the rug, which proposed a tryst outside the Municipal swimming pool in Abadan. This is where she would be waiting, from dusk to dawn if necessary, on the day of Mr Conroy's departure, which had been revealed in all the newspapers.

And later that week, when they were sitting in the bazaar teahouse, her father enquired on the progress of Mr Conroy's carpet. She simply told him it had been completed and delivered. During which the anxiety within her was so intense she feared it would glow on the outside of her skin. But her father appeared impervious. He was, as usual, immersed in his world of principles. And he proceeded to frantically beckon Dr Azizi who, at that moment, had entered the teashop in which they were sitting.

"I presume you have heard the United States government is now wading into the nationalisation argument?" said Hajji-Hossein with a grin as the Doctor approached their table with a glass of tea.

"Ha yes. By all accounts they have despatched a special United States envoy. It is his role to put the British neck in a vice, and force them to accept the nationalisation in principle."

"Well it is about time," said Hajji-Hossein. "Thus far, every time that particular lion has opened its jaws, we have heard nothing but the squeak of a mouse! Are you telling me the beast finally speaks with a roar?"

"It speaks with a roar indeed. But I fear its teeth are more interested in pulling out the entrails of our communist party. Incidentally how are the wedding preparations going?" he asked, turning to Parissa.

For once she was thankful to hear the sweet sound of honesty in her own voice as she recounted the preparations for the Aghd. It would take place at the social club and a bus had been booked to take relatives to Abadan. Mrs Dashti would be travelling a few days earlier to assist in setting up the wedding spread.

"Well, exciting as it all sounds, I must depart. I have a variety of medical appointments this morning," said Dr Azizi as he finished the remains of his tea.

"You will not believe this but I'm on my way to see the darvish who entertains at the north end of the bazaar. A colony of bees has taken residence in his bushy beard. Every time the poor man moves he suffers a hundred stings!"

"Why, in God's name, does he simply not shave the thing off?" asked Hajji-Hossein.

"He refuses to do it on religious grounds and has vowed to endure the pain until his beard is evacuated," said Dr Azizi as he departed. "In the meantime I'm applying daily poultices to try and prevent his face turning into a giant raspberry!"

"Well come to me if you need something for the pain," called Hajji-Hossein winking at him in the doorway.

Dr Azizi was not amused. "Show some prudence with that substance Hossein, and take heed," he said in a serious tone. "One of these days *the dream of the beautiful* might well conclude in the *sleep of the dead*."

He closed the door behind him with such purpose that a water-pipe on the shelf next to the door fell to the floor, smashing into tiny pieces at his daughter's feet.

23

Tehran, 1951

She was running through the scarlet poppy fields, laughing and breathless. Tall green stems thumped against her face. Her father was chasing her. Endless freckles of crimson flowers bled across the green horizon. Jags of mountain pierced the cobalt sky. Nearby, her mother washed the dishes in an untroubled ripple of water heading towards a meaningful river. A consummated picnic offered nature its remains. Those were days of perfect form. Pleasures were untamed and conduct had no conditions attached.

How misshapen life had become since then. Distorted and dangerous. And as their vehicle pulled into Abadan bus station, she was engulfed by a sense of foreboding. What if Mr Conroy had changed his mind? Or she was refused entry to the ship? She forced herself to swallow back the pessimism which intensified the storm of sickness brewing in her stomach. She began to repeat to herself the only gem of comfort she knew. That Mr Conroy had taken delivery of the carpet and requested it be conveyed to her that he *understood her message and was delighted with it*. This is what Hassan had told her. It was surely a sign that he intended to meet her as arranged. After all, it was essential that he remained discreet, to prevent her father from finding out.

Hassan had confirmed this again when she sought him out behind the bazaar warehouse. And although she wanted to shake his arms and wrench out of him: whether Mr Conroy had examined it; or what his expression had been; or if he had enquired after her, she restrained herself.

Apart from this speck of assurance, there was only one other thing she knew to be certain. Her wedding was destined to be a lavish affair. It had swelled and luxuriated to the point of disproportion. No matter how often she had begged for a humble event, it was not to be. A modest bridal tunic had evolved into an extravagance of ruffle and lace. A token room had ballooned into a large hall. The refreshments had turned from a light morsel to a feast. And with each exaggeration, her conscience became more ulcerated with dishonour.

Truths had so entwined themselves with lies; and lies with truths that even she was struggling to discern fact from fiction, or fiction from sincerity, or sincerity from sham. And the whole issue had become so aggrandized she was convinced she would trip over her own complicated conspiracies.

She would not be seeing Karim before the ceremony for which she was grateful. He had sent word that there had been some unrest resulting from tension between the British and Iranian workers. Thankfully things had become more tranquil on their arrival.

Her family had arranged to lodge at the home where she had stayed with Yasmin the previous year, as the ceremony was not for two days. Her father and brother were allocated their own room and Parissa shared a bed with her sister.

The first evening was spent with the host family over an evening meal, discussing the various preparations that would be taking place the next day. Her sister's simmering excitement began to gnaw at Parissa's morsels of hope. That night Parissa caught hold of her sister's hands as she jumped around on top of the bed in their room.

"Raya, you need to keep calm. I cannot endure this," she said.

"Why? Are you not happy? I cannot believe you are not excited! I am so happy for you. And I am happy for myself. I will be the female head of the family. "

"Yes you are right. But how will you manage without me?"

"I will be-e-e-e, quite fine," said Soraya bending down to look in a mirror that was on a small table next to the bed. She pulled her hair up at the sides, as if to tie it in a bun. "Does this make me look older?" she asked.

Parissa squeezed out a stiff smile. "Yes, it does a little. But I need to let you know what is to come, Raya."

"I *know* what's to come Pari," said Soraya wagging her finger in front of her sister's face. "I have been watching you for a long time remember?"

She had jumped off the bed and was now holding up one of her sister's dresses to her chest and looking sideways at herself in the mirror on the wall.

"Come here. Sit down."

"Just wait a minute. I want to see what…"

"Come here. I have something to say."

She came over dragging her feet in exaggeration.

"Soraya I am going to tell you something that only *you* will know."

She gasped. "Is it a secret?!" she said, paying attention for the first time.

"I suppose it is."

Soraya clapped her hands.

"Soraya, you have to take this seriously. You may not like what I have to say. But I am telling you because you are the head of the family now and you need to be responsible."

There was a silence as her sister realised the importance of the moment. Parissa lowered her voice to a whisper as she pulled something out of her pocket. "Come here," she said to her sister holding up a gold chain on the end of which was a round gold locket. She opened it. Inside was a small picture.

"This is a chain which has a picture of our mother inside. I want you to have it. I am giving this to you because I think you are old enough to wear and look after it. Do not take it off for anything."

Soraya stood still whilst Parissa put it around her neck. "As long as you wear this, she will always be looking after you from wherever she is."

"Is she here now?"

"Yes."

"But if I wear it, who will look after *you*?"

"A married woman is cared for by her husband. And I need to tell you something else. I will be going away for a while."

"I don't understand," said Soraya. "Going away? Where are you going? To be with Karim?"

"No. You see, Raya. I shall not be marrying Karim," said Parissa stroking her sister's cheek to ease her frozen expression.

"Did you hear me?"

No response.

"Raya, did you hear what I said?"

Her sister cocked her head in slow motion, confused wrinkles spreading across her forehead.

"Why are we here then?" she whispered. The fresh bloom of adolescence in her face had melted into a childlike stare of vulnerability.

"I cannot explain it to you now. One day, when you are older, you will understand. There is an Englishman, you see. He wants to marry me and take me to live in Great Britain. And Raya, I want to go with him."

A fat tear emerged from her sister's eye. It rolled slowly down and balanced itself for a while on a collection of fine hairs on her cheek.

"But what about Karim?" she whispered through her clogged throat. "Has he done something wrong?"

"No, my dear. He has done nothing wrong. He simply needs to find another."

"I don't understand then. Why are we here? Does father know?"

"He does not. No one knows."

"Will you ever be coming back?"

"I hope so Raya. I really hope so. That depends on father."

"But if you tell him he will understand and then you can stay."

"He will not understand. And you must not tell him, on any account. He will find out for himself soon enough. And when he does he might be angry. But you must remember he is not angry with you – only me. And others may well be angry with me too. Perhaps for a long while. You need to understand this."

"I won't be angry with you Pari. When are you going?"

"Tomorrow, very early in the morning."

"Tomorrow! But it's so soon. What will Ali say?"

"Ali will understand I think. He may not approve. But he will understand."

"Do you have to go? I will miss you."

"Of course you will. But you could come and visit?"

"Yes. Who would look after us? Would father get himself a wife?"

"I suppose he might do. But you are thirteen now and you are a grown young woman. You need to stay and get an education. Don't end up like me with nothing."

"I want to be like you," said Soraya.

"That is nonsense Soraya. You need to think of the future. Carpet weaving is not the way of the future."

"But father says that I am the fastest knotter he has ever seen."

"Father says many things, for many reasons."

"Oh."

"As soon as I am settled I will write to you. I have taken the address of Nargess Shabi, Dr Azizi's friend at the university and I shall write to her and give her news of my progress. She will let you know how I am. I will miss you all so much." Parissa stopped and started to cry.

"Please don't cry Pari!" said Soraya putting her arm around her sister and drying her eyes with her sleeve.

"I think we should go to sleep now, But when you wake in the morning I will be gone. When father asks where I have gone you will say you do not know."

"I will not be able to sleep."

"We will both try. Come, get into bed and I will read you a Mollah Nasredin story," said Parissa getting out a small book.

They prepared for bed and Parissa lay by her sister's side flicking through the book.

"The Sermon. Read The Sermon!" said Soraya closing her eyes.

Parissa read from the small book. "So, one day Mollah Nasredin went up to the pulpit to give a sermon. And he said to the congregation who was sitting cross-legged before him, '*Do you know what I am here to talk to you about today?*' And the congregation shook their heads in bewilderment. The Mollah threw up his hands in frustration. '*Well, if you don't know what's the point of me being here?*' and he stormed off in frustration. So the poor confused congregation rubbed their beards in puzzlement and one of them said 'Next time, we had better say we know – or he will disappear again!' So the next time Mollah arrived to deliver his sermon, and asked, once more, if they knew the topic of his sermon, the congregation were prepared. They chimed 'Yes, Mollah – we do!'"

Soraya started laughing beneath the blanket .

"So," continued Parissa "The Mollah said: 'Well, if you *know* – you certainly don't need me to tell you. So my work is done.' And he left the mosque.

By this time the congregation was getting upset, and during a conversation between themselves as to what to do one man had an idea. "Next time he comes to preach," he said. "Half of us must say 'yes!' and the other half 'no!' He will have no choice but to give the sermon!" This pleased the crowd enormously.

Soraya had the pillow over her mouth and between her knees to stifle her laughter.

"The next day – the Mollah arrives once again and this time the congregation was truly prepared. As planned, when the Mollah asked if they knew what he was going to talk about, half said yes and the other half no. Well that surprised him. He scratched his head and for a moment did not know what to say. Then he pointed to the left of the room and said…."

Soraya interrupted, imitating a man's low voice "Well – in that case I suggest the half that knows, tells the half that doesn't. And we won't say anymore about it!"

Parissa laughed and smoothed down her sister's hair. She continued reading the Nasredin tales until her sister had fallen asleep in her arms. And then she too fell asleep dreaming of the morning and what was to come.

****

At first morning light Parissa woke with birdsong in her ears. The house was still as she gently rose from her bed, a thunderstorm brewing in her chest. From her bag she took a small pair of scissors and sat down on the chair in front of the long mirror on the wall. She began to cut off her long ebony hair. Each tress fell silently to the floor like a flake of black snow. It was, she had decided, the most inconspicuous way in which to undertake the journey. As soon as they discovered she had fled, her father and brother were sure to follow her trail, and question locals about sightings of her. She could not risk being recognised. She was sure Mr Conroy would be expecting her to be in some kind of disguise.

When the deed was complete she scooped them up and put them in her bag. From another sack she withdrew a crumpled suit; one of Ali's old ones. She put it on and examined herself in the mirror. How simple it was to be mistaken for a male! And how peculiar. Standing there was the very son her father had always wished for in those early days.

After packing what was left of her bag she kissed Soraya lightly on the forehead. She climbed out of the open window onto the grassy bank below, sending a few reptiles scuttling underfoot. The light of the newborn sun united with the morning sulphur fog to concoct a warm, low lying, haze. Thankfully, it would aid her disguise. She crossed the road and briskly turned the corner, where she took a small map from her pocket. It was the map given to her by Karim on their previous trip. And the irony of the moment was exaggerated by the bright glow bouncing off the white surface of the paper as it caught the morning sun.

She commenced her journey to the municipal swimming pool and before long passed the large English house that she and Yasmin had peered into on their last visit. It appeared different. Empty. Shutters banged themselves angrily against the window frames with the help of the passing wind. Waste bins bursting with discarded, imported, packaging lay upturned on the immaculate grass. Items of children's clothing had been tossed on the porchway stairs. The occupants had clearly left to return to England, she supposed.

The small shop at the end of the road was open and she went in to get herself some bread, to rid herself of the anxious and thumping heart which was making her dizzy. She felt mostly naked without her scarf, which added to her apprehension.

It took her by surprise when the shopkeeper greeted her with "Good morning young man." Her disguise had succeeded, and for this she was grateful.

She left the shop and walked a little further, eating her bread, and before long arrived at the swimming pool complex. It was deserted and the pool was drained. A scrawl of white paint on the green fence said: *Oil from Iran, for Iran!* She took a watch out of her pocket. It was Ali's which she had borrowed the night before. The time had just passed six. She had another six hours to wait.

She noticed a small alcove nestled between the swimming pool gates and the adjacent fence. In it was a small olive tree circled by a low wall. She sat. Her head was spinning with fear or excitement: she was unsure which. She felt nauseous with trepidation. From her bag she withdrew a small brown packet and unravelled it. The nugget of opium she had stolen from her father looked like a chocolate marble in her palm. She put it to her nose. It smelled like a pickled walnut. She had taken it on a whim. A collection of thoughts had compelled her perform the deed. She might need it for bribery. Or to sell it for money. At this very moment it seemed to offer every answer to her trembling body which cried out for calm. She broke off a tiny lump and put it in her mouth. The bitter taste made her wretch. She forced herself to swallow it. Then, with vigour, she drank the whole bottle of water she had bought.

The relief, when it arrived, did not fail her. It unbuckled her from the misgivings. It deposited her on a cloud. It helped her mind dance with joy. It muffled her bleating conscience. And, in the dream that followed, she sought and received absolution from her father. Again. And again. And again.

She was awoken, it seemed minutes later, by the sound of loud chanting. Her arm was numb where she had fallen asleep leaning against the wall. A procession of men passing by in the street were chanting: "Down with the British!" The sun was hotter than it should be for that time of the morning. She looked at the watch. It was twelve fifteen. She snatched her bag and jumped up. Had Alec come and gone? Perhaps he had not seen her tucked away under the olive tree! She approached the vociferous crowd and asked one of the men where the British ship would be setting sail from.

"The Southern Dock. That's where we are going –to celebrate their departure!" said the man.

Why had he not arrived? "I was clear in my instruction," she said aloud.

She repeatedly dissected her conversation with Hassan, squeezing out of it every undertone. She combed every nuance of the exchange, in the hope of unearthing a hidden connotation. Something to guide her next step. The exercise gave birth to nothing.

Finally she concluded he must have come to meet her, and passed her unrecognised, assuming she had changed her mind. Perhaps he had returned to the docks. He would be waiting there instead. She was frozen to the spot for some minutes as she considered her options. She avoided a hundred times the small voice within telling her to return to the house.

The procession of chanting men with their pounding arms and oscillating banners began to seep away. She picked up her bag and merged her body into the stern crowd, her head still weightless from the opium. Her limbs felt like rubber bouncing in tandem with the regiment of surrounding male brawn. It was as close to unfamiliar as she would ever be. She was grateful the opium had deadened the largest part of her inhibition. Those male bones would stiffen for sure, if they perceived a woman was amongst them.

They passed a building she recognised as being the Gymkhana Club. The window through which she and Yasmin had spotted Mr Conroy was defaced with red paint. 'Free Iran' was scrawled over it. On the grass outside, a collection of farangi women were sitting with their husbands and children, mostly on suitcases. As the demonstration passed there was a tense exchange between some men at the front of her procession and two British men in the garden. She was thankful to see Mr Conroy was not amongst them. It was broken up by the leader of the procession and they continued on their journey.

Before long, Parissa caught sight of the smoke stack of a gigantic ship above the heads in front of her. As they grew near the colossal grey beast sounded its authoritative horn upon the miniature mankind frolicking around its iron hide. To its right, a crowd of joyous natives waved a multitude of flags. And upon them was being showered an avalanche of high-spirited words by a megaphoned man on a platform. Parissa caught only the tips of the phrases which ignited the crowd's approbation. "Full control", "rightfully ours", "end of imperialism".

For she was elsewhere, with her new found confidence, pushing through the crowd of excited men towards the ship, a few hundred yards in front. With every approaching step, the three tall funnels seemed to emit a stronger smell of disapproval.

She crouched behind a collection of large oil drums, a convenient location from which to watch boarding passengers and to scour the ship's deck. It was swarming with little people. After a while her neck began to ache from looking upward towards the terraces. Forlorn faces peered over the railing edge. And spaces between the metal rails encased the frozen and perplexed expressions of children.

Above them from the main mast, a British flag fluttered its farewell in the wind. And along the dockside, an orderly line of reconciled families waited to board the ship. Mr Conroy was nowhere to be seen. It occurred to her for the first time: he may have admitted defeat and already boarded. And she felt sick at that thought. With every passing moment she could feel opportunity slipping through her fingers. Without further deliberation she leapt from her spot. She ran toward the plank where people were waiting to board. A woman in the queue gasped and clutched her baby close. Parissa grabbed her arm. The woman screamed.

"You know Mr Conroy?" stuttered Parissa in broken English

"No!" she cried.

Parissa ran along the row of waiting passengers, frantically repeating her question. All shook their heads.

She began to cry. A faint and melodious call to prayer launched itself in the distance. Two seagulls swooped and screeched their claim to a stray piece of bread on the ground. A fleeting aroma of roasted corncob skimmed the air. She brushed aside her hunger. There was a tap on her shoulder. She jumped and turned around, ripe with expectation. An official looking man, in a white suit and cap, inspected her gravely and asked her to explain herself.

Words did not offer themselves. She felt her lips trembling; her eyes drowning in their own sorrow. The man gently led her to the other side of the ropes which had been put by the docks to cordon the area off.

"I'm afraid you need to have official permission to enter this zone," he said firmly.

She nodded. He returned to his post. And she was reduced to bystander.

Henceforth, she beheld, through the distortion of her tears, a performance in which she was not, and never would be, a part. Misty and disfigured British personnel in procession up the ship's plank. The blue silhouette of the ship's boarding officer blowing the final whistle. The hazy jumble of men disassembling the walkway. A young man, late to board and running breathless, jumping onto the gangway before its final fold.

An orchestra on the top deck played a jovial, departing, tune. The ship creaked and whined as it pulled away. A cluster of men behind her cheered and clapped. All too quickly, the steel leviathan melted into a miniature blemish on the skyline. Its only legacy was a question-mark of black smoke, contrasting starkly against the cyanic sky. A pelican encircled the whipped-up dockside waters, beating its wings on the water and scooping up fishy remains with its bill-tip.

Parissa continued to gaze from her spot until the sun was perched like an orange wheel above the sea. Then she raised herself from the dock nail on which she had been sitting and turned around. Not far away, sitting on a collection of timber pallets in the shadows, a figure was watching her. She gave a small gasp when it stood up and walked in her direction. And as it stepped into a shaft of sunlight the shape was drenched in colour. It was her father.

The final and blunt stroke of defeat punched her chest. And each of her swallows had the smart of a blade.

He approached and put his hand on her shoulder. "I could not allow you to do it my girl. You would have suffered immeasurably."

She looked at his face with horror. "What have you done to him?!" she cried frantically.

"I did nothing to him my dear. Perhaps you're surprised that I have even noticed, of late, how changed you have become? I asked Hassan to show me the rug when it was ready. And of course I saw your woven message. Although I wasn't sure of its meaning, I noticed the instruction on the reverse. My dear, I simply intercepted its journey. For your sake. You would decay in that world."

She set free a small sob that had been trapped in her throat for what seemed an eternity.

"Come, let us return to the house. We have a wedding to prepare for. "

She complied wretchedly. And she departed with him, empty and soaked in sorrow. But most of all with the very kernel prised from her soul.

24

London, 2003

"You were in love with an Iranian carpet weaver girl?" Manu's tone exposed the somewhat frantic pitch of a twenty-first century prude. Why, he wasn't quite sure. After all, had he not been waiting for some kind of revelation such as this?

He stood in Alec Conroy's living room, next to the hanging Persian carpet, which had been the subject of their conversation for the last ten minutes.

"You're clearly shocked," Conroy said as he wheeled himself slowly over to a small wooden table, on which sat a silver teapot was encircled by a smattering of crockery.

"Not so much shocked. Surprised maybe."

There was a silence. It was cut through by the stark and spindly sound of pouring. The old man picked up the cup and saucer. His buckled hand extended out a rattling cup of tea. A teaspoon fell onto the floor. Manu bent down to pick it up. He met Conroy's cloudy eyes on the return.

"You're the first person I've told in fifty years," said Conroy "and I suspect you'll be the last."

"So, who was she exactly?" said Manu, eager to dive into the meat. He sat on the sofa and took a sip of his drink. Disappointingly, it tasted of nothing. He hastily put it down to the housekeeper's poor tea making skills. If this whole senseless affair had taught him one thing, it was that brewing, stewing and infusion were qualities that modern day cuisine had shunned at their peril. In their quest for fast food they had normalised both the insipid and the over-seasoned. It was a mutation too far.

"Her name was Parissa," said Conroy, interrupting his thoughts. "And she was the daughter of a carpet seller in the central bazaar, in Tehran. The father, Mr Forooshi, was an interesting character – extremely political and a highly intelligent man actually. He had a small shop in the bazaar.

And this is where I met his daughter." Manu recognised his referral to the carpet-seller, whose daughter had married Karim Dashti, the man he and Cyrus had visited recently.

"You say you were in love with her. That must have been fairly controversial at that time and in that society, surely."

"Yes of course. Absolutely."

"And did she feel the same way?" asked Manu, realising he was starting to stray into dangerously emotional waters.

"I'm not sure."

"You're not sure?"

"It's rather more complicated than that," said Conroy. "She was, of course, very shy and in any case her father would not tolerate her being in a room with a man on her own. The only saving grace was that her father was rarely around. And her brother was rather lax in his sisterly protection duties."

Conroy stopped. Then he clarified.

"I didn't take advantage of her – just to be clear!"

"It's not what I was thinking" said Manu; though that very notion had been pecking at his mind for the last few minutes.

"I would never have taken advantage of her. I realised my position entirely. That's what made it so difficult. I struggled with myself for a long time over this. And at all times I acted entirely appropriately."

Manu recalled the woman in the teahouse who maintained that the Englishman had brought shame on the family. There must be something Conroy was not telling him.

"She was a Muslim, and undoubtedly torn between her traditional culture and the western liberal ideals that many of her new friends in Tehran were espousing," continued Conroy. "But regardless of her feelings, her father was having none of it. In retrospect, I should have spent more time cultivating my relationship with him and demonstrating my love for the culture."

"So her father was the obstacle to your feelings?"

"Her father knew nothing of my feelings at the time – though he claimed there had been gossip in the bazaar. But my ultimate obstacle, as it turned out, was Parissa's betrothal to a man called Karim Dashti. I was unaware of this and would never have compromised her position, had I known."

Manu raised an eyebrow above the china cup he held in front of his lips. He had assumed Parissa's relationship with Karim had been formed *after* Conroy had left the country. No wonder the community had been distressed. All was beginning to fall into place. He faced the dilemma of whether to admit he had recently been in Parissa's company.

"So you must have declared your feelings to her?"

Conroy nodded his head sadly as he recounted the melodramatic finale in the carpet shop and his proposal. It had, evidently, in both equal and opposite measure, been keeping his passion alive and crushing his hope to death. And, as he told it, his creased lips re-lived each word and sentiment. His pupils darted to and fro as if catching glimpses of her face. And his hands caressed the air, touching her abstract skin.

How remote it seemed from Manu's own memoirs of passion. As expansive as the gaping stretch between north and south. Only one solitary peak existed between those poles. Isabella Plantation, one Saturday afternoon in 1998: the blood red sprays of gigantic tropical flowers, the metallic tinkle of the stream, the nodular bark scratching the back of his forearms. Strands of her caramel hair in his mouth. Her hot breath on his cheek. The controlled explosion that stunned them both and which was quickly put aside for ever. Would she ever return from Cogolin?

There was a loud sigh. Conroy was wiping his forehead. A pristine white minibus was struggling to park outside the window. The grandfather clock in the corner discharged three orderly chimes.

"Perhaps you thought she would go against her father's wishes?" asked Manu.

"It was unthinkable of course. Although part of me – the irrational one I suppose – hoped she may decide to do just that."

"And you never saw her again after that?" asked Manu rising from the sofa and walking towards the carpet which hung on the wall.

"No. I had a visit from her father before I left the country. He came to my house to deliver a carpet I had commissioned. He presented me with a carpet she had woven for me. And her sentiments were quite clear."

"I'm not sure I understand."

Conroy pointed to a small rug at the corner of the room. Its green and mustard hues bounced devilishly off the wall which ran along the side of it.

"Her parting gift to me it seems."

Manu walked over and crouched down to examine it. Amongst the patterns was woven a line of poetry in Farsi. He looked over to Conroy for a translation.

"*However deep your grief may cut you, do not surrender to it; but let it ferment and season you as few mortal or celestial ingredients can.*"

"Oh I see. It seems pretty final," said Manu.

"And it did hurt. It hurts still, in many ways."

"Are these the only two carpets that are woven by Parissa, in your possession?"

"Yes. Why do you ask?"

"It may seem like an odd question, but did she ever weave her poetic inscriptions in English?" asked Manu.

Conroy appeared confused. "Not as far as I'm aware," he said. "I can't imagine why she would!"

"No," said Manu slowly, "of course." The answer, though still evasive was, he sensed, written all over him.

"Did you ever marry?"

"I didn't no."

"That's sad."

"Yes I suppose it is. I just never found the right person."

"And you never traced her after that?"

“I did try on a number of occasions. I even went back to Iran at one point before the revolution in the early seventies. But I was not able to trace her.”

“Oh, I’m sorry to hear that.”

The intimacy of their conversation was severed once again by the opening of the door and the tactless intervention of the housekeeper. She thrust a coat in Manu’s hand and drew Conroy’s attention to the community centre van waiting for him outside.

Manu walked along the corridor to the front door, with Conroy following him in his wheelchair.

On the way out he noticed a small mosaic wooden frame on the wall. Under the glass was simply a small parchment of paper that had been ripped out of a notebook. Upon it was scrawled in blue ink, in English. ‘To Mr Conroy. Lovers are killed by those they love so well….(Saadi)’ . And below it at the bottom of the page it said: ‘I like to write in English!’ It was signed Parissa.

Conroy noticed him looking at the frame. “It was the biggest regret of my life you know.”

“What?” said Manu.

“That I was never able to say goodbye. I asked her brother to tell her the date I was leaving, but for all I know, he didn’t pass it on. I never heard from her.”

Manu shook Conroy’s hand and opened the front door. The liquid sun poured itself into the hallway. And as he departed Conroy’s final declaration resounded in his ears. The date the boat was sailing was *the fourth of October 1951*.

25

London, 2003

It was quite remarkable, and rather embarrassing, for the truth to alight from such unexpected quarters.

How was it possible for two middle-aged, adequately intelligent men not to have seen what was in front of their faces for the longest time? Inclination had led both of them by the nose and presented them with clue after obvious clue. And still the penny had not dropped. Instead they had allowed the wish to become the father of the thought. At this moment, Manu felt himself a lone figure, standing mid-pitch in a sold-out Highbury stadium, bearing the butt of a disparaging Arsenal chant.

At least now there was a thankful clarity in the air: no link to any intrigue; no scandalous documentary; and plenty of reason to get back to their ordinary lives. Cyrus was due home next week. He wouldn't be pleased to hear the ending of the story. *All things End in Yes* was the carpet weaver's message to Conroy, her response to his proposal. But he had never received it. Either way, the poor man had been left waiting and disappointed at the docks. It was a simple and sad tale of everyday Middle Eastern folk. One of a multitude of ordinary lives, shattered by cultural restraints, family values and modern imperialism.

He empathised with Alec. How difficult it must have been for him to bury his affections when he had been so smitten. He wondered whether he should have told Conroy his love was still alive. The man had lived through decades of pain. He surely deserved a modicum of joy before he died. After considering it he decided his decision was the right one. Conroy was a frail man and it might make him frailer still. But surely it would do no harm to show him the inscription; the ultimate proof of Parissa's feelings for him. Manu sank into his armchair. He sat at his dining room table.

He gazed out of his window. He paced around the carpet which had spawned so many fanatical thoughts.

If Laure was there she would know what to do. Why had she not been in touch since he left his message? The chocolaty smell of her hair wafted into his mind.

Manu descended on the fridge. It was fully stocked for once. The return of his sense of taste had brought with it a new found vigour and a proclivity for stockpiling. On the shelves, where once Sainsbury's Chicken Dhansak (for one) had resided, Persian lamb cutlets and aubergine pickle had taken its place. A regurgitation of his culinary past had come to pass. A new-found pride in ancestral recipes had, seemingly, recharged his appetite. And as he had begun to appreciate these things it was as if his sense of taste was also slowly being re-born.

He whipped himself up a Kookoo sabzi, appreciating the extra time it took to mince the coriander and add it to the egg – where a quick omelette had always taken a couple of minutes. That was one of the contrasts, it seemed. Iranian food was dead slow. It took its time; was a culinary sloth. But, he figured, that could be cool and contemporary too. Slow food was all the rage these days. He contemplated writing a Persian cookery book. There were hardly any on the market. The British would, no doubt, find it quite peculiar. Even seasoned food editors would turn their noses up for sure. Perhaps he could adapt the menus to a western palate? It was an excellent idea which enthused him no end. And he remembered how Laure, after tasting his mother's Aash soup had, for months, pestered him for the recipe. He had consistently denied her that basic request, saying she should not inflict such a concoction on her fellow British citizens. And he realised, during that short trip to Iran, how much he had evolved. Wised-up. To the world and to himself.

He sat at the table to eat his lunch and flicked through the latest copy of BBC Good Food magazine. Yes, a Persian cook book was a hip idea. Jan Jackson might well go for it. In fact she was just the sort of editor who would appreciate such a venture. She was used to risks. She took them every day – wearing those skirts.

He wondered if he had Laure's father's number. She must have given it to him at one point. After lunch he looked through various boxes and books but could not find anything. He opened his wallet, which bulged with receipts and business cards fraying at the edges. He emptied it on the table. A small blue piece of paper caught his eye. He picked it up and turned it over. On it was a telephone number written in Farsi. It was Karim's number, passed to him by Cyrus the day when they had visited him. He stared at it for a short while. Should he pass it to Conroy? Let him decide whether to ring and speak to her after all these years? It would be a last hurrah before he left this earth. He was in two minds. He knew from experience there was a pointlessness in stirring up old sentiments. They could be as destructive as they were emancipating.

He looked at his watch. It would be just after four in Tehran. He walked over to look out of the window. People beneath were fussing their way through life. From that vantage point, on the fifth floor, the streets looked like a network of human veins. Small cars scuttled through them like blood cells. On the frame of the window pane before him, a fat ant was attempting to climb over a large flake of dry peeling paint. It was failing miserably. The flake would not allow it to progress the journey. It was a sticking point. Similar to his own, more human, hurdle. If Parissa had not taken up Conroy's offer why did Karim, and the woman in the teahouse, insist Conroy had shamed their families?

He rotated the piece of paper with Karim's number in between his fingers. Then he walked over to the telephone on the shelf, picked up the receiver and dialled the number in his hand.

"Hello can I speak to Karim please?" he said in Farsi.

"I'm sorry he is asleep. Can I take a message," said the woman who answered the telephone.

"Is that Parissa?"

There was a pause before she spoke again.

"Who is this please?" she said, in a frightened voice.

Manu apologised and explained his recent visit to their house with Cyrus.

"Karim will be awake later. This evening," said the woman, a little more reassured.

"It is you I wish to speak to," said Manu. "You must be Parissa, his wife."

"No this is not Parissa, no. This is her sister Soraya. Karim will be awake later this evening or tomorrow morning. You need to call back another time. Sorry."

"Oh okay. Is Parissa not at home?" asked Manu.

"Why? Why are you asking these questions?" said the woman, in an anxious voice.

He apologised again and took the time to explain that he had recently visited a Mr Conroy who had asked after her sister.

"Are you working for Mr Conroy?" asked the woman in a frightened whisper.

Manu was surprised and he laughed unintentionally. "No, no – I'm not. But I have recently met Mr Conroy, who mentioned a carpet that Parissa had woven for him which he never received," Manu lied.

He could hear her rapid shallow breath on the other side of the phone.

"I do not know of any carpet," she said eventually.

"When will Parissa be back?" asked Manu tentatively. He could not allow himself to relinquish the moment, even though it was beginning to feel very uncomfortable.

"Parissa is no longer with us."

It was said in a harsh and fierce whisper and was not what he expected.

She had died. Something had happened to her. He needed to know what it was. The only solution was to introduce some honesty into the conversation. Pleading with her not to hang up, he told Soraya his story from beginning to end, including his recent dealings with Mr Conroy.

The woman's attitude softened somewhat. She told him that although Parissa had intended to accept Conroy's offer, her message to him had been intercepted by their father.

"The heartbreak was that, the night before her wedding, Parissa took her own life. Our father never recovered. For it was his opium she had used to do it."

"Dear God. I'm sorry. I'm so sorry," said Manu, genuinely shocked.

"It was, of course, I who married Karim," said Soraya.

It all made complete sense now.

After his conversation with Parissa's sister, Manu sat on the rug, cross-legged, for some time. Now every little thread and knot spoke volumes. He turned over its corner and looked at the seeping black ink scrawl. He was not imagining it. There was a cold atmosphere in the room. As though a young woman was standing behind his shoulder implying the carpet did not belong there.

What followed was a good few sleepless nights, a variety of bizarre dreams, a few visits to an empty soup café and a rapprochement with Alice where they agreed to remain friends before Manu woke one morning with a hefty headache and some clarity.

After breakfast he rolled up the carpet and tied it with a piece of string before calling a taxi cab in which he made his way across London to Kensington.

A short while later he was standing outside Conroy's front door, with the rolled up carpet in his arms. He was greeted by the housekeeper.

"Yes? Oh it's you. What are you doing here?"

"I wondered if I might see Mr Conroy, just for a moment," said Manu

"Of course you haven't heard. Why would you?"

"I don't understand. Heard what?"

"I'm afraid he passed away the day before yesterday. He had a seizure from which he could not recover."

"Oh God. That's terrible."

"Yes it is. Now can I help you with anything else?" said the housekeeper.

"No. No. Thanks," said Manu turning to go. Then he stopped and looked back, just as she was about to shut the door. "When is the funeral?" he asked.

"It has not been arranged yet."

"Could you please call me – if I give you my number – and let me know the details. I would like to attend."

She eyed him suspiciously as he wrote down his number and handed it to her. She took it without a word and put it one of her many pockets.

He picked up the carpet and put it on his shoulder. The weight of its narrative, coupled with his own guilt, was heavy on his back. He had allowed the poor man to die without knowing the truth. How could he have done such a thing? He had practised repeatedly his conversation with Conroy. And now it was too late. It was the story of his thick-skinned existence. Life had consistently passed him by. And he had, time and again, failed to pick up the golden threads. Failed to distinguish the vital signs. To sift out the essential from the immaterial; the worthy from the insignificant.

He walked down Kensington High Street passing the three adjoining Iranian grocery shops. Outside on the pavement, the shadow of the New Year celebrations lurked amongst boxes of broken coloured eggs and plates of dying lentil sprouts.

After taking the tube to Hampstead, where he disembarked, he opted to take the Willoughby Road route home. He couldn't hack a conversation with Reg the Veg about why he had a carpet on his shoulder, or what was in season, at this hour. It was nearly time for lunch – and he was famished.

As he neared the junction between Willoughby Road and the High Street, he experienced a strange and instant waft. He dismissed it and carried on walking. But it would not let go of his nostrils. It hung like a nosebag from his muzzle. Was that really a fragrant mixture of herbs which was flooding his nasal passages? Or had he finally succumbed to the madness which he had been expecting all his life. The shock was intense enough for him to stop, place the rolled carpet vertically on the pavement and rest his arm on it. His disturbed mind was intent on playing havoc with his senses. He lifted his nose into the air, to catch another whiff. And there it was. Again. He picked up the carpet and began to walk at speed, in anticipation, towards the end of the road to where the aroma was coming from. He turned the corner with expectation. And for once it did not fail to deliver. A few yards ahead of him, a blackboard sat stridently on the pavement. On it, in white chalk, was written: Today's Specials: Carrot and Apricot Soup; Persian Aash Soup.

Through the steamy window he could see Laure giving instructions to Phyllis who was leaning with one hand on the table and the other on her hip. He watched the movement of her generous mouth as she spoke and the gracefulness of her gait as she skipped behind the counter to answer the telephone. The hanging menu board bounced to and fro in the wind. There was a blur of a small boy whizzing past in front of him on a scooter. He heard his mother apologise as she went past. He mumbled an acknowledgment as he watched Laure replace the telephone. She looked up and recognised him through the pane. She waved. It was an excited wave. And it excited him. Of all the appetites he had been suppressing only this one remained un-tackled. He opened the glass door which pinged with joy as he entered. The two ladies looked up.

"A bowl of Persian Aash soup, please!"

******

About the Author

Lily Barker is a British novelist and a member of the Society of Authors. For more information please visit **www.lilybarker.co.uk**

Anglo Iranian Oil Co Ltd

Memo: To all British staff from the Secretary of State for Foreign Affairs

I am addressing you on behalf of his majesty's government and in agreement with your directors.

In the critical situation which has now arisen in Southern Persia we, here at home, fully appreciate how difficult and unpleasant your situation has recently become, and are proud of the manner in which you have carried on in these trying circumstances.

As you know, we have made repeated attempts to negotiate with the Persian government but their intransigence and their insistence in attempting to apply a law which was passed without proper reflection, or consultation, has led to a situation in which we have been obliged to withdraw from Abadan the tankers under our control. This means the oil refinery and field operations will have to be closed down, at any rate for the present.

We know what a blow it will be to you all to see this great industry built up by your efforts and those of your predecessors thus brought to a standstill with all the harm which must result to Persia and the countries which have hitherto benefited from this great enterprise.

We must earnestly hope that, when faced with the consequences of their action, those who are responsible for this situation will change their attitude and agree to negotiate a settlement. We for our part will take all practical measures necessary to protect you until you are able to resume normal operations. You may rest assured that you all have our sympathy and regard. And your welfare and safety are foremost in our minds. Good luck to you all.

29th June 1951
Secretary of State for Foreign Affairs

Herbert Morrison

(copy of letter sent to British staff at the Anglo Iranian Oil Company in Iran.)

Acknowledgements

Many historical works were consulted in the writing of this book. But in particular I would like to thank the following academicians, authors and individuals – without whose material or assistance I could not have written this novel.

J.H. Bamberg
Manucher and Roxane Farmanfarmaian
Stephen Kinzer
Ali Ansari
Jane Kelsey
Judy Swank
My Faber Academy colleagues, in particular Rachel Clare who bravely suffered the first draft

Lightning Source UK Ltd.
Milton Keynes UK
UKOW04f1431110913

217013UK00002B/14/P

9 781782 994572